The
Goddess Lounge

Margaret Finnegan

Lucky Bat Books

The Goddess Lounge

Published by
Lucky Bat Books
LuckyBatBooks.com
978-0-9849154-7-7

To my village

"Sing to me of the man, Muse, the man of twists and turns driven time and again off course."

—Homer

"Oh, grow up!"

—Joan Rivers

Chapter One

Ok. So I'm on my way to The Goddess Lounge, the coffee house/knitting salon/menstrual palace that Fox News calls, "A man-hating elevator to hell, another example of debauched LA, a sinful hideaway for modern-day polytheists and the Hollywood types who forever confuse spiritual wholeness with liberal narcissism."

Yeah. It's not a good morning.

Plus, it's raining—crazy raining. Water is falling in thick sheets, like it does maybe once every five or six winters in LA. Naturally, we Angelenos are so stunned by the sheer presence of water under our tires that we can barely drive. It's taken me an hour and a half to get here from Altadena, and that's not even twenty miles. I'm feeling it, too. My calf is stiff. My foot is restless. My whole body wants to go all crazy Mel Gibson, and if I have to hear one more morning DJ make another joke about Noah's Ark I'm going to jump out of my car and dive under an MTA bus.

Of course, this being Hollywood, there is no street parking either. When I finally reach The Goddess Lounge I have to pull into a lot half a block down, which means my loafers get soaked through as I make my way to the oversized brass doors carved with ornate reliefs.

Outside the doors stand three women. Protesters. Damn. I forgot there would be protesters.

Now, as the daughter of a left-wing Hollywood celebrity, I actually know a thing or two about dealing with protesters. For example, do not engage protesters. Treat them like your child's messy bedroom. Walk away—just walk away—and know that one day, maybe eighteen years from now, that room will be turned into a guest room and the mess will be gone. The more you engage in the battle of the messy room, the more tension you will feel and the more misery you will endure. Similarly, the more you try to talk to protesters, the more people will call you names and throw things at you. It happens to Georgie every time. You'd think she'd learn, but when it comes to keeping her mouth shut my mother's an addict. She just can't stop herself.

Unfortunately, this apple doesn't fall far from that tree. When I see the protesters, I assume my best road-rage fueled 'don't fuck with me' stride. I look straight ahead, I set my jaw, and then, right when I reach the door, I go all stupid. I hesitate, just for a second, and my armor chinks right up. Forget it. It's over. They know I'm marshmallow.

"God sees you," says one of the women. "You can't hide your shame from Him."

I look down at the sidewalk stars bearing the names of actors and actresses that even I've never heard of, and, knowing all I know about ignoring protesters, I stammer, "My mom made me come."

Snarl. Curse. Moan. "It's your eternal damnation."

With that friendly invitation, I enter The Goddess Lounge. And…surprise. Relief. This place seems nothing more than a funky/alternate universe sort of Starbucks with oak tables and chairs and a purple velvet couch. Women sit relaxed, chatting and knitting. A few of them browse a shelf full of colorful yarns. Really, it's all very *Small Worldy*. I definitely don't see how it could have spurred that Orthodox rabbi to say, "What over 5,000 years of Jewish law and tradition have done for monotheism, that viperous den threatens to destroy in one fell swoop."

As for the famous red tent, maybe that's just a myth.

Three young servers in bright-colored saris smile at me and, almost in harmonic unison, say, "Welcome."

"Hi," I say. "I have an *appointment* with Tamara." This place may not be as bad as I thought, but I'm still not saying the words "goddess consultation."

The tallest of the servers picks up a clipboard from the counter. "Name?"

"Penne Armour."

She slides a finger down her page. "Hmmm…I'm not seeing you…you said Penny?"

"Actually, Penne, with an e, like the noodle."

The shorter servers knit their brows and give matching tilts of the head, so I say what I always say, "Hippie parents."

They smile. Honestly, they're like little dolls. I want to enroll them in my preschool; they're that adorable. I look back at the server with the clipboard. "You might look under Georgie Wile."

"Ah! Geooooorgie," says the girl, stretching my mother's name out the way people do. "We love Geooooorgie. Of course, Georgie *is* on the list. You must be her daughter. We've been expecting you."

She introduces herself as Uzume and her companions as Freyja and Bast. "We've each taken goddess names. Some of the more committed devotees do that," she explains. "But you can keep your original name. The goddesses believe in choices."

They lead me through a swishy beaded curtain and into a room the size of a backyard swimming pool. There, surrounded by potted palms, blooming orchids and maybe twenty enormous candle stands, each fitted with a gigantic, burning candle, is a scarlet tent.

Well, what do you know? There really is a menstrual tent. "Wow. *People* didn't do it justice."

"It is difficult," says Uzume admiring the sight before us. "There's no photography allowed, you know."

"And what words do it justice?" asks Freyja.

"You could say it's red or shiny or round—but so is a yo-yo," says Bast.

"Words fail. You know?" says Uzume.

I know. But let me try. Think little baby circus tent. It's about six feet in diameter. A bright bronze ball stands atop the highly pitched center of the tent, which is, otherwise, entirely covered in thick layers of gleaming, red silk that undulate softly as the air warmed by the candles rises and falls.

"May I take your coat?" asks Uzume. "We don't want to get the tent wet, at least with ordinary LA rain water. We'd have to re-sanctify."

"And we'll need your shoes," says Freyja.

"And your camera, cell phone, any kind of electronica. Those things are really toxic to good chi. We'd definitely have to re-sanctify," adds Bast.

Far be it from me to toxify a tent's chi. I hand my wet things to Uzume and begin pawing through my purse. Now, I know dusty pink is not the most fashionable color for purses these days. My daughter Grace Claire tells me that all the time. And I know some people would see the size of my purse and think carry-on luggage, but here's the thing: I like my purse. I like how the shortish straps fit neatly into the crook of my elbow yet can slide up and rest on my shoulder. I like the spaciousness of my purse; I mean, if I found a Chihuahua on the street, I could plop it inside and still have room for all my stuff. Sure, my bag may cause me to list a little, but many women list. I'm not the only one. The point is, it's a great bag, but it's not always easy to find things in this bag. It's a job less for the eyes and more for the fingers, which have developed a sort of sensory memory of the contents. I do my usual spider-crawl over the wallet, under the checkbook, behind the sunglasses and the mini first-aid kit and the anti-bacterial lotion and the Kleenex and the water bottle and the various crumpled papers and receipts, lipstick, sunscreen, Tic Tacs, and loose change. I search every inch of that bag: no phone, but I never leave home without my phone.

Uzume glances at her watch. "Isn't your watch 'electronica?'" I ask, adding a visual scan to my search.

"Oh, no. We all use wind up watches," she says. "Better energy."

"Tamara carries a whole line of them. All goddess inspired," says Bast.

Freyja holds up her wrist to show a large-face analog watch attached to a silver chain bracelet. Painted in the center of the watch face is a blond woman wearing a fat gold necklace. "Freyja. See?" she says pointing to the necklace. "The gold necklace gives it away. Gold necklaces are her symbol. All goddesses have symbols. You'll see."

I close my purse and pull it up to my shoulder. "I guess I left my phone at home." Then, more to myself than the others, I add, "I hope Grace Claire doesn't need me," because—after all—what's the point of having a phone if Grace Claire can't get a hold of me?

From the front room comes a door chime. Freyja and Bast nod and head back through the beaded curtain, which means only Uzume gets to escort me to *the tent*.

"Oh, my," I say stepping inside.

"Is there a problem?"

"No. It's just…there are a lot of burning candles in here. I'm just wondering…I don't mean to be difficult, but that's a lot of fire for a silk tent"—I look around—"especially one filled with big pillows."

Uzume laughs. "Oh, Penne, you're so funny. You must get that from Georgie."

"Yeah. You know, silk is actually highly flammable."

Uzume laughs again before stepping back outside the tent. "You just wait, Penne," she says closing the door flap. "This will change your life."

And thus I am dimmed to a plaintive red hue. The combustible-looking pillows are stacked around the edges of an oriental carpet, and in the center of the carpet stands a black lacquered table, oval and low. I step over the pillows and sit behind the table. I wait for maybe twenty minutes. Of course, since I do not have my phone, it could be five minutes. It could be an hour. Who's to say? All I can really say is that, without that phone, I am totally disconnected from my life. At this exact moment, gunmen could be ransacking Grace Claire's school. My dogs could be drowning in what I'm sure is now my waterlogged backyard. Who knows? Not me. Because I have no phone.

Just when I am really getting inventive predicting all manner of disasters going on without my knowledge, the beaded curtain gives a rattle and I hear the soft padding of feet. The door flap flutters and in walks an older woman with a short-cropped Afro and fantastic cheekbones, high, tight, and the color of cinnamon. She wears loose-fitting, apricot-colored yoga togs that match her neatly manicured apricot toenails. She even smells like an apricot. Extending her hand across the lacquered table and clasping mine, she says, "Penne. Penne, Penne, Penne, Penne, Penne. So nice to meet you. Finally. I'm Tamara."

"Nice to meet you. Yes. It's taken a while, hasn't it?"

"It has," says Tamara smiling her apricot lips. "So many cancellations. I'm glad your daughter is better, and your dogs. I didn't know dogs could get the flu."

"Well, we're not exactly sure it was the flu, but they really suffered for a while. Fortunately, everyone is fine now."

"I'm glad." Tamara sits across from me. "You know, you're not at all what I expected."

"No," I answer, returning to one of the conversations I've been having all my life. "People always expect me to look like my mother, but, you know, genes. Always two sets."

"Oh," says Tamara. "And your father is…?"

"No one famous. He died a long time ago. I didn't really know him, but he was kind of a big guy. Good farmer stock. Big bones."

Tamara narrows her eyes a little.

"You know, this is such a nice table. I've been looking for something like this for my daughter Grace Claire. She's always leaving her nail polish lying around the house. I thought if she had a nice place for it—"

Uzume enters with two chamomile teas in pretty china cups and saucers. "Ah," says Tamara. "Thank you, dear."

Tamara takes a sip. Then, as Uzume leaves, she says, "So…where is Georgie?"

Now for the other conversation I've been having all my life. I speak quickly and with what I know sounds like forced good cheer. "Georgie's— what—about twenty minutes late already, so that probably means she's about ten minutes in any particular direction from here. Time is a relative phenomenon in my mother's life. She runs thirty minutes late as a rule, but I've known her to run one or two hours, even one or two days, late."

The words take control, as they so often do. I bite my tongue and try and stop, but still the words spill out. Worst yet, they are joined by anxious giggles that give every third or fifth word a high-pitched cackle. "I call it

Georgie-time. It's sort of legendary. It used to drive her directors and producers crazy, which is not to say that my mom is not a good actor. I'm very proud of her. Anyway, I'm sure this is just a routine case of Georgie-time. Like I said, I'd give her another ten minutes. Tops."

Tamara's apricot lips purse themselves into a round little apricot pit. I swallow and manage an unconvincing smile.

"I suppose we can begin without Georgie."

And off I go again with the crazy, happy voice, "Hmmm. I wonder if that's a good idea?"

Tamara's apricot lips purse themselves into an even smaller apricot pit. "It's your choice, of course."

And now I must look like one of those perversely happy game-show people. I nod and pull my cheeks and eyes wide. Tamara sips more tea. "Your mother told me about your situation," she says putting her cup back on the table.

"Oh, really?" That's a little deflating. Not that I'm surprised, but still, Georgie promised.

"Please don't blame Georgie. She meant well. The more I know, the more I can help. And you are menstruating right now?"

That deflates me even more. I look deep into my teacup and nod.

"Good. Our bodies are more open to the wisdom of the goddesses when the blood of life flows through us. It's hormonal."

"Hmm."

"Because their hormone levels are more steady, postmenopausal women have an open channel to goddess knowledge. That's why they're comfortable speaking their minds. They implicitly understand that their opinions are informed by the divine."

I study a thin, feather-like crack in my cup.

Finally, the tent flaps open once more, and there she is, my mom, Geooorgie Wile, a twig of a woman with buoyant breasts and a smile that melts glaciers. "How fucking fantastic is this?" she says.

Georgie's arrival changes everything. That's just what Georgie's presence does. That's just who Georgie is. Where once the tent induced a quiet lull, now the silk sparkles like it's been doused in ruby red glitter. Then again, that may be the reflection that Georgie's mammoth silver pendant casts in the candlelight. It's a flat disk the size of a fist, and it hangs from a chain of big silver beads.

"Fuck-a-duck," Georgie sighs. "I thought you'd back out again, Penne. I thought maybe the goldfish would be sick this time—and you don't even have a goldfish—but fuck-a-duck you're here." She grins, and, as if exulted by the good fortune of their sheer proximity, the candle flames shoot even higher. "I hope you haven't started," she says settling down next to Tamara.

"No," says Tamara with only the slightest tone of annoyance. "We were waiting for you."

"Crap! Am I late?"

"No matter," says Tamara. "We're all here now." With a wooden mallet the size of an emery board, Tamara hits a silver gong, which calls to us Uzume, who enters with a silver tea tray. On one side of the tray burns an incense stick sticking out of what looks like a wad of Silly Putty. One inhale of its clovish-orangish-potish scent and I start to cough.

Her eyebrows raised, Tamara says, "Does the incense bother you?"

My mother waves. "Penne loves incense."

"Georgie." Tamara waits until my mother turns to face her. "This is Penne's consultation. Penne can speak for herself."

"Of course. You're right," says Georgie. "Sorry."

"Does the incense bother you, Penne?"

"I'm fine."

"That's not what I asked. I asked if it bothers you."

I mean to say, "No." I mean to say, "I love incense." Because, really, I mean to just get through this experience so that I can go back to work, watch over my little preschoolers and know that thirty miles west of me, in her beautiful Santa Monica home, my crazy but well-intentioned mother is no longer scheming to improve my fucked-up life and is, instead, scheming to improve her own fucked-up life. Instead, unwittingly, thrown off by a steely glint in Tamara's eyes, I blurt out, "Incense makes me a little nauseous."

"No," scoffs Georgie. "You love incense."

Tamara turns to Uzume. "Why don't you take the incense, Uzume. Just leave the cards."

Uzume hands Tamara a thick deck of what look like over-sized playing cards, deep red with shiny golden edges, and retreats from the tent.

"Penne," Tamara says placing the cards on the small lacquered table. "What do you know of the goddesses?"

"We studied Greek myths in junior high."

"And that's all?"

When I reply with an apologetic shrug, a hard look etches itself across Tamara's face. "Typical. For over two thousand years, patriarchists have denied the golden history of womanhood. Fundamentalists. The religious right. So-called 'traditional values' sheep can't stand to imagine a world that does not revolve around the all-precious phallus.

"The Goddess Lounge returns to women their sacred stories. It gives back to them their goddesses, the ancient and universal figures that glorify our eternal female power. All women are invested with this power. It grows out of our very bodies. It is made manifest monthly with each woman's cycle—with the blood paid in holy tribute to our sex's fertility. This Menstrual Tent: it is a holy place. It is the place where we join in communion to honor that tribute."

Over the years, my mother has dragged me to more kooky places than I can count or remember, although several stand out for their sheer bizarreness. Last year's "aura surgeon," who waved her hands frantically around my body for forty-five minutes in order to cut out the "cancer of unhealthy energy that had insinuated itself into my karmic field" remains particularly noteworthy. But I think it's fair to say that the menstrual tent is beginning to seem like the weirdest one of all. The weirdest and the grossest. Blood paid in holy tribute? Power made manifest in women's periods? Ewww. Ewww. Ewww. No one wants to hear that.

I swear, Tamara reads my mind. She freezes. Disappointment washes across her face. "Penne, you don't want to be here, do you? You think the Red Tent is vulgar…embarrassing." Tamara speaks as serenely as ever, but this time with a sense of wonderment, a pitying disbelief that anyone could find her menstrual tent less than inspiring. "Did Georgie force you here against your will?"

"Penne loves this," says Georgie. "She couldn't wait to come. Once she realized how fun it would be."

"I couldn't wait. I'm very happy to be here."

Tamara narrows her eyes. "I should warn you. I cannot help you find your inner goddess if you do not want me to. Goddesses are proud. If you are not committed to finding her, she will keep herself hidden. Worst yet, she'll choose someone else. So, what will it be? Do you want your goddess?"

What can I say? I took a morning off of work for this. I drove an hour and a half in the rain for this. My mother, who lives for putting me through this sort of shit, is sitting right in front of me, her eyes so bright that you can see why strangers still send her valentines. What else can I say: "I do."

And if I don't really mean it, well, what harm done? My mother is happy and my life is simpler. In the end, white lies are a small price to pay for peace. Anyone who tells you otherwise knows nothing about family.

Chapter Two

Imagine a set of tarot cards. Now re-imagine them with hand-painted goddesses on them and pretend that an apricot-scented gypsy is telling you your fortune.

There you go. That's a goddess consultation at The Goddess Lounge.

"Take these cards," Tamara says to me. "Now, choose twelve of them—any twelve—and put them face down on the table."

I put my twelve cards on the table.

"Very good," says Tamara caressing the cards with her fingertips as she turns them over and spreads them out like pillowcases on a clothesline. The cards are richly colored and gorgeously illustrated, but don't think that means the goddesses pictured on them are a bunch of glamour girls. They come in all sizes, shapes and colors, and while several look relaxed and happy, most seem worn down by daily life. They look flustered, angry, tired. They do not look heroic or attractive, and I may not know much about goddesses, but I do know that they are supposed to look heroic and attractive.

Tamara studies the cards slowly, clinically, nodding occasionally and twice uttering "interesting."

Georgie cocks her head. "Indeed."

Tamara says, "Each goddess has her own power, which means that each goddess speaks to a different aspect of the female experience. Love. Loss. Pain. We're not the first women to feel these. The goddesses know that, and they offer guidance. We call this guidance intuition. Some people dismiss intuition as irrational, but intuition is a gift. It is the gift of the goddesses. We ignore it at our peril."

"So true," mumbles Georgie, resting her fingertips just barely at the point of her chin.

Tamara spreads her hands over the line of cards. "These cards show the goddesses that have been attempting to guide you. Usually, two or three predominate."

"Such blessings," whispers Georgie.

Tamara points to a deep blue card featuring a woman in a saffron-colored, empire-waist gown. She has broad shoulders, wide hips, and a crescent-shaped layer of fat at the curve of her belly. Actually, she looks a little like me, except that her eyes are wide, desperate but determined, and mine are just sort of brown and demoralized.

"This is Demeter," says Tamara. "The Greek goddess of the harvest. She's a powerful mother figure."

Wow. "Actually," I say, and I have to admit, I'm sort of impressed, "mothering is very important to me."

"Um-hum. You have the miserable Demeter."

"What? I love being a mother. I live to be a mother."

Tamara leans back and looks at me. "I see." Then she points to another card. It shows a stern-looking woman in a powder-blue pantsuit. She stands before a thick wall of flames that extend to the tips of the card. "This is Kali. You've heard of her?"

"No."

Georgie sighs. "And I sent you to such good schools."

"Kali is the Hindu goddess of life and destruction. You have the destructive Kali. The angry Kali.

"You have her here too. But here she is even more angry, even more dangerous." This time Tamara points to a card with a sea-green woman dressed like a cowboy. In each hand she holds a pistol. The background consists of naked male cadavers piled one on top of the other. "My goodness. You are full of rage, aren't you?"

"Me? I never get mad."

"Everyone gets mad," answers Tamara.

"I may get annoyed, frustrated. But I'm very good at keeping perspective. I realize that, in the scheme of things, I am extremely lucky. Even blessed. I focus on that."

Tamara squints. Georgie does too.

"Hmmmm," says Tamara. "Let's move on. What I find interesting are these cards." Tamara waves at the other cards lined in front of me. "Surprisingly, these cards all signify the same goddess."

"They look so different," says Georgie.

"Goddesses can be chameleon-like. It's how they adapt." Tamara fingers a card featuring a punked-out teenager. She looks so punch drunk happy that I smile, until I realize the girl's about to walk off a cliff. Another card shows an old woman gazing at her feet, which stand on a sheet of cracked black ice. Other cards verge on the pornographic. In one, a woman opens a daintily wrapped penis-shaped package. Another shows a naked woman lying face up on a bed of roses. A third depicts a woman in a French maid's costume licking an ice cream cone and holding a whip.

The last card, however, is different. It shows a pretty little girl kicking up from a wooden swing. Her pink legs stretch out in front of her and the soles of her black patent Mary Janes shine face up in the breeze. She seems to represent nothing less than pure joy. This card I like.

Tamara can tell. She says, "Yes, that is a nice one. Some would say the best in the deck."

"It's a mother goddess too, isn't it? It's a happy mother goddess," I answer.

"Oh, no," replies Tamara. "Motherhood is not a Hallmark card. Motherhood is hard. It's full of anxiety and worry. It has its pleasures, yes, but look at this child's face: When was the last time caring for your daughter left you feeling like *that*?"

She has a point there. "Then who is she?"

"You mean, who are they? I told you, these cards represent the same goddess. I've never seen a reading so dominated by one goddess. It's very...unusual. Especially for this goddess. She is discriminating and elusive. Very." Tamara stops. She seems lost in thought.

Georgie gives a soft cough. A moment later she clears her throat. Sounding like someone about to be diagnosed with a serious medical condition, she says, "So, Tamara, which goddess is it?"

Tamara looks up. "Oh, yes. Penne, I have exciting news." She pauses dramatically. "Venus—Aphrodite, as the Greeks called her, the most illustrious of all the goddesses—is willing to share her wisdom with you."

With a gasp, Georgie throws her hands over her mouth. "Venus! Holy crap! How fucking brilliant is that! I knew it, Penne. I knew this was what you needed. Venus. Holy shit. I knew it was your turn for something good."

As for me, the whole thought makes me let loose such a bitter snort that the inconceivable happens: My mother's face glows red from embarrassment—this in a tent where we all look like strawberries. I watch as the corners of my mother's mouth begin to twitch as she glances from me to Tamara, who has allowed a slight frown to crease her peaceful face. Finally, Georgie crawls around the table. Despite her appearance of eternal youth, my mother's knees are not what they used to be, and their soft creaking echoes throughout the tent. "Penne," she whispers in my ear. "Honey... sweetie. I'm not sure if that was the response Tamara was looking for."

A Grand Canyon-sized silence fills the tent. Clearly, my goddess consultant is awaiting an apology, but all I can do is stare at my fingernails. I mean the jig is up. With one snort, I have outed myself as the goddess atheist that I am. I didn't mean to, and I will definitely pay for it because Georgie is like the coastline. She works and works and works until she has carved a groove into a person's very soul. I can only imagine what this particular groove will look like. But what can I do? A snort is a snort is a snort. My shoulders slump forward. I puff out my cheeks and let out a long stream of air.

"I'm sorry," I say. "I'm sorry. It's just that...I don't think so. I mean... Venus? The goddess of love? And me? That's just...not very likely. Not that this morning hasn't been great. It's been a revelation. It's just that...well, the mother goddess: sure. I take parenting very seriously. The angry goddess, maybe. Like you said, everybody gets mad sometimes. But there is no way that Venus"—this last word comes out way too bitter—"has anything to say to me."

The frown on Tamara's face is now barely a shadow, but her eyes betray a despotic fervor. At this moment, Tamara isn't anybody's sunshiny apricot. She's more like the green cowboy goddess, the one with all the cadavers. "The goddess chooses the woman, Penne. Not the other way around."

"Ok," I say, my lack of faith showing like a cheap bra strap. "Still, I just think that...in my situation...in my case...maybe there's been a mistake."

"Venus is not some airy beauty rising from a clamshell."

Now I snicker. The sound just pops out like a gopher from a hole.

Tamara shoots me a cool glance. Georgie shrinks back. "Venus is not pop love songs and Viagra-free sex," says Tamara. "Yes, Venus is the goddess of love, but what is love but momentary ecstasy shot through with loss and pain—and that's if you're lucky. Don't you think that's a story that might resonate with you?"

Georgie squeezes my hand.

"My situation isn't quite like that."

"How so?" asks Tamara.

I look around the tent seeking the words that have now abandoned me. "It's just...it's hard to explain."

"What's so hard? Your husband left you," says Georgie. "Owen got a loft in Silverlake, moved his fucking-skanky-whore-bitch-shitboobed girlfriend into it, and barely makes time for his own daughter. It's been a year, and you are so still so fucked up that you won't change the message on your answering machine so that it doesn't say Owen's name. You made him cookies last month."

"The cookies were for Grace Claire, and I only had Grace Claire bring them on her visitation because they had flaxseed and wheat germ, and Owen always feeds her junk food."

"You need to move on. I've been divorced three times. You think I don't know what I'm talking about?"

That does it. Now the words come flooding back. "Maybe I don't want to rush things *because* you've been divorced three times."

"Wah, wah. Cry me a river. Now we're back to this. No one gets the childhood they want, Penne. Get over it."

"Ladies," says Tamara. "Ladies, let's find our divine energy. Breathe in—deep—and let it out. Good. Now, all I know is that Venus is calling you, Penne. She is, for the time being, your inner goddess. True, Demeter and Kali tug at you. However, Venus is in command here. She has chosen you, and she doesn't choose many. I wouldn't reject her so easily. Her gifts are incalculable, and, of course, so are her punishments. Just look at Atalanta."

"Who?" asks Georgie.

"Atalanta. Very pretty girl. Rich too. All these men wanted to marry her, but she said she would only marry the man who could beat her in a foot race, knowing that she was unbeatable and the losers would be executed. One day, a young man named Hippomenes took up the challenge, and he wisely prayed to Venus for help. Venus gave him three apples. Every time Atalanta took the lead, Hippomenes would roll an apple in front of her. Each time, she would stop and pick it up, and Hippomenes would pull ahead. In the end, he won the race, and he won Atalanta, who, thanks to Venus, loved him in return."

"But that's a happy story," says Georgie.

"So far! Atalanta and Hippomenes forget to thank Venus. So, she compelled them to have sex in another goddess's temple fully knowing that that goddess would feel offended and turn them into lions. Now, for eternity, they have to haul that goddess around in her chariot."

"You don't want to slight Venus, Penne. The consequences would be disastrous." Tamara shakes her head.

"I'm sure Penne won't slight her," Georgie says. "Right, Penne?"

Blah, blah, blah. Anything to let me go home. "Yes. Absolutely." Ha! Not even a smirk.

Tamara points one of her apricot fingernails at me. "Well, you better not."

"I won't. I will think long and hard about all of this."

"You can't just think about it," says Tamara. "You must invite Venus into your life. You must reach out to her."

"Oh, she will," promises Georgie. "She wants to. This will mean so much to her." My mother is crying now. Crying! Tears are running down her face.

"Oh, Mom," I sigh turning to embrace her because, really, as much as I dread this new age stuff, she just does it because she wants to help. Georgie flings her head in front of mine, and there I am, back in third grade, breathing in her soft hair, which doesn't smell all movie star, like you think it would. It's more like fresh lettuce and maybe a little sunscreen. She lifts her head slightly, and I think she must catch a glimpse of Tamara's watch.

"Shit." Georgie pulls herself up. "I was supposed to be at a UNICEF Brunch at the Beverly Hills Hilton twenty minutes ago. Meryl Streep is going to be there, and it doesn't look good for fucking Meryl Streep to be the only *mature* actress anyone in this town ever sees. Crap. Crap. Crap. I gotta go." With that, she blows us kisses. "Bye, darlings. Tamara, thanks so much. Penne will grow so much from this."

"You're leaving?" I say.

"You sweeties finish without me. I don't mind. Kisses." And she's gone.

It's not my imagination. The inside of the tent really does grow dimmer. Dark maroon settles over Tamara's face, but it can't hide her irritation. "Well," she says banging her mallet against the gong. "I suppose we should move on to your goddess initiation ceremony."

Are you kidding me? "There's more?"

"Now we must invite Venus into your life. Uzume will need to fetch some supplies."

"Uzume," says Tamara, when the tall girl opens the tent flap, "we will need you—"

A soft, high-pitched ring erupts.

"What's that?" asks Tamara.

The ring sounds again.

Damn! I rifle through my purse.

"Is that your phone? Electronica in the tent?"

"She swore she left it at home," declares Uzume.

"I thought I had. Here it is. Darn it. They hung up. I hope it wasn't the school."

Tamara appears about to wilt. Her apricot lips turn inward as she picks up each of my goddess cards. "Penne. Penne, Penne, Penne, Penne, Penne. I'm afraid we'll have to re-schedule. Your phallocentric device has despoiled the tent. It has filled it with negative energy, which goddesses, of course, abhor."

"My what?"

"Your phone! Your phone!" She's all green cowboy goddess now. "Your tool of male oppression. Cell phones, laptops: the latest tools for integrating male hegemony into personal spaces and private relationships."

I try to speak, to apologize, but Tamara silences me. "There's nothing more to say. We'll simply have to re-sanctify. Uzume, please get Penne her things."

Uzume rushes away as Tamara and I step outside the tent.

"I'm sorry. I thought I left my phone at home."

Putting a hand on my arm, Tamara sighs and tries to recover her poise. "Penne, dear. You are guided by Venus. Who am I to judge you? Still, you will have to return for the rest of your consultation. Can you do that?"

For godsake, how can I say no? I've toxified an entire tent.

From the front of The Goddess Lounge comes the sound of loud, angry voices. Uzume must have told everyone about my phone. In one instance, I have become the scorn of modern-day polytheists, which hurts a lot more than you would think.

Then, another sound. A man's voice. Angry and sharp. "No. I want to see her, and I want to see her now."

A tall man with dark chocolate hair and a black trench coat glistening with raindrops slices through the beaded curtain. Uzume, Freyja and Bast run after him, shouting and flailing their arms. Little Freyja grabs his wrist. "You can't come in here. Men aren't allowed in the sacred space."

"And he's got an iPhone," wails Bast.

He shakes Freyja off like so much marshmallow fluff and hovers over Tamara. "You Tamara?"

"I am. Who are you?"

"William Browning."

Tamara opens her mouth and a dawning look of comprehension drains the sparkle from her eyes. "Ahhhhhh," she sighs. Then, collecting herself, she says, "Yes. I expected you might turn up. Alas, I'm afraid I can't help you. The goddess chooses the woman and, when she does, she seldom worries about collateral damage. As Caesar said, 'the die is cast.' Fate is fate.

"Now, I am delighted to meet you, Mr. Browning, but your male energy poisons this zone of sacred female chi. Fortunately for you, a client has already despoiled the tent; otherwise, we would have a serious problem."

The man takes a step back. He blinks and, for the first time, seems to take in his surroundings. He looks at the tent and the candles, and the corners of his mouth turn down. Then he looks at me. Wrinkles begin to crease his forehead. "Penne?"

Damn. "William," I say. "Hi."

"You know each other!" Tamara's eyes start to brighten.

"My hus-…I mean, Owen and William work together. I mean, William is Owen's boss."

Tamara's apricot-pit pout widens into a rueful little smile. "I did not know that."

William hesitates before saying, "You're looking…better, Penne."

There's an understatement. I laugh. "Well, I guess it wouldn't take much." Let's not go there. "But how are you? How's your—oh, gosh, what was her name—the cheerleader?"

"Ashley," he says with the briefest glance at Tamara.

"Right. Ashley." Yeah. Like I didn't know that, but there's no reason for William to think I would be so pathetic as to remember the names of everyone even barely associated with Owen. "Ashley is William's girlfriend," I explain to Tamara. "Just adorable, as I recall. She is a cheerleader, right? You know, Grace Claire is a cheerleader this year. She's at a new charter school. Really fun. Terrific principal. Lots of extra-curriculars for seventh graders—like cheerleading. She's having a blast. Much happier than at the private school. We're both great by the way. Super good."

William's eyes soften. He takes a step toward me. I think: maybe he can tell I'm not crazy anymore, maybe we can be, not friends, but two people who, on the odd occasion they run into each other, don't automatically assume that the other one should be locked up in a mental hospital. Then he seems to change his mind. His look grows harder, and I remember that he has found me at The Goddess Lounge so how sane can he think I am? He motions to Tamara. "Do you mind?"

Goodbye. So long. I titter my farewells, grab my things and race outside.

Just one problem.

The protesters are breeding. At least a dozen men, women and one glassy-eyed little boy now stand with blurry, faded signs reading "There is but one God" and "Honk if you love Jesus—not whore-mongering idols."

One of the men points a dripping finger at me. "Heed the commandments: Though shalt not worship other gods."

"I just…my mom made me come." Damn, damn, damn. I engaged!

"You're going to hell, you demon bitch," shouts an older woman with tight gray curls.

"SINNER! SINNER!" spits the little boy.

I try to explain. "You don't know my mother…."

Forget about it. I'm toast. The protesters hurl insults like fraternity pledges hurl beer. The boy calls me "Satan's fucking spawn." His mother whacks him for it, smack on the back of his head, right after she calls me a femi-Nazi bitch.

Ha! Doesn't matter! I'm not listening! Let them hurl away. Why? Because I am free! I am delivered. The Goddess Lounge is history. Not even seeing William Browning, not even knowing that he considers me as unhinged as a crack house door can spoil that, although, inexplicably, it does take a little helium out of my balloon.

Chapter Three

In my experience, many people express interest in alternative spiritual traditions. They say that they want to know all about your Astral Planes retreat or your Shaman's Journey. They say that they have often thought of doing something like that themselves. They don't mean it. They think they do, but really they don't. They're like tourists who go to foreign countries and see the sites from buses. All they want is a safe distance from which to collect funny stories.

This is exactly why I resist Nancy when she presses me for information about The Goddess Lounge. Nancy is my co-director at the pre-school. I like her a lot, but she's persistent, that Nancy: Persistent and nice, with this very laid-back-mahalo, native-Hawaiian vibe that matches her soft brown eyes and Hula-girl hair. Good luck refusing her. She's deadly. "I want to know. Just tell me who your goddess is? I won't laugh, I promise." Blah, blah, blah, blah, blah. For three days she goes on like this, and what does she do when I finally tell her one afternoon after all the kids are gone and we're cleaning up? She laughs. Of course, she laughs. She laughs and then turns around and tells the rest of the staff, and they laugh. "Oh, we're not laughing at you," she reassures me. "We're just laughing because it's so funny. I mean, Venus!"

"I know," I say.

And then one of the assistant teachers—a young gal still working on her BA—adds, "It's just that Venus is the goddess of love and your husband totally screwed you over. So it's ironic."

"I get it."

"Plus," the gal adds, "Isn't Venus the one that slept with all the gods and just, like, basically, slept with everyone?"

"Yeah," says Nancy.

"And Penne," the assistant teacher thinks for a minute and seems to realize this can go nowhere good and mutters, "is so not like that."

"That's not a bad thing," I say.

"Of course not," says Nancy wrapping her arm around me.

"There's nothing wrong with not sleeping around," I say.

"Absolutely," says Nancy squeezing me tight. "No one is saying otherwise."

"Of course not," says the assistant teacher. "It's just, you know, some people...go out."

"I do have a daughter at home."

"You have to think about her," says Nancy.

"I do," I say looking at the young woman. "I do. I have to make careful choices. I have to make choices that will boost up Grace Claire, not bring her down. I need to show her that even though her father left and started a new life with a new, practically adolescent girl who sells shoes, I haven't. I am still putting Grace Claire first. It's called being a good mother."

This little exchange is proof of the fact that when life—or your mother—forces you along a different path, it is best to seek solace not in humans but in dogs. Personally, I have four dogs. I say the more dogs the better. Here's why: dogs don't give you grief. They do not laugh at the thought of Venus choosing you. They do not call you 'Satan's fucking spawn' when you try to be a good daughter. They do not leave you for slutty Venezuelans or make fun of your favorite purse or sigh in disappointment when your phone toxifies their precious tent. And they do not—repeat, do not—leave messages like *this* on your answering machine:

"Penne? Owen. I know I'm supposed to pick up Grace Claire on Friday, but William's out of control. I'll be working all weekend again. Talk to Grace Claire for me, ok. I'm sure you can make her understand. You're so much better at that kind of thing than I am. Thanks."

Make Grace Claire understand? Make her understand what? That her father is cancelling out on her *again*? How am I supposed to make a thirteen-year-old girl understand that? I sink down to the floor.

And what about my dogs? What do they do? Do my dogs laugh? Do they tell me to 'move on'? No. They sense my pain and surround me with love. They lick my face, my neck, my hands, my sweater. They nudge me with their wet noses and knock into each other in desperate attempts to find space on my lap. Then they chase after a fly that got in the house because they know how much I hate flies.

Yeah. That's love. That's what every relationship should be, but you don't get that with humans. With humans everything is drama. Drama and excuses and broken promises and empty words. Well, you know what? I've had enough of it. I will not make Grace Claire understand. Owen can make her understand. This is Owen's mess; let him clean it. I call his cell phone. No answer. I call again. No answer. I call another eight times. Finally, I leave this message: "Answer your goddamn fucking phone, Owen! Call me!" Then I hang up and add, "Fucking shit. Fucking, fucking shit."

It is a cruel fact of nature that, when faced with difficulties, children often channel the worst of their parents. Violence begets violence. Alcoholics raise alcoholics. I channel my mother's dirty mouth. It's horrible. I know. I hate it. I always vow that I will try to do better, but some patterns are too deeply ingrained to abandon, and this is one of them. In times of crisis, I have the potty mouth of a seventh-grade juvenile delinquent. "Piss. Piss. Piss. Dammit. Dammit. Dammit. Owen, what are you fucking doing to me?"

I need to talk to Owen, see him. "Don't do it," says an annoying Georgie voice in my head. "This is what divorce attorneys are for." But here's the problem. Attorneys take days. Friday is just a few days from now. More importantly, Grace Claire is very fragile about anything that has to do with her father, and what does my mother know about the emotional fragility of seventh graders? Shit. That's what she knows. When I was in seventh grade, my mother promised that I could spend the summer at a horse ranch braiding manes. Only when I got there—rolls of ribbon in hand—did I learn it was really a fat camp, and that the closest I'd get to an equestrian vacation was when we rolled ourselves onto the pommel horse. So, let me tell you, that internal Georgie voice isn't really sticking. The voice that's sticking is the one that keeps dialing Owen's cell to tell him to fucking pick up the goddamn phone. When a half an hour of that doesn't work, I call his office, and guess what? That bitchy receptionist that treats me like I'm invisible because I haven't had a boob job and a tummy tuck tells me to "try Owen at home."

HA! AHA, HA, HA! At home! He's not at the office! He's not working this weekend! He's lying. He's probably taking stupid Rosa to Hawaii or Tahiti or France or someplace warm and beautiful and expensive! He just doesn't have the balls to admit it. Well, if he thinks I'm covering for him for that he can—wait.

Let me think about this a minute.

Goddamn it.

It's not just that Grace Claire is fragile when it comes to anything involving her father. That's not the only issue. It's that Owen's throwing Grace Claire under the bus. Again. He's blowing her off. I can't tell her that.

Shit.

The dogs come back and settle around me. I look at my oldest dog—the only girl—Lucy, who I've had even longer than Grace Claire. She's arthritic and practically deaf, but she gives me such a soulful look that I know she understands. "We can't let her find out, can we?"

Lucy rests her head on my thigh. I rub her neck. The other dogs—my boys—nudge my hand so that I can rub them too. They're sweet. They would never choose Tahiti over us.

By the time I go to pick up Grace Claire, I've decided what to do. I will lie my ass off and buy her whatever she wants. So, basically, I will do what Owen asked in the first place, but it will cost me money. Bastard.

It's raining pretty hard by the time I reach campus. Poor Grace Claire is running across a long quad and getting soaked. She's wearing a thin pink tee shirt—why? why?—and she's cradling a stack full of binders and folders. I race over with my umbrella.

One look at me, and Grace Claire's eyes grow all squinty as she telegraphs me in a language decipherable only by seventh grade girls and wolves. I can't translate it directly, but I'm pretty sure it means that I'm in trouble. She runs past as I say, "Don't you want the umbrella? Grace Claire?"

A tiny woman—very thin—her face partially obscured by a wet Dodger cap, approaches. She walks tentatively, as if she's crossing a desert of Legos. "Excuse me," she calls in a voice too loud and annoyed for such a slight body. "You're Grace's mom, right?"

I guess I nod because she adds, "I'm Xinran Dong. I need to talk to you about Pei."

"Pay? Is it a fundraiser?" I reach inside my purse and start feeling for my wallet.

"Pei. My daughter." She points to a girl in a dull green nylon jacket. The hood is pulled so tight that only a pair of metal-rimmed glasses stick out.

I glance behind me. Grace Claire is already in the car. Now I don't need a translator. She's got her wolf eyes set on dismember.

"I'm sorry," I say. "Do you think you could call me? I've got to go."

She shakes her head and sends a cascade of water flying across the bottom of my neck. "Why all you fancy rich ladies treat your girls like royalty?"

"I…I beg your pardon?"

"Never mind," she says before shoving a knobby index finger into my chest. "I will call you. You bet."

Experiencing such an encounter, a smarter mother would get in the car and just drive. She would say nothing about her daughter's predatory eyes. She would not ask why small Asian women were poking her in the chest.

She would turn on the ignition and, later, try and hide in the laundry room. But, as I think it is so important to understand, I am not the smarter mother. I am the poke-a-sleeping-lion-with a-stick-to-see-if-it's-dead mother. So, naturally, as soon as I get in the car, I say, "Who's Pei? I haven't heard about her."

The strain in Grace Claire's voice bespeaks a healthily unrepressed anger. "Don't do that again."

"Excuse me?"

"Don't run out to meet me. Parents wait in their cars. That's what they do."

"Of course. My mistake. I'm sorry."

She says, "Humph," but it sounds like a forgiving "humph," so I think I've survived that landmine. We must be good. Right?

"About this Pei girl," I say. "Her mom seemed kind of mad."

"God. It's like you don't know me at all."

Hmmmmm. Not so good, after all. "Um-hmmm. That must be hard to feel that way."

"You're so embarrassing sometimes."

So now I will just shut up because, really, sometimes too much talk is worse than too little. Believe me, mothers who spend all day swatting the ball of who-did-what-to-whom end up with full body bruises.

At least the dogs are happy. They scramble toward me as we walk in the house. My pit bull, Pedro, pushes me to the floor, and the other dogs, anxious to show their delight, flop on top of me. It's at this moment when I remember that I haven't actually deleted that message from Owen. Up I go, but it's too late. Grace Claire pushes the button.

Armageddon begins: The wailing. The crying. The moaning.

"He was going to buy me boots."

"I'll buy you boots."

"He was going to take me to frozen yogurt."

"I'll take you to frozen yogurt."

"You don't understand. You don't know what it's like. I was excited."

"I hear that you are very disappointed."

"Stop it. You're treating me like one of your fucking preschoolers. I fucking hate it when you do that."

"We don't talk like that in our family, Grace Claire."

"Georgie fucking does."

"But *we* don't."

"I do."

"I'd rather you didn't."

"I'd rather I fucking did."

I take a deep breath. "The point is, sweetheart, that your dad loves you. He works hard because of you, so that he can keep you safe, so that he can provide you a good education."

"Ha! Then why is he making me go to public school? I liked my old school."

"Private school is expensive. This is a good school too."

"You don't know anything. You're just a fucking preschool teacher. And none of this would even be happening if it weren't for these damn dogs. I hate them, and I hate you."

And there you have it: Full body bruised in two minutes flat. That might be a record.

Chapter Four

"Look, Penne. It's Venus! She's calling you." This from my mother. She's pointing to an aquamarine billboard on the side of an MTA bus. It features a photograph of a finely carved marble head and reads, "Venus: Say Goodbye for the Very Last Time. January 3 - May 12."

"Mom," I say. "That's not Venus. That's a banner for the Museum of Antiquities."

"But the photo. It's a sign."

"It's a two thousand year old marble statue that was looted and is now being returned to Italy. It's been in the news for years."

"Ah! But after all those years, it is only now that it is hanging from buses, pointing you to your goddess."

"Those bus signs have been out for weeks. I only saw Tamara a few days ago."

"It's a sign. You'll see."

We are having lunch at a place my mom likes in Pasadena. They have excellent mojitos and people always tell her how much they love her, and it is very important for Georgie to feel loved, even by total strangers. We are strategizing about Owen. Actually, I am strategizing. I've decided to confront Owen, and I need her to watch Grace Claire.

Her response? "That's why you have a divorce attorney, Penne. He does the talking; you do the demanding."

But I've been expecting this and know exactly what to say. "Grace Claire doesn't think she needs a babysitter. You're the only person she'll let stay with her; you know that. She adores you. She wants to be just like you."

With a pleased-looking bat of the eyes, Georgie crosses her legs and sits back. "Well. I sense that my inner goddess thinks you're right. I should be the one to help you."

"Hold on. You never told me you had a goddess."

"I did tell you. I've told you many times. This is your problem, Penne. You don't listen. You're barely present in your own life."

"I am present in my own life. I am very, very present."

"Flip, flop, flip: past/future, past/future, past/future. You're either moaning about Owen or worrying about Grace Claire.

"And I did tell you about my goddess. Actually, I have several, but I'm focusing on my relationship with Ishtar, a great Babylonian goddess. A mother figure, like Demeter."

"*You* got a mother goddess?"

"Yes," says Georgie sounding defensive. "And don't even go there, Penne. This is not about you. Besides, it makes sense at this time in my life—when I feel such maternal responsibility toward our fragile planet. I'm thinking about installing solar panels. Did I tell you?"

With great effort, I restrain myself and manage a smile. "You know who would be interested in that: Grace Claire. They're studying global warming at school."

My mother is coming at Georgie-time seven. Meaning sometime before eight. Probably.

Even before the doorbell rings, the boys announce her arrival. They run down the hard wood floors, their nails clickety-clacketing, their barks throaty, their bodies jostling into each other, into walls, into furniture. I don't think I've ever felt so enthusiastic about anything in my life, and they're like this every time a car pulls up. The only down side is that you can't cork this level of excitement. You can't just say to the dogs, calm down. It'd be like trying to tell a toddler to chill after opening birthday presents. Dogs are not faucets. You can't turn their emotions on and off.

So here's what I do. Here is the system I have devised. I check the peephole to see who it is. I undo the deadbolt. I grab the dogs' collars and pull them back about four feet. Then I say, "Come in." Then, whoever it is enters. They slowly approach the dogs for a routine sniff as I pet the dogs' heads in a soothing, calming fashion. It works very well. Plus, believe me, if it's a suspicious person or one of the assorted missionaries that sometimes drop by, I usually don't even have to look through the peephole before they're back on the sidewalk.

Georgie comes in, like always, but guess who she's hiding on the side of the porch, who she didn't even say anything about when I checked the peephole? Tamara and her little goddess helpers. In they come, totally surprising me so that I let go of the collars. The dogs lunge forward—not their fault, again, think toddlers and presents—and they herd Georgie and her minions into a little circle and start jumping on them and licking them and sniffing them and drooling on them.

Some people, even people who claim to like dogs, even people like Georgie, don't always appreciate that this is how dogs make friends. These people need reminders. Every time. I say, "Don't mind these guys. They're just saying they like you."

"Are these female dogs?" asks Tamara, but what I'm really hearing is that she thinks my dogs are untrained, which is not true.

"You know, some people like to say that they adopted their dogs, but our dogs adopted us. They showed up, one by one, on our doorstep. Somehow they just knew that this was a safe place. And that's what it is. A safe place. That's why they are so especially happy and friendly. You don't meet a lot of dogs like these."

Tamara raises her hands high as if half expecting the dogs to burglarize her. Really, she must not be hearing me. Loudly, I add, "Honestly, these guys are full of love."

Tamara says again. "Are they female?"

"No, no. These are my boys: Pablo, Casanova and Jude," I say grabbing for a collar. "We have a girl too, Lucy, but she's upstairs." I get a hold of Pablo, but he swats me with his tail and I let go. "Look how sweet they are." I nod at Jude, whose rusty forepaws are on Georgie's waist and who is licking her twisting, wincing face even though I have told her many times that licking is a sign of affection and there's no need to get all Bette Davis on me. "They like her."

"Well, they'll have to go. Their energy is toxic to the work we have to do," says Tamara breaking free of the dogs and walking to the living room, followed quickly by Georgie, who brushes dog fur off her coat as if she's just been pawed by a pack of drunken sailors. Honestly, she is not helping at all.

The servers remain surrounded by canine affection. Bast is frowning.

"Don't worry about Pablo," I say. "Pit bulls are very misunderstood."

"It's not that," she says. "It's just that my goddess is half cat. I don't think she'd like me, you know, cavorting."

I finally get a hold of all three collars and pull the dogs away from the girls.

Uzume takes a step forward. "You never can be too sure with goddesses, but I don't think they'd mind. What do you think Freyja?"

"No. You never can tell. But it's not like you went looking for these dogs, Bast. You sort of found them—and you're here for a good cause, after all."

"I guess you're right," says Bast. "Actually, I really like dogs. My mom has Yorkies."

I wish Tamara were so easily appeased. She does not seem pleased at all. "And this room is all wrong," I hear her saying. She points at the television. "Too much electronica. We'll try the bedroom. She doesn't have a television there, does she?" she asks Georgie. "Or a computer?"

"Grace Claire," I holler.

Grace Claire comes in and freezes, her eyes fixed on Tamara.

"Grace Claire, I'd love it if you could put the dogs in the garage. Ok? Grace Claire?"

Grace Claire doesn't always admit it—she's thirteen after all—but she loves these dogs. Truly, deep down in her heart, she cherishes each one and would probably throw herself in front of a bus before she ever let any harm come to them. That being said, Grace Claire tends to be more of a big picture kind of person than a detail person, and the actual work of caring for the dogs does not much appeal to her. So I'm a little surprised when she does what I ask. Her eyes still soaking in Tamara, she nods and drags the dogs to the kitchen.

I smooth out my sweater and take several deep breaths before sucking in a wide smile and taking everyone's coats. "What a surprise to see you all. Are you guys helping Georgie babysit?"

No one has any idea what I'm talking about. Of course not! I knew they wouldn't! Yet, as with dogs, I guess hope springs eternal because I am nodding my head up and down half-convinced that this movement alone will make it true.

A good mom might at least try and indulge me here. But Georgie says, "Oh no, dear. Tamara's here to finish your consultation. We've decided you can't wait for the tent to be re-sanctified. If you're seeing Owen, you'll need your goddess. Then, when we're done, you can take Tamara and her helpers back to The Goddess Lounge. We carpooled, Penne. Carpooled. It's so eco."

"Excuse me?"

"Environmental. Green."

"I know that. It's the other part. I have to drive them back? To The Goddess Lounge?"

"It's basically on your way."

My shoulders inch up my neck. It's kind of painful, actually. I may be having an aneurism. "I'm sorry?"

"Well, you can't expect them to stay here. I mean Bast is half cat."

I rub my fingers along a lump the size of an English muffin at the base of my neck—ow, so ow. It's seeming bigger than normal, the lump. I'm thinking not just aneurism, I'm thinking also tumor. "But…"

Grace Claire comes back in. With two quick fingers she flicks her hair behind her ears and says in the overly calm voice I've heard her use with cute boys, "Hi."

Georgie couldn't be happier. She nods and says, "Gorgeous, I want you to meet my spiritual advisor, Tamara, and her beautiful *goddess* assistants. Ladies, this is the delightful and perfectly fabulous Grace Claire."

Grace Claire is vibrating. She's a shiver of excitement, but in a cool, unimpressed voice she says, "You're the goddess lady. I read your blog."

Oh my lord. "You do? I feel uneasy about that. I'm not sure it's safe to read strangers' blogs. I think I saw a *Dateline* about that."

"I liked the one about Lindsay Lohan," adds Grace Claire.

Tamara wilts, and the servers slump their shoulders and shake their heads. "Yes," says Tamara. "A sad case, that one. A little Morrigan would do her such good, but…the woman must be willing."

Georgie leans in and gives Tamara a hug.

"Still," says Tamara looking at me and allowing a small smile to creep onto her face, "at least we have one woman willing."

"Mom? You're going to find Mom's goddess? Can you do me too?"

Wrapping Grace Claire's small hand in both of her own, Tamara says, "Oh, we've already found your mother's goddess. It's Venus. Now we need to properly invite Venus into your mother's life. As for you…are you a woman yet?"

Grace Claire blushes and gives Georgie a quizzical glance—and damn it all to hell if I don't know exactly where this is headed.

"Have you started your period yet?" whispers Georgie.

The warmth drains from Tamara's face and voice. The servers each take a step back. Tamara frowns. "We do not use that term at The Goddess Lounge. Too patriarchal. Like menstruation is a *curse*—another word we don't use, by the way—like it's something you have to wait out or suffer through every month. When, in fact, it's a privilege. It's life itself. We prefer 'flow,' like a life-giving river or stream. 'Flow.' 'Cycle' is also acceptable because of its non-linearity."

Grace Claire stares down at her feet and shakes her head. 'Flow' is something Grace Claire is a little embarrassed about. All her friends have already started.

"That's all right, dear," says Tamara. "I'm sure it will be your time soon."

I put my arm around Grace Claire and pull back until Grace Claire's hand plops out of Tamara's. I say, my lips practically affixed to my teeth, "This is very nice of you, Tamara, but I have other plans right now."

"Ha!" says Georgie walking toward the stairs. "You have loads of time. The bedroom is up here," she says to Tamara. "I think it's fairly electronica-free."

Tamara, the servers and Grace Claire follow Georgie upstairs. Honestly, all I can do is stand there and watch. I should have known Georgie agreed to babysit too fast. A loud scraping sound from above wakes me from my colon-squeezing misery and sends me plodding upstairs.

The servers are dismantling my room. They've cleared off my desk and centered it beneath my window. A pile of electrical devices—a digital clock, a cordless phone set, an iPod docking station, and a lamp—have been piled on the bed next to poor Lucy, who lies half-buried under my pillows. A word from Tamara sends her helpers scurrying to the car. They come back with fresh roses and about a half dozen other flowers and herbs that look familiar, but, to be honest, could be hemlock. Uzume sets a periwinkle silk cloth embroidered with silver triangles on the desk. On top of it, Bast and Freyja put two crystal bowls, one filled with rose quartz and red juniper berries and the other with apples and pomegranates. Tamara puts half of the flowers and herbs in a crystal vase, which she sets on the desk, and lays the rest of the foliage on the blue silk. Then she makes a large circle with dozens of votive candles. She sets a larger candle—white, about ten inches high—in the center of the desk.

"What is all of this stuff?" whispers Grace Claire.

"Goddesses are particular. You've got to prove that you deserve their wisdom," says Tamara rummaging through one of the boxes until she finds a long, thin, black velvet box. She takes the box and places it in front of the large white candle. "Each goddess needs to be called in a unique way. For Venus, we need roses, laurel, juniper—basically everything we have on our altar." She lights the candles and motions for us to sit down within the circle. Then she turns off the wall sconces so that the only light comes from the flickering flames encircling the room and the moonlight shining through the window. With an elegant pinching movement, Tamara picks up a sprig of sage from the table and holds it over the tall, burning candle. She brandishes the burning sage high in the air and walks trance-like around the room.

The servers close their eyes and begin to chant. They might be saying, "Ama." Or it might be "Omah." I can't really tell because the burning sage is making this white, sweet-smelling smoke that is making me cough. Of course, Georgie and Grace Claire join in, even though I'm pretty sure they can't tell what the exact chant is either.

"First we cleanse the room of negative energy," Tamara says. She steps inside the ring of candles and drops the sage into the crystal bowl filled with quartz and berries. The berries begin to blacken and burn, releasing an acrid smell. The chanting stops. Georgie squeezes Grace Claire's hand, and Grace Claire starts vibrating again.

The fire extinguishes itself and Tamara pulls the black velvet box from the top of the table. She opens it to reveal a pearl necklace from which hangs a sapphire pendant the size of a thumbnail. At the top of the sapphire is a triangular ring, platinum, through which the jewel attaches to the pearls. Tamara puts the necklace on me.

"It's for you," Georgie whispers. "A present from me."

"Venus," says Tamara standing and lifting her hands to the sky. "Goddess of love and beauty, you call on this woman. Now, at this altar filled with your delights, reveal your wisdom. Tell her what you want her to know."

Slowly, Tamara sinks to the ground and faces the altar.

Having endured many strange ceremonies, I know that when the high priestess sinks to the floor, you're not supposed to upstage her by doing anything. Nobody moves. Nobody speaks. People wait. So...I wait. I sit stock-still and follow Georgie's example by staring up at the large white candle on the desk.

After about ten minutes, at which point my knees are grieving for their lost youth, Tamara turns and gives my hand a pat. "Ok," she says.

"Ok?" I answer.

"Um-hmm. We're done."

"Really?"

"Really."

"Ok. So great." I turn to blow out the votives.

"Don't do that," says Tamara pressing her hand on my shoulder as she stands up. "The candles must be allowed to burn themselves out."

Uzume leans toward me. "It's part of the ritual."

"Yeah. Plus candles always make a room look cool," adds Bast.

"Totally cool," adds Freyja.

I nod, because I am polite, but believe me, once everybody's gone these candles are going out. Tamara may lack a healthy respect for fire, but I don't.

Georgie must know me better than I realize because she points her finger at me and says, "Don't worry. They'll be ok. I leave candles burning around the house all the time."

"Also," says Tamara, "you must wear the necklace continuously. That's very important."

Georgie points her finger at me again. "Promise you won't take the necklace off."

"She won't," says Grace Claire. "I'll make sure."

"I won't." Sure, I'm lying. And you know what? I'm happy about it. Two days, three days max, and Grace Claire will be wrapped up in some new social drama. She will forget all about her promise. Then guess what? The necklace is coming off. Because who goes around with the same necklace on for, like, forever? And I'm supposed to shower in this thing? That can't even be good for it. That's just crazy. This night is crazy! This night is...Georgie.

Chapter Five

There are many good things about living in LA, but few of them compare to the rush of driving on a free-flowing freeway. When the gods of traffic shine on you in glorious, unpredictable ways, you feel a sense of power and giddiness that's akin to really good flirting. And the gods of traffic do shine on me as I drive Tamara and the servers back to The Goddess Lounge. For one thing, the rain stops. It's been pouring for two weeks, and I step on the gas and—poof—clear skies. Plus—get this—the interchange between the Pasadena and Hollywood Freeways is completely open. When has that ever happened? And right as I pass Echo Park a giant screech and crash erupt behind me. I have no idea what happened; I will never know, but that's ok: it's behind me. The road ahead lies clear.

Instead of putting me in a good mood, however, the open road is pulling me down. My stomach is hurting. I feel nauseous. And it's not just that I have to stop at The Goddess Lounge, which is inconvenient but not nauseatingly inconvenient. It's the Owen part. What am I doing? I'm going to ambush him about missing visitations? Like I'm Laura Croft? And what's he going to say? What's his girlfriend going to say? I mean, they're probably having sex right now. I'll probably walk in on them naked. And Owen will really want to talk about Grace Claire then. This is no good. It's not going to work. I should have told Owen I was coming by. I should have left a message. Or I should have listened to Georgie and called my divorce attorney. Why am I doing this? Why, why, why, why, why?

I'd turn around at the next exit except that I've got Tamara with me. She's sitting shotgun and droning on in her special calm-like-a-pond way while her helpers fill the backseat and bob their heads up and down in agreement with every thing she says. I can barely look in the rear-view window anymore without feeling like I've been tossed into the waves.

Tamara says, "Goddesses communicate metaphorically, not directly. Be prepared. Watch out for Sobriety and Despair: they're Venus's enemies. Be on your guard. If they find you, follow Venus's lead—do what she would do."

"She would drink," says Freyja.

"Probably wine," adds Bast.

We approach The Goddess Lounge and Tamara grabs my wrist. In an urgent tone she says: "I almost forgot: Heed the lesson of Paris."

"There's really no way I can go to Paris."

"Nooo! Not the city!" frowns Tamara. "Paris! The man." She speaks quickly now. Already I can see the shadow of protesters, their picket signs rising and falling in front of The Goddess Lounge. "Paris was a shepherd— actually, he was a prince, but that's a different story. This was before the Roman Empire. This was when Venus was called Aphrodite. Anyway, the goddesses Aphrodite, Athena, and Hera commanded that Paris choose which of them was the most beautiful, but they each also tried to bribe him. Hera said that if he chose her she would make him the king of Asia; Athena promised to make him an unbeatable warrior; and Aphrodite promised him the love of the most beautiful woman on earth."

"Of course, he followed his penis," says Uzume.

"He did," explains Tamara. "So Venus gave him Helen—as in Helen, 'the face that launched a thousand ships.' He stole her away to Troy. Her husband—the king of Sparta—followed suit, and wham: the Trojan War. The point is: gifts have consequences."

I pull up to The Goddess Lounge. Tamara and the others get out. They seem completely un-phased by the protesters, all of whom are waving picket signs and yelling, "Devil Worshipper!" "Sinner!" "Witch!"

Just as I'm pulling away, Tamara rushes back to the car. I put down the window, and she says, "The greater the gift the greater the consequence."

I look out the rear-view window. Uzume, Bast, and Freyja are standing in the middle of the street waving goodbye. A street light shines straight down on them. I swear, they almost glow.

Without Tamara's yammering you would think I'd be able to re-center myself, find my inner kick-box fighter, but that's not happening. Now I'm completely nauseous. And also sweaty. Now, not only will I probably throw up when I see Owen, but I'll stink too.

Still, I am trying, and I have renewed my determination because, hell, I'm almost there. Plus, if I turn back now, Grace Claire will hurt me. I promised to pick up a jacket she left at Owen's. I am thinking good thoughts. I am thinking about the moment I am in right now. The moment of me passing a beat-up red Mazda that won't even go the fricking speed limit. The moment of me passing another after another after another of those goddamn Venus banners that are hanging every two hundred feet on every goddamn street. "Say goodbye for the very last time." Easier said than done. That bitch won't leave me alone so shut the fuck up already.

I am not thinking about my dogs. I am especially not thinking of the day I pulled into the driveway and found Casanova lying on his side, too bone tired and miserable to sit up. Collarless. Covered in fleas. So thin and dirty that he looked like a skeleton wrapped in tar. I am not seeing the six-inch gash across his muzzle and one swollen-shut eye, proof that he'd either had a run in with a coyote or a shovel. I am not remembering that he was the sorriest thing I'd ever seen since…well, since Pablo had shown up looking much the same. I am not remembering how I took him to the vet, bathed him, fed him, and put "Found" notices around the neighborhood. And I am definitely not fixating on how the blood drained from Owen's face the moment he saw Casanova lying on our bed, or how, five minutes later, Owen packed his suitcase and left, or how a week later he had a loft apartment in Silverlake and had started spin classes, or how two months later he had a live-in girlfriend named Rosa Luna, who was twenty-five and sold shoes. No. I am not thinking about these things. Those thoughts are just like little annoying gnats that, maybe, occasionally, flit through my consciousness, but they are so inconsequential that I barely even notice them. Those thoughts mean nothing to me because I am blaring the radio and singing Donna Summer's "Last Dance," and I am so enjoying myself that I drive four blocks past Owen's street, only realizing it when I pass the big Gelson's Market on Hyperion.

I circle back, drive to the top of a narrow road and park in front of a new loft development with an angular, block-like construction and yellow-tan concrete walls. As I approach the lobby, the door opens. Two glassy-eyed women in wool skullcaps and tight-fitting tee shirts and jeans shuffle outside. They move in a daze, all but their suddenly hard nipples nonplussed by the cold night air. Frankly, I am a little worried about them. I wonder if their mothers know they're walking around without coats.

I slip in the lobby and look around. A row of mailboxes along with a long bin for oversized deliveries hangs on a wall. Just because I am a naturally curious person and not because I am a psycho-ditched wife, I finger through a pile of unclaimed catalogs. Victoria's Secret, American Apparel, Lucky Brand, Abercrombie and Fitch, Sephora, Hello Kitty…all addressed to Rosa Luna. Then I stop cold: Tiffany's, Barneys, Apple, La Maison du Chocolat, Dolce and Gabbana, Fendi, Lux Getaways, Blue Parallel Travel,

Galapagos Island Cruises—all marked Owen Armour. *Stupid jerk. Stupid me. Stupid my life.*

I go over to the elevator. Inside stand a man and woman dressed much like the glassy-eyed girls. Their mouths are slack; their faces blank.

"Excuse me," I say. When they neither move nor respond I try a more forceful approach. Smiling, I ask, "Are you getting off?"

The man cocks his head. He's thinking. Hard. "Are we getting off, Lena?"

"Ummm," she drawls. "You wanna get off?"

The man considers this option as the elevator door slowly closes.

After a moment, a chuckle echoes from inside the elevator. "Get off," he says. "That's funny."

"No, no, no, no, Sean," replies the girl. "'Jack off' is funny. 'Get off' is, like, an insult or something. It's like: 'Where do you fucking get off?'"

"Hey, man, don't tell me to fucking get off."

"No, no. That was the lady."

"The lady?"

The elevator opens again and the couple gives me a lazy, questioning stare.

I say, "I'm just trying to get to the third floor."

Sean narrows his eyes and curls his pale fingers into tight balls.

I lift my big pink purse from the crook of my elbow up to my shoulder. Pointing to the exit, I say, "The lady went that way."

"Right!" With a sudden burst of energy, he pulls the girl by the hand and they run outside as I step onto the elevator.

I have never actually been to Owen's apartment. I have dropped Grace Claire off at the building, but Owen always waits on the curb in a determined effort to keep his old and new worlds apart. It surprises me, therefore, to arrive on the third floor and discover that Owen—who insisted we paint every room in our house Navajo white—has a wasabi-green door. It surprises me even more to find that door ajar.

I am polite. I knock gently, and, when no one comes, I take a single finger and push the door open. A strange smell wafts into the hallway. I know this smell. I've known it my whole life. It's pot, something I naively believed I would never have to smell again the moment I moved out of Georgie's house and into my college dorm. And now here it is…coming out of Owen's apartment. Any nausea I may have felt driving instantly vanishes because this is weird. The one thing Owen will not put up with is drugs. He barely even drinks. That's one of the things I've always liked about him. He's very straight and narrow. Very law and order. Very un-Georgie.

I walk inside—and then I walk out: I simply cannot believe Owen lives in this pit, but it's Owen's unit number all right, the same one printed on Owen's child support checks. I enter again and, this time, simply stare at what might be described as a global-warming version of Narnia. The loft itself is large and square. It has beamed ceilings and glossy purple concrete floors. Plants fill the apartment. So many green and growing things stand so thickly together that I can barely see ten feet in front of me. The walls, violet except for an exterior wall painted black, are covered with a series of black and white photographs of a tall, thin woman with hard, silo-like breasts and in various stages of undress. I can only imagine that these are of Rosa. She appears to have silver eyes that looked vampirish from one angle and strangely absent minded from another.

How much more obvious can it be? Rosa is a drug-addicted whore. That's why Owen's never let me meet her. He doesn't want me to know what kind of skanky Blair witch project bimbo he's sleeping with.

"Hello?" I say. "Owen?"

To my right, above softly swaying vines, stands an elevated deck with semi-transparent rice paper walls. I climb what definitely do not look like permitted or up-to-code stairs. "Owen? It's Penne. We need to talk." There is no door, so I simply enter the paper-walled room.

Ok. I'm making a reassessment here. Strike zombie. Instead, think Disney princess vampira. This room is incredible. It has a lavender shag rug upon which stands a circular bed—king-size—covered in a satiny purple bedspread. Surrounding the bed is fine white netting that hangs like an inverted ice cream cone from a single point in the ceiling. The only other furniture is a cushioned stool and a white vanity table covered in about one hundred bottles of nail polish.

"Anybody?" I say approaching the table, where I open a shallow drawer near the top. It contains an empty tube of lipstick, some old eyeliner, and snapshots of Rosa, who, it turns out, actually has hazel eyes. But she's pretty, I'll grant Owen that.

"Wha?"

There's someone downstairs, and it's not Owen.

"What?" says another voice.

"Did you hear something?"

"No, I was just, like…you know…"

"Well, yeah, maybe, but I think there's somebody upstairs."

"In the bedroom?"

"Yeah, cause like, I totally see a shadow and shit."

"Dude," says the second voice, "maybe it's Rosa." His words turn slurry and breathy with excitement. "Maybeshe'sback. Rosa?"

"Rosa?" yells the first voice. "Rosa, we're here. We waited. Just like you asked. We waited."

Now there are other voices, a bunch of voices, talking.

"Rosa?" they say.

"Where's Rosa?"

"She's here?"

"Where?"

Owen I think I could handle. Even Rosa I could probably handle. But weird-sounding, word-slurring Rosa groupies? I don't know. They give me a bad feeling.

A wave of feet shuffles toward the stairs.

"Are you up there, Rosa?"

"We waited. Will you try on the shoes now?"

A sweaty hand on my purse, I walk down the stairs.

Five men and two women, all in their early twenties and each with stringy, dirty hair, bare—almost blue—feet, and dark circles under their eyes wait at the bottom. Their bodies, so joyfully expectant, melt into disappointment.

"You're not Rosa," says a girl with more face piercings than I have ever seen on one person. Her ears are covered in rows of small gold studs. Silver hoops hang down from her eyebrows and nose and a thick silver bolt sticks out from her bottom lip.

I am strong. I am confident. I say, "Hi. I'm looking for Owen Armour. He lives here."

They groan and shuffle back through a wall of plants towards the front of the loft.

I follow them to a seating area walled in by bamboo shoots sprouting out of gigantic blue and white porcelain pots. The Rosa groupies cram onto matching floral couches and stare at a square, glass-topped coffee table covered in pansies, four bongs and a heaping platter of joints. One man lifts a flowering pot of pansies from the table. With the speed of a turtle, he plucks a petal from a flower and pops it in his mouth.

"So," I say. "You guys know Owen?"

Only the woman with the piercings looks at me. "Owen. Pish."

"Exactly. Owen. You know where he is?"

"Who remembers that kind of shit?" says the woman.

"I know what you mean. Gosh. How about this: anybody know when he'll be back, or"—I swallow—"Rosa? Anybody know when she'll be back?"

The man holding the pansy plant plucks a full flower and places it petal by petal into the open mouth of the second young woman, who smiles at the young man as she slips her hands down the front of his pants. "She said to wait," says the man.

"How long?" I ask, because I am being very calm even in the face of some really weird stuff.

"I don't know," he says.

"Who remembers?" says the woman with the piercings.

I turn to find another man, this one freakishly tall and thin and wearing only Lycra biking pants, looking at me. He has this startled look on his face, as if I've just materialized in front of him. "Hey," he says. "Wanna flower?" He plucks a yellow pansy from a plant and holds it out to me. "Here."

"No thanks," I say. On the other side of me, one of the men has now taken off all his clothes except for a man thong. I didn't even know there was such a thing as a man thong, but I guess there is because that looks what he has on. "You know what," I say. "Maybe I'll come back. Ok? Enjoy your flowers."

"Don'tworryaboutit, man."

It's the thin man, the one I heard in the loft.

"Youcantotallyhaveone. We're like…communal or something."

I take a step back. "That's nice of you, but I don't eat flowers. I'll see you later."

"You'vegottaliketryit. S'like…shit…reallyawesome." The man steps toward me before realizing that the coffee table blocks his path. "Just a sec," he says, confounded.

"Next time." I make for the break in the bamboo shoots, but, before I can get there, an icy hand squeezes my shoulder. It's Sean, from the elevator. He's glaring at me. Lena stands shivering next to him. She's pulling down on the sleeves of her tee, as if this will keep her warm. "Hey," he says in a dangerous rasp, "Are you sure that lady went outside?"

I slip my shoulder away. "Definitely."

The thin man, having crawled over the table, drapes an arm around my waist. His skin is cold and though his arm looks weak and bony, I am pulled tight to his side. His other hand dangles a purple and yellow pansy in front of my mouth. "G'ahead. Reallygreat. Try it."

"This a friend of yours?" asks Sean.

"Yeah," the other man answers, now puckering his lips and brushing the flower against my face. "Get your own babes."

"Ok, ok. Just don't be sharing our shit with nobody."

"I really should go," I say. With a clumsy pirouette I pull away from the thin man.

"No, no. Stay. You know Owen?"

I should go. I know I should go, but I turn around. "Yes. I'm looking for him."

"Owen's awesome. Owen's the best."

"Yeah," says Sean. "Owen's like...the Man. Except for, you know, he's a total drag, and he's old, and he's like, kinda boring and shit."

"That's true," nods the thin man.

"Do you know where he is—or when he'll be back?"

"Pish," sighs the girl with the piercings. "It's only been, like, a week."

"Owen's been gone a week?"

The thin man blocks the opening in the bamboo and bumps my hip. With a pink-faced leer, he motions me to the other girl, who is now making out with one of the men. The man-thong guy is doing jumping jacks.

I push the thin man away, break through the bamboo, and make my way to the door.

"Dude," says Sean, "I think your girlfriend's dumping you."

"Who?" says the thin man.

I am out the door. I am down the elevator. I am in my car, and I am driving on autopilot, and I am shivering. Ohhhh. Creepy, creepy, creepy, creepy, creepy. Weird, weird, weird. I finger the sapphire pendant. What the hell was that? Who were those people? Why were they at Owen's—and where was Owen? Where was Rosa? Shit...shit, shit, shit. Is Owen using drugs now? But Owen doesn't do drugs. I know he doesn't. Shit. Had he really been gone for a week? Was he ok? Oh my God! Was he dead? He couldn't be dead. He left that message.

I pull into my driveway. Then I see it. A dark mass on my doorstep. Owen? I stop the engine and run to the door. There, in front of me, slumping in a pool of black mud lay an enormous, panting dog. It's a hundred and thirty pounds, at least, with matted blond fur and hopeless, wet eyes.

"Oh my goodness. Oh my goodness. You poor boy." I sigh. "Let's get you inside. You're safe here."

Chapter Six

What a morning! The rain is gone. The sky is blue with cotton candy clouds. It's seventy-four degrees, and it's winter. Look north: Joggers in sunglasses and skimpy shorts are running uphill. Look south: Bicyclists are flying by in their little Lycra outfits.

You think people in Michigan are doing this?

This is California living.

I am appreciating all of this because I am keeping perspective. Sure, I spent most of the night caring for an abandoned Newfoundland, and sure my husband has disappeared and his apartment has been overrun by hipster drug addicts, and sure, I seem to have developed a tic in my right eye that might be related to that tumor I'm working on in my neck, but hey, everyone has problems, everyone has pain. In the scheme of things, I am lucky. I'm not being burned alive in Afghanistan because I teach girls. I'm not starving to death in Africa. Globally speaking, my problems are miniscule. In fact, when I think about world suffering, I can barely remember what my personal problems are, and I try and think a lot about world suffering. I'm just caring that way.

Grace Claire, however, remembers my problems. She doesn't know the exact magnitude—still very small—of my problems, because I don't see the need to share the fact that for all I know her father is lying dead in a gutter somewhere. But Grace Claire remembers the general outline of things.

"So is Daddy coming today or not?" It's probably because I'm tired that I seem to be picking up on a squeaky Styrofoam quality in Grace Claire's voice. We are on the way to her school, and she is sitting in the backseat and punishing her long, white hair by stretching it as far as it will go with the pull of her brush.

For the fourth time, I try to explain. "Daddy wasn't there, so I don't know. I will call him at work. I know he wants to come, but, like he said, he is very busy."

"It's no fucking fair."

"We don't talk like that, Grace Claire."

"Go to Dad's office. Tell him he promised."

"That's a good idea. Maybe I'll do that. Yeah. I will do that."

"Good. Hey! Are you wearing the necklace Georgie gave you?"

"Of course." Goddesses and necklaces are now the least of my problems.

"Oh, my God!" Grace Claire suddenly starts laughing. "Look at that lady at the bus stop. Her ass looks like a chair. Like somebody could sit on it. Why would you dress like that if you were so fat?"

Grace Claire points to large woman dressed in a bright yellow tube-top dress. She has balloon-like legs and arms and her butt does, unfortunately, stick out like the rounded seat of a cushiony chair.

"She's probably a very nice person," I say. "We don't judge people by the way they look. You know that."

"She's a whale."

I pull into the school drop-off zone. "Still—"

A small fist whacks into my windshield. It takes me a second to recognize the person attached to the fist, but then it comes to me: It's the lady in the Dodger cap. Pei's mom.

"Hey," she yells. "Rude lady. I keep calling. Why don't you call back?"

Man, oh man. She has been calling, and I have meant to call her back, but I can hold only so many thoughts in my distracted mind, and I simply do not have room for this lady too. I roll down the window. "Sorry. I've been busy."

Grace Claire pinches my shoulder. "Drive! Drive! That lady's crazy."

Oh my gosh! My sweetheart! So supportive! "Oh, sweetie, it's ok. I *should* have called her back."

"No. Really. She's crazy."

"Noooooo."

The woman points at Grace Claire. She says, "Your daughter is the one!"

A woman in an orange safety vest is scurrying toward us, her arms rotating in large circles. "You're in a drop-off zone. Drive on. Drive on."

Get this! Pei's mom jumps in my front seat. Grace Claire grabs her things and flees, yelling, "Don't listen to her, Mom. I didn't do it. And don't take off that necklace!"

I look at the woman. "You drive," she says. "I talk."

With an eye on the orange-vested woman, I pull forward, but slowly because I have to think about this. I mean, I don't know this woman and she seems very hostile right now, and even though she is very small and rather sickly looking, my mind is quickly cataloguing the numerous ways she might try and hurt me. But then I think, why would she hurt me? She's a mom, and if she hurts me she'd have to go to jail—witnesses have seen her hijack my car—and if she goes to jail that would totally mess up her daughter and what kind of mom would want that? I try appeasing her.

"I'm sorry I didn't call. Xinran, right?"

"Yes. You can take me home. I'm tired."

Letting her in the car and driving forward a few feet seems one thing. Driving her home seems another. "Actually, I'm on my way to work."

"Lucky you with your exciting career life and your special popular daughter. I need to talk to you, and I am tired. Drive me home. I'm just around the corner."

She sees me give her a wary glance. "What? You think I'm a serial killer?"

"No. Of course not," I say, but secretly I sort of wonder. Still, just because you can't put a plug in stupid, I let her direct me to a small duplex.

"Come in," she says. "We'll talk."

I hesitate. She really is sickly and weak looking. How bad can it be? She probably does just want to talk. We are both mothers of teenagers after all. We have much in common, probably.

She leads me to a back unit where an elderly woman, even shorter than Xinran, stands outside sweeping the wet sidewalk. The old woman's back is bent and buckled, and her neck is draped with folds of liver-spotted skin. As we approach, she starts to offer a toothy smile, but then Xinran says something in what I think is Chinese and the old woman scowls.

We get in the apartment and Xinran flops onto a sagging couch that stands underneath a cheap print of The Last Supper. Next to it hangs a portrait of a big-eyed Jesus, and next to that hangs a huge family photo, the kind you might get at JC Penney, blue background and all. There is a man, presumably Pei's father, in a dark blue suit and red tie. Next to him stands Xinran, looking much more vital. She's at least twenty pounds heavier and she wears bright red lipstick the exact shade of the wool dress she has on. Finally, there is Pei, maybe a year or two younger. She stands in front of her parents, and they each have a hand on one of her shoulders. She is smiling. They are all smiling. They look happy, sincerely happy.

Xinran pulls off her coat and closes her eyes. Her face is pale, Camille-pale. "Are you ok?" I ask.

Xinran opens her eyes. "Now you are Miss Nice, huh?"

The elderly woman puts a brown blanket on Xinran. She mutters something and bangs my thigh as she heads for the kitchen.

"That your mother?"

Xinran nods. "She does not like you."

I try to smile "Why?"

"She thinks you are a bad mother. Cause your daughter is so mean."

"Grace Claire?"

"Oh, yeah. She's a mean girl. Very mean girl. You gave life to a mean girl. You did not know that?"

I am willing to admit that Grace Claire can be a little high strung. Bright, creative—some might say gifted—children often are. Everyone knows that. And it is true that Grace Claire has issues about the separation, which she is working out on a weekly basis with a qualified therapist. It is even true to say that Grace Claire can be—occasionally—demanding, rude, and hurtful to me, her own mother. But the parenting books make it very clear that many precocious young teens focus all their anger on their families because they know their families will love them anyway. In fact, it stands to reason that the meaner such adolescents act toward their families, the nicer they can be to everyone else. Allowed that safety valve of orneriness, they can shower their natural loving personalities on the general community. So, really, Grace Claire has no reason to be a mean girl; she has a safe, healthy space to express her age-appropriate fury at home. Without trying to offend Xinran, I try to explain this.

Her English might not be as fluent as it seems though because she says, "That's not it. Your daughter is mean. Don't worry. It might not be your fault. Some girls are mean. That's how they are, like some kids are left-handed. You cannot always blame the mother."

"I wonder if you're thinking of a different girl?"

Xinran's mother returns from the kitchen and hands her daughter a mug of tea. Her eyebrows drop down as she scowls at me again and sits next to Xinran.

Xinran says, "No. It's your daughter. She's mean. Bitchy. Evil. She calls Pei 'fat freak.' Says she smells. Says her teeth are green. Now no one will sit with Pei at lunch. No one will do group projects with her. Every morning before school, Pei gets diarrhea; she is scared your daughter will do something worse."

"Hmmm," I say. "Hmmm." I look at Xinran's tiny carcass of a body slouched on the couch. I look at her mother hovering over her. "Hmmmm. I know you are looking out for your daughter, and, as a preschool teacher,

I think that's great because it's tragic when parents can't be there for their kids.

"You know, I'm very close to Grace Claire, and this just doesn't sound like her. I wonder if…hmmmm…I don't want to say that maybe your daughter is lying, but I wonder if she could possibly be stretching the truth. Maybe she has some other cause for anxiety…maybe something at home, for example, something she's worried about…and she's acting out, for some reason."

"No," says Xinran.

"Really? Because Grace Claire is very sensitive, very caring. We have many dogs."

Xinran hands the mug to her mother and closes her eyes. Her breathing becomes shallow and her pale skin begins to glisten. Finally, she says, "Listen. Your daughter is mean. I'm sorry. It's true. I do not have the energy to worry about this anymore. I have my own problems. It's your turn. Your daughter made this mess. You clean it up."

The elderly woman adjusts Xinran's blanket and gingerly removes the baseball cap from her daughter's head to reveal an eggshell-like skull marked by thinning tufts of short black hair. With a gentle, delicate touch her mother strokes Xinran's head and starts to coo what sound like endearments but then I realize are songs. In a low, almost monotone voice Xinran's mother is singing to her daughter. She sings, and as she sings she sways her buckled back, back and forth, in time to her tune.

It seems too private, too intimate for me to witness this, but I look down and then up again because it's sort of mesmerizing. I want to say, "How do you do that? How do you hand yourself over to your mother like that? Do you have to be dying? Do you have to be so weak that nothing matters?" I can't imagine. And that's sad because what if Grace Claire can never imagine it either?

Xinran is done with me, that much is clear, so I make my way back to my car and sit for a minute. It's a lot to take in. Too much to take in. Luckily, however, I find that worries are like accordions; tweak them just a little and they fill voids one never knew existed. Hours earlier, I could not have imagined my brain holding more distress than it already did. It just goes to show how much we women underestimate ourselves. Without even trying, my brain has opened an entire warehouse of space so that I can now worry about Grace Claire, Owen, the new dog, Xinran's accusations against my daughter, and Xinran, who really does look sick. My globally insignificant worries and anxieties brew together into such a heady potion of stomach-churning stress that by the time I reach work I have to throw up, which I do, in the preschool's half-sized toilet.

"Go home," Nancy tells me. "Half the class has called in sick already."

"I'm ok."

"You don't want to infect everybody else."

"I'm not sick."

Nancy puts down the clipboard and crosses her arms. "Grace Claire?"

"Sort of. A little. Partly."

She sighs. "Well, you could be sick. Maybe you just don't know it yet. Why don't you go home anyway?"

I nod and hang up my apron.

She walks away and then turns to me. "You know, if you're up for it later, a few of us are going out to happy hour tonight. Wanna come?"

"Oh." I stoop to pick up a handful of Legos one of the kids has dropped on the floor. "I would, but...I was just out last night and...you know...two nights out in a row...I don't think Grace Claire or the dogs would like that."

"Well, next time then."

"Sure. That sounds great." And, in theory, it does.

I do not go home. I go straight to Owen's office in downtown LA. Why? Because Grace Claire is right. Maybe Owen's there, except the bitchy receptionist seemed to say he wasn't, but maybe he will be because I have a new theory. Maybe Owen has left Rosa. Maybe he's left her because he's realized that she's a drug-addicted prostitute who uses her own doped-up Charles Manson followers to commit heinous crimes. Maybe Owen has realized this and, afraid to admit what a mess he's made of his life, he's moved into his corner office, where he has been hiding for a week because he's afraid that evil Rosa is out to kill him and steal everything he owns. That would also explain why he has missed his visitation. He isn't being a dickhead, like Georgie thinks, he's just trying to protect Grace Claire—and me and even the dogs—from a band of clammy psycho killers.

Unfortunately, this scenario—while hopeful in its own way—does not do much for my unsettled stomach, which is starting to feel kind of strawberry frapped.

Also, I'm remembering that I think I might be banned from Owen's workplace because, the last time I was here, the dogs and I camped out in Owen's office until the security guards—who I once made Christmas cookies for—threw me out saying something like, "Sorry Mrs. Armour, but if you try that again we'll have to call the police," which maybe constitutes banning, but maybe only if I'm with the dogs. Hmmm. This isn't good for my stomach either, so I throw up again, right in the lobby restroom.

But good news! The old guards are totally gone. They have two new guys, and they can't possibly have memorized the faces of every ex-wife who's not allowed to come here anymore. Right?

More good news: I'm rinsing my mouth out with tap water when I hear a voice. "Hi! Wow. Long time no see. Wow!" It's Ashley, William Browning's cheerleader girlfriend, who doesn't seem to think I'm supposed to be blocked from the building. At least she doesn't cartwheel over to the guards. She says, "Have you lost weight? Are you lunching with Owen? Still friends? Wow. I would never forgive someone for dumping me like that. You are so super nice." She's dressed in tight jeans and a black hoodie. The hood is up and a few golden hairs peek out from underneath it. It's kind of a dark look for someone who makes a living with pom poms, but, hey, this is LA. Dark is more a fashion statement than an attitude.

"How are you?" I answer as I plaster on the respectable smile of someone who is exactly where she is allowed to be. "I was thinking about you recently. I ran into William and—"

"Really? The goofball. He never mentioned it. Where were you?"

"This funny place in Hollywood: The Goddess Lounge. My mother made me go."

"The Goddess Lounge! I love The Goddess Lounge!"

"You've been to The Goddess Lounge?"

"I love it. Did you see Tamara? Tamara changed my life! I love her."

"Really?"

"And you saw William outside?"

"No. In the tent room. I don't know what he was doing there, actually—"

"Weird. I'll have to ask him. Hey, by the way, you're going up, right? You think you might run into William?"

"Maybe." Shit. I hope not.

Ashley's eyes narrow and she tilts her head to one side, "But you're here for Owen."

"Yes."

"Good. I mean you and Owen probably have a lot to talk about. Anyway, if you do see William, I wonder if you can do me a favor? Don't mention you saw me. Ok? Cuz I totally have a surprise planned. Ok? We like to do little surprises for each other."

"No problem."

I wait a few seconds—ok, maybe twenty minutes—and make my move for the elevator. I can do this. I have this under control. "Damn." It's that guy from human resources. What is his name? Well he's not getting on this elevator. I push the close door button.

I'm good. I'm allowed to be here. It's a free country.

The doors open and I slip past the bitchy receptionist and hide myself among the maze of cubicles that swallow the floor space. As vice president of finance at Global Financial Services, Owen actually has no cubicle. He has a glass-enclosed office—a corner office no less, an office with a glass-topped desk and a Herman Miller chair that invites stares of longing and envy. So I'm a little surprised that none of the many skinny, glossy-haired administrative assistants trolling the cubicle mazes try and stop me from walking right into Owen's office. But no one does.

I guess it doesn't really matter though because there's no Owen hiding under the desk. There's no sign of him at all. But here's what's weird. It's not like Owen is the neatest man I've known. He doesn't line his shoes up in the closet or wash his own dirty dishes, but he's no slob, and he's professional enough not to confuse his office with a dormitory. So why is his office a pigsty? Stacks of paper lay everywhere. There are crumbs on the desk and a bottle of tomato juice; Owen doesn't even like tomato juice. And—strangest of all—there's a picture of some guy and his six kids on the file cabinet. Then the guy in the picture with the six kids actually comes in. He looks at me and says, "Can I help you?"

"I'm looking for Owen Armour. It's ok. I don't have any dogs with me."

The guy points his finger at me. "Penne, right? Doug Lister. We met a few years ago at the holiday party."

"Right. Hi, Doug. Nice to see you." I swear I've never seen this guy in my life.

"Nice to see you," he says as he walks past me and sits down in Owen's chair. "Don't tell me you're looking for Owen."

"I'm looking for Owen."

He pulls down on his earlobe and begins to scratch it. Then he rubs his neck and looks down at his desktop. "Why don't you check in with William? You know where his office is?"

I nod. Damn, damn, damn.

"I can't really say any more," Doug says looking up at me, "but—just so you know—there have been some changes."

"Changes?"

"Ask William."

"We let Owen go. A few days ago." These are the words William Browning says to me. He says them all Brooks Brother's professional, his eyes as soulless as his three hundred dollar tie. He won't give me details. He won't tell me why. He says it's an internal matter and that he is 'legally obligated' to keep the truth from me, the mother of Owen's child. All I can get out of him is that Owen has seemed distracted.

"What do you mean?"

He looks down at his desk and hits a few keys on his computer. "Well, frankly, he stopped showing up for work."

"What?"

He taps a few more keys and clears his throat. "On Monday. He stopped coming. He didn't call. When someone finally got a hold of him, he said he was busy and couldn't come in—that he didn't know when he'd be able to come in."

"What was he busy with?"

He doesn't even look at me. "No idea."

"Didn't you wonder?"

William shakes his head. "No. Owen can be difficult. You must know that." He looks at me for just a second and then sits down and studies his computer. "How are your dogs?"

I straighten up a bit. "It was my understanding that only the dogs are no longer allowed here."

"I beg your pardon?"

"I don't remember exactly what the guards said, so I could be wrong, but it was my impression that the problem was the dogs, not necessarily me."

Finally, William looks at me. He closes his laptop and puts his hands on his lap. "What are you talking about?"

"What are you talking about?"

"The last time you were here you had dogs. How are they?"

"They're fine. Look. About that day with the guards. I know that every-one here saw me looking all *Fatal Attraction* meets *101 Dalmatians*, but I had a very good reason to do what I did."

William leans back in his chair. "What reason was that?"

"You really want to know? Ok. When Owen left us, he said it was because of the dogs. Basically, he said I would choose any lost mutt over him, that I was nicer to the dogs than I was to him, and that he was tired of living with the Mother Teresa of the canine world. But—the thing is—he lied. I know he lied. He left me for someone else—"

"Rosa."

"You know Rosa?"

"Everyone knows Rosa."

"Oh. Anyway, like I said, he lied, and I just felt that I—and the dogs—had a right to the truth. We had a right to know, and we had a right to be told the truth to our faces."

He opens his laptop again. "I only meant that I like dogs. I have two myself."

My legs feel a little wobbly. I sit down. "What kind?"

"Pit bulls. Found them in Studio City. They were stranded in the middle of Riverside Drive."

Something stirs inside me. It's...I don't know. I feel funny, almost dizzy. "They're a very misunderstood breed."

"Yes. They are." He stands up. "Well, I'm glad you dropped by. Sorry about Owen. I wish I could help—"

My head is still spinning. "Really?" Oh my God. No one ever offers to help.

"Um...of course."

"Maybe you could help me find Owen." I quickly tell William what happened at Owen's apartment. Why? No idea. But the words are flowing out of my mouth. He twists in his chair. His mouth sort of half opens as his brows knit closer together. The lines in his forehead etch themselves deeper and deeper into his skull, and I try to shut up, but I can't shut up, and now his skin has turned sort of gray, and I say, "Can't you talk to the people here? Maybe they know where Owen is. Maybe they know what's happened to him and if he's ok."

William leans forward in his chair. He presses the tips of his fingers together and taps his chin up and down on them, and I know, I know before he even starts talking, that I've managed to convince him that I am even more spastic crazy than he ever imagined.

Finally, William says. "If you're really worried about Owen, you should call the police. If he's missing, you'll want experts."

"The police?" Damn. I stroke the pendant at my throat and begin twisting the pearls around my forefinger. "But...what if Owen is involved in something...ugly. I mean, I don't know if I could put my daughter through that."

"A private detective then."

"Maybe." I stand up, and it takes real effort too. I feel dizzy and queasy and when I reach out to shake William's hand I realize how clammy it is. "Ok. Well, thanks for your help. Good luck with your dogs."

He walks me out of his office. "Are you ok?"

"Yeah. It's just...what if Owen really fucked up. Sorry. I mean, I think I need to figure out what's going on."

Chapter Seven

Good news. Nancy was right. I have the flu. I feel like shit, and I'm pretty sure that I smell really bad because I haven't showered or brushed my teeth in three days, and my only true friend in the world is Advil. Lucy's been good too. She barely leaves my side. The boys won't come upstairs. I smell too disgusting for them, and that's saying something because they eat cat shit and their own vomit. The point is that I'm not all crazy psychosomatic throwing-up-in-office-buildings because I have the spleen of a worm but because my body has been taken over by a serious virus. And now excuse me while I turn onto my side and cry for a while.

I am Medusa. My hair has turned into greasy snakes; at least this is what Grace Claire tells me. Her social studies class started a unit on Greek myths. In a few months they get to go to the Museum of Antiquities and say goodbye to fricking Venus "for the very last time." Apparently, I will be chaperoning because that way Grace Claire can get ten extra-credit points and perhaps avoid a C- in her class. But it seems to me, even in my current incapacitated state, that maybe those teachers are A-type personality perfectionist jerks because Grace Claire clearly knows who Medusa is so she must know something. Maybe they're just testing her wrong. When I am better I will email her teacher.

Feeling worse. Georgie good mommy. Brought groceries and dry shampoo. Gave me tapioca. Love her.

On the mend. Found out that Georgie's "groceries" consisted of olives and tapioca. Grace Claire's been surviving on cereal and delivery pizza. Georgie bad mommy.

Tomorrow I go back to work. Today I luxuriate in clean. I wash every part of me and then change my sheets and open the windows to air things. No rain—yet—but more is expected tonight, and I can already smell the humidity that's collected in the sidewalk. My iPod is in its docking station and I am listening to Diana Krall because Diana Krall is the only goddess I believe in, although I'm starting to like my necklace. When I was sick all I could do was run my fingers across the smooth, warm pearls.

The phone rings and—bleh—my fever might be coming back, at least it feels like it when I hear Xinran's voice and she reminds me that my "mean girl is still mean." Then she goes on to say, "Yesterday your mean girl said to Pei, 'Why do you wear stripes when they make you look so fat.' Everybody laughed at Pei and today she had to go to school half an hour late because of her diarrhea. Now I think that you are a bad mother because you don't do anything."

"I'm sorry. I've been sick."

She says, "You don't know sick," and then hangs up.

So piss, piss, piss. Not every mess can go in the goddamn washing machine.

Then—get this—as I'm headed out the door to pick up some real food, William Browning starts walking up my sidewalk. He says something, but it's hard to hear him because the boys are at the back fence showering us with artillery barks and, possibly, spit, for which I blame the Newfoundland. He's very drooly. I bring William inside, but then the boys run in through the doggy door and just when I think they are about to jump all over him in their friendly way of greeting they slow down, sniff at his heels and trot all calm as can be over to the couch. It's kind of weird, actually. Maybe they are reassured by the smell of his pit bulls.

He follows the dogs into the living room. "I heard you were sick. Are you all right?"

"I am now."

"Good."

"How did you know I was sick?"

"I called the other day. Your mother told me. She said you were very ill. She said you would likely have to go to the hospital."

"She said that? I had no idea she was so worried."

He sits down in an armchair.

I worm my way in next to the dogs. "It's nice of you to check in on me."

"I was worried about your dogs."

There are not a lot of reasons I can think of for William being here—even the idea of William wanting to check in on me seems a bit of a stretch—but the dogs?

"I just thought, if you were in the hospital, your family would be worried about you, and then what would happen to your dogs? Would you have someone to feed them…walk them?"

"You came here to walk my dogs?"

"Your mother called yesterday and thought it might be helpful."

"My mother. Hmmm. Well, she's just always thinking of me, isn't she? You know, I appreciate your wanting to help, but I'm sure I'll manage."

"Pneumonia can be deadly, you know. I had an aunt who died from it. I'm here. You might as well let me take your dogs around the block. You don't want to rush into too much physical activity."

I look at the dogs, who are surveying William with easy eyes and tucked down ears. Well, if they want to go with him…

Forty-five minutes later, William's back claiming that the dogs didn't give him any problem. They didn't pull on their leashes. They didn't clamor after squirrels or other dogs. William says they were "perfect."

Even I wouldn't use the word perfect with my dogs.

I offer William some tea because, really, when a person walks your dogs so that you can recover from the pneumonia you never had, it's the least you can do. He says he can't stay long, but he sits down, and I can't help noticing that his cheeks have gone all pink from the walk and that he has really, exceptionally, good-looking hair. It's like a chocolate bar: deep, dark brown and just a little shiny. It's wavy too, kind of like the sea, the chocolate sea.

"I also have cocoa," I say. "It's good with whipped cream."

"Tea's fine."

"Oh. Ok. Tea."

"Listen," he says, and he leans toward me so that his chocolate hair is right at eye level. "I need to talk to you. The reason I called in the first place was that I felt bad about our conversation. Of course, you're worried about Owen, and, of course, you want to be discreet. To be honest, the company has a vested interest in your discretion also. I don't know what Owen is involved in, but I don't want any personal mistakes he's made coming back to haunt Global Financial. I asked around to see if Owen had talked to anyone lately. Our director of human resources says Owen called a while ago. He wanted to set up a meeting to talk about his severance package. I guess before he hung up he started crying, sobbing really. Then, when the meeting came, Owen never showed up."

"That doesn't sound good. That sounds bad. Really bad."

"I'm not sure about that. Maybe it's just a mid-life crisis. These things happen."

"Maybe." Maybe not. Maybe it's something worse. Much worse.

William stands up. "I'm sure that's all it is, but I'll let you know if anybody hears from him." He smiles and turns on this confident, man of industry, man of action charm. I've seen it at Global Financial parties. It's almost hard not to believe him when he says, "I'm sure everything is fine."

I get up to let him out, but, having been sick, maybe I get up too quickly, because I instantly start to wobble. William's arm wraps around me and he sits me back down. He slides round to face me. Gazing at me like I've got a thermometer hanging out of my mouth, he says, "About the dogs: I can't come tomorrow or the weekend, but I can make it Monday. How's that sound?"

I finger my pearls and somehow hear myself saying, "Ok." And it is ok, right? I mean, I have been pretty sick, maybe not with pneumonia, but I am still a little weak and congested.

William's long gone by the time I serve Grace Claire her own hot chocolate topped with mini-marshmallows, just the way she likes it. While she takes a sip, I settle down next to her and give her a look of deep compassion. It's not so hard. What you do is you tilt your head and kind of swallow your lower lip while you crinkle your eyes. Grace Claire's therapist calls this "cultivating a demeanor of active listening." The woman's writing a book on this topic so I guess she knows what she's talking about, but I'm the one who added the mini-marshmallow component, because I don't need a book to tell me that sugary and fat-laden treats create a bond of mutuality between all people.

Grace Claire knows only too well my look of deep compassion, which must be why she has her eyes fixed on the bottom of her cup. She slides from one side of the kitchen chair to the other, as if this might help her dodge my interest, but it's not going to work. I am more determined in my compassion than she is in her distraction. Finally, she yells, "What? What?"

I tilt my head a little more to the right. "I'd like to hear about Pei."

Grace Claire slams her cup on the table. "I should have known the marshmallows weren't free."

"I'm concerned about the choices you seem to be making."

Well, that's it. Grace Claire collapses into tears while she vomits up a long, sorrowful story about how hard it is to be the new kid at school, how hard she's trying to fit in, how everybody thinks Pei is weird, how everybody thinks Pei is a freak, how—honest to God—Pei does stink and does have green teeth, and how, really, Pei is the one who picks on *her*. Pei hates Grace Claire because Grace Claire is new at school and already has lots of friends, while she, Pei, has known these kids her whole life and they still don't like her. It is hard, Grace Claire cries, to be pretty and popular. Everyone blames things on her because they are jealous. Everyone expects her to be cool and to say the right thing and to wear the best clothes. It's a burden—almost a disability. It weighs so heavily on her slight shoulders that sometimes she doesn't know what to do or who to turn to; it's like she's paralyzed. Are her new friends really friends? Or are they using her—building their own cache of popularity by their proximity to her own good looks? What can she do? She says she does not know what to do.

"Poor baby," I say, wrapping my arms around her. How much clearer can it be? Grace Claire. Pei. They are both victims of a ruthless middle school culture built around pecking orders and one-upmanship. It is the system! The system has turned one girl into a golden-haired Brahmin and the other into a fat, smelly Untouchable. And while common sense and experience tell me that the top of the mire is always better than the bottom, I can see that Grace Claire has suffered too. Just as I suspected, Grace Claire never—NEVER—meant to hurt anyone. She is just trying to find her way in a new environment. Maybe she jumped on the punish-the-outcast bandwagon too eagerly—and yes, I can admit Grace Claire has done that—but wasn't Grace Claire acting out of fear and peer pressure? Doesn't that prove how insecure Grace Claire really is?

"How about a few more marshmallows?" I say. "Those are good, aren't they? And what if I call Pei's mom and tell her your side of the story—not the bad parts about Pei, just how hard it is to be the new kid?"

Grace Claire sniffles, and her long hair shakes behind her with a wave. "I guess. Maybe. If you think it will keep that freak from spreading lies about me."

"She's not a freak. She's a girl, just like you. I'll call her mom. I'll see what I can do. Hey! And I have an idea: why don't you invite a few of your new friends over for a trust-building sleepover? Doesn't that sound fun?"

Grace Claire licks her lips. "That might be fun. Can we get gelato from Bulgarini's?"

"That's kind of expensive, and right now—"

"But one of my friends is lactose intolerant and they have goat's milk ice cream."

"It's nice of you to think about your friend. I guess I can probably get some."

Now, it would be easy right now to think I'm caving in to Grace Claire—who, remember, is also a victim here—but, actually, I am not all sweetness and roses. Oh, no. Grace Claire has been mean, and she needs to face some consequences. "Pretty, popular girls may feel a lot of pressure," I tell Grace Claire. "But remember that popularity comes with responsibility, especially to more awkward kids, like Pei. You have it in your power to make lives miserable or bearable. Maybe Pei will never be your friend. Maybe she is a little weird, but maybe what she needs most of all is compassion. For goodness sake, the girl is so afraid to go to school that she has diarrhea every morning. You can't want that. No one wants that. Now listen: When I was young, I was much more of a Pei than a you. I had three chins. I had a mouth full of braces. And my hair—oh my God—you don't want to know what my hair was like. Think scouring pad."

Grace Claire laughs a little and her eyes begin to shine.

"Ok. So be nice. You're a nice girl. Don't be afraid to let people see that."

Monday rolls around and, with it, William. He drops by early in the morning, before I've even taken Grace Claire to school. Get this: the dogs don't forewarn me. I just hear the doorbell. When I get downstairs the dogs are sitting at the door, waiting, calmly.

"How are you feeling?" he asks.

"Better every day."

"Good." He looks down at me, man of action, man of industry. I smile. "Ok."

"Ok."

"The leashes?"

I see Grace Claire's towel-wrapped head peek down the hall. "Right," I say. "Here you go."

Together, we attach the leashes to the dogs' collars, and then I watch William walk the dogs toward the street. I'm telling you, he's very tall. Good tall.

Grace Claire comes up behind me. "Why is Daddy's boss walking the dogs?"

"Georgie told him I had pneumonia, and I guess I'm still recovering."

"I thought you had the flu?"

"I did."

"So why'd Georgie say that?"

I take Grace Claire's pretty little hand in mine. Her nails are bright pink and have little white daisies painted on them, a remnant of the weekend's sleepover. "Always remember this," I say. "Georgie has good intentions, and

Georgie loves us, but Georgie believes that goddesses take our personal calls and IM us through flowers and trees."

Grace Claire pulls her hand out of mine. "They do."

Hmmm. I worried less when I thought she might be mean.

At work I am happy. I do not have to think about delusional daughters or mothers or missing husbands. In fact, I do not have time to think about those things because I am busy with Play Doh and picture books and Band-Aids, which is good because when I check my messages before heading home I find a message from Owen. Apparently, he is stranded in Iceland, where William has sent him on business, even though, of course, he no longer has any business because he's been fired. "I guess I won't be able to make this weekend's visitation," he says, his voice wobbly. "Tell Grace Claire I'm sorry. Tell her I mean it. God. I think I've really messed things up."

"What do you think that means?" I ask William when he calls later.

"That he's stranded in Iceland?"

"Owen's not in Iceland."

"Then I don't know, but I wouldn't over think it."

"Trust me. It's too late for that."

"Listen," he says. "I have something I want to give you. If you're feeling up for it, you can drop by the office, or I can bring it by the next time I walk the dogs, but you might want it sooner."

How can I resist? I go to his office the next day after work. No throwing up this time. No sweaty palms. I am recovered, and I don't know these security guards so I'm totally calm when I take the elevator up to William's office and I see the bitchy receptionist.

"Hello," I say sounding all professional. "I'm here for William. He's expecting me."

"Go right ahead," smiles Little Bitch. "Nice tennis shoes."

"My job changes lives," I answer. "Have a good day."

When I find William, he's talking on the phone, and he's got that man-of-industry, man-of-action vibe going. He motions me inside his office and points to a stack of postcards on his desk. I sit down and take one. They're for a designer shoe store on Robertson called Ojo.

"Ah," I mutter.

I'd forgotten all about Ojo. That's where Rosa works, as I learned during the time in which I did nothing but Google her name, which was not obsessive of me, by the way; it was merely educational. Most of what I found out about Rosa I learned on a sleazy blog devoted to ranking LA's sexiest retail clerks. "Hot Westside Retail Babes" called Rosa the "most highly sexi-licious" employee at Ojo. On a scale of one to ten, it ranked Rosa's features thus: "tits—10!!!!!; legs—9.8; ass—9.6; long-lusty black hair—9.2; throaty Venezuelan accent and pouty lips—off the charts HOTTYHOTHOT!" But, you see—and this is why the democratic nature of the Internet is so help-ful—Blogger "Big Dick Likes to Shop" warned that guys trolling for good-looking shop girls should beware Rosa's surprising martial arts skills. Luck-ily, commenter "Shock Cock," explained that there was really no reason to worry. All you had to do was bring Rosa a box of ice cream bon bons from Milk's on Beverly Boulevard and you could watch her try on high heels—as long as the owner was gone and there were no customers around. Tuesday nights were best.

You see? This is information any mother would want to know.

Yes. I remember this all now. It's sort of like how you block out how bad food poisoning feels and then you eat a bad shrimp and remember. You blocked the memory, but you didn't really forget.

William hangs up the phone and looks over at me. "Doug Lister—you might have met him the other day, he's taken Owen's position—found these in a file cabinet. I thought they might help you."

"Maybe they do." I look at the clock on William's desk and then performed the mental drive-time calculations instantaneous to southern Californians. Downtown to Robertson: Ideal conditions? Twenty-five minutes. Visit to Ojo? Thirty minutes, maybe. Robertson to Altadena: Forty-five minutes. Total time: About an hour and a half, which is doable because Grace Claire has cheerleading and gets out late today. But counting on ideal conditions in LA is like counting on the tooth fairy to pay your mortgage. So I per-form the second set of drive-time mental calculations instantaneous to southern Californians. I double all traffic times to fit real world conditions. With luck, I can do it. I stand to go.

"You're leaving?"

"I'm going to Ojo."

"Wait. Do you think you're well enough?"

"I'll manage."

"Maybe I should take you."

"Oh, William," I sigh. "You are very nice, but you don't want to do that."

"Well, no," he admits, "but I would."

Nonetheless, he doesn't. It's one thing to let a guy walk your dogs; it's an-other thing to drag him to the esteem-sucking syringe of a Westside fash-ion boutique.

In the parking lot someone chirps my name. It's Ashley, who is looking a lot more bubble gummy in a tight white tee shirt, a blue tennis skirt, and little pom pom socks. "Hi! Wow. You're back. Why is that?"

"Long story." I fish in my purse for my keys. There's my phone, there's my sunglasses, there's the pile of lose change…

"A long story involving William? Cuz I hear Owen's not even working at Global Financial anymore."

"William's been very helpful. You're lucky." I feel some more. Got them!

"Don't you forget it." She squints and then darts behind a Ford Explorer. "Hey! Hey, Penne. Is that William right now? Coming toward us?"

I look behind me. "Yeah. I think it is."

"Listen," whispers Ashley. "Do me a favor. Don't tell him I'm here. It's part of the special thing I'm working on. Ok? Ok?"

"Penne," calls William.

"I'm not here. Remember," whispers Ashley.

"I'm glad I caught you," says William as he walks toward me. "Your mom just called."

"My mother? Called you?"

"I gave her my number when you were sick. Listen, she says you really are not well enough to be driving out to the Westside."

"Ok, William, I didn't want to tell you this because, well, I don't really know you, but my mother is…dramatic. She is…larger than life, and, as a result, everything she says is dramatic and larger than life. Listening to my mother is like holding a magnifying glass up to your eye. Things look bigger than they are."

"I don't know, Penne. You do look a little pale."

I do?

"Why don't you go home and take a nap? Head out there another day."

I'm need-a-nap pale?

"Thank you, William," I say. "Maybe I will."

"Good. Let's talk tomorrow, when I come by for the dogs." He takes a few steps back.

"Ok."

"You're not pale," whispers Ashley when he's farther away. She stands up. I look over at her. The shadow of the SUV has turned her skin a bluish-gray, and her eyes…what is it about her eyes? I don't know. But all of a sudden my stomach feels a little queasy. Maybe I am still sick.

"In fact," she says. "You're very pretty. Good hair. Nice skin. You didn't use to look this good. What happened?"

"Take care, Ashley," I say, walking to my car because sharing my recent calorie-burning history of marital drama and influenza will only bring me down. "Good luck with your surprise."

"Don't you worry," she says stepping into the light. "I've got it all under control."

Maybe a smarter me would go home about now. Maybe a wiser me would worry more about a relapse than the disappearance of my soon-to-be ex-husband. But this is what I know: Grace Claire has cheerleading once a week. Thus, she comes home late from school once a week. I have done my mental drive time calculations. This is the time to go to Ojo. Right now. So I am going.

I make good time to west LA. Very good time. I make a slight detour to Milk's and pick up the ice cream bon bons Rosa likes. It slows me down a little, but I've still got a good cushion of time when I reach Robertson, which, I am sorry to see, has been invaded by those damn Venus banners. I'm really beginning to hate that museum.

I find Ojo easy enough. It's right between an uppity dress shop and a vegan restaurant, and is, as I suspected, a joyless arena of tall, skinny nightmares and ghouls. Small. Spare. White. What it lacks in actual product—it has maybe four shelves of shoes—it makes up for in cold, crisp snobbery. I only see one worker: six foot tall, cracker thin, coiffed platinum hair, six-inch heels. She stands behind a glass-topped desk near the back of the store and seems very determined not to look at me, even as I clear my throat and say, "I'm so sorry to bother you." Instead, the woman holds up a manicured index finger and types something into her phone. Finally, she looks up, at which point I give her my widest, brightest, most sincere smile, for only then do I realize that she's wearing a skin-toned eye patch over her right eye, and although part of me knows that—eye patch or no—this lady will be an evil bitch to anyone larger than a size four and not carrying a $2000 Fendi handbag, another part of me feels compelled to let the woman know that I would never hold an eye patch against someone.

It's a moment of weakness I soon regret. As always, thinness trumps. And now it trumps in the face of sucker-patsy bourgeois geniality, which is, of course, an almost deadly error to bounce back from. Honestly, I'm a little disgusted with myself. I spent countless hours of my youth hiding behind Georgie in stores like this—and not just in LA but New York, Paris, places that make royalty feel like gutter-dwelling rodents. I should have known better. I'm like a cheap-cut of beef; she's searing me with her one good eye.

Then she notices the Milk's bag in my hand and sneers, "Not another one! How many times do I have to tell you people, Rosa doesn't work here anymore—and don't even ask. I'm not trying on any shoes, you sick-o."

I take a step back. "Oh, no. I'm not one of those people."

"You can't possibly want to buy anything. I think you'll find we're beyond your price point. Try Payless."

It's times like this that I really appreciate Georgie. First of all, no one would ever say this to Georgie, but if they did, Georgie would have about twenty creative variations on the words bitch/bastard/asshole to sling at them. Me? I've got nothing. Slights from perfect strangers shut me like a Ziploc. "Oh, gosh," I finally stammer, and even as I'm talking I seem to be digging myself deeper into a pathetic state of simpering spinelessness. "Wow. Maybe we can try this again."

The woman raises a penciled-in eyebrow over her patched eye. It's possible that I've lost the ability to create spit.

"You're right. I am looking for Rosa, but it's nothing fetishistic. I just need to ask her some questions."

With a wag of a long finger the woman says, "LAPD?"

"No!" My knees lock and the spit comes rushing back. In fact, it might be darting across the room as I shout, "Why? Are the police looking for her? What did she do? Is it bad?"

"I think you should go." The woman practically floats to the door. It's like the air conditioning is slowly pushing her, which maybe really happens when you're the human equivalent of a praying mantis.

"No. Wait," I say. "I don't want to get Rosa in trouble, I just—"

The door opens—and unbelievable—who walks in? William. The man is kudzu; he's everywhere I turn, but he sure makes an impression on ol' one eye.

She drinks in his tall, lank frame and his expensive business suit and purrs, "I'll be right with you, sir."

I don't think William even sees her. He's pointing at me. "You," he says. "I thought you were going home. You look very pale."

"Why are you here?" I glance back at the one-eyed woman whose one-eye brow is almost touching her hairline.

"Your mother called me back and made me promise to do this for you. She was worried you would come out here before you were really better—and it looks like she was right."

"Ok, William. Come here." I drag him outside. "Listen. I had the flu, not pneumonia. My mother lied to you. She is still lying to you. She is lying to you because, for some reason, she has decided that you are a new player in the sparkling reality show that is her life. I am very sorry."

A man walks by with a black Standard Poodle. William follows the dog with his eyes, and then looks back at me. "Then why did you let me walk your dogs?"

Shit.

I feel my face color. "They like you."

William nods. "Ok." He points to the window, through which I see the one-eyed woman watching us, her arms crossed in front of her. "Then I guess you have this under control. I should get back to work." He looks down at the pavement. "Keep me posted. About Owen, I mean. Global Financial will want to know if everything is all right."

"You bet."

You know how sometimes you look in the refrigerator for a snack and there's nothing good so you check the freezer and you find, like, a two-year-old ice cream bar and you know it's going to be pretty blah but you hope that maybe you're wrong, and so you eat it and it's even worse than you imagined, and you're left feeling kind of disappointed and hollow and even ashamed? For some reason, that's what it's like watching William walk away. I pull on my necklace, which suddenly feels kind of tight. The pearls have gone overly warm and the sapphire pendant dark, but then I peek up at the sky. It's covered in rain clouds. Everything's darker, which says it all.

When I return to the store, the one-eyed woman won't even look at me. She just texts away on her phone.

I wander over to the shoes, which are pretty amazing looking. They're like exquisitely wrapped presents with high heels. Sort of Christian Louboutin meets Alice in Wonderland. Elegant yet whimsical and with lots of embellishments. The heels must be six inches. I think they could kill people. Still, I was not raised by my mother for nothing. In my preschool teacher duds I may not look like a fashionista, but I can talk the talk. I have American Express.

I hold up a black patent pump with a thin ankle strap. It's the most minimalistic shoe in the store. "Do you have this in a size eight?"

The woman puts down her phone. "You do realize that those shoes are handcrafted in Barcelona and cost $995."

"Really? Well then I'll try both the black and the gold."

The woman narrows her good eye and twists her mouth into a mean smile—I'm telling you, Grace Claire could never even begin to make a face this mean—and says, "Fine."

She comes back a minute later with two boxes and escorts me to a chair. "These run a little small," she says, "but let's see how we do."

I put my Milk's bag down, take off my shoes and start to squeeze my foot into the pump. Already it feels tight. "Are you sure these are eights?"

"Oh, let me help you," she says grabbing my foot and somehow squeezing it in the shoe and tightening the strap around my ankle.

"Ouch!"

"Oh, does that hurt? I'll be more careful with this one." She rams my other foot in the shoe. "Aren't they pretty?"

"I think they are a little small."

"Oh. But you liked them so much. Give them a try. Walk around. See how they feel."

She pulls me up and pushes me forward. I lurch and reach out my hands for support.

She pushes me forward again. "Some people say they take getting used to, but you're doing fabulous."

It's like my feet are being Panini-ed at a sixty-degree angle. They burn and pinch and pound. They've turned an ugly fleshy red color, except for the tops of my feet, which are blue because I think the ankle straps are cutting off my blood circulation. "Ouch," I say again, and, again she pushes me forward, hard this time, so that I fall to the floor.

In an instant, a zebra-striped stiletto is planted on my chest.

"I told you," she says standing over me, her good eye diluting. "These shoes are beyond your price point. You think I stand here all day to babysit déclassé, hausfrau, posers like you?"

"I have American Express."

"It better be fucking Platinum."

"It is." (It's not.)

"And you better be taking both pair."

"They are a little tight."

"What does beauty care about tight?"

"Nothing. I'll take them."

She lifts her foot off me and smiles. "Well then, madam," she says undoing the ankle straps and pulling the shoes off me. "Let me help you."

"And Rosa?" I say.

She looks at the Milk's bag.

"It'd be a shame for them to melt," I say.

She opens the bag and plops a bon bon in her mouth. "She took a job a few months ago at some club near Staples Center. Dashed Sails I think it's called." She stands up and brushes the hair away from her good eye. "Now please tell me you would also like some silk stockings with these."

"Absolutely," I say. I stand up and slip on my old shoes.

The woman walks over to a shelf of stockings at the back of the store.

I pull my purse up to my shoulder.

Like a top, the woman spins around. "I have my eye on you."

"Uh-huh," I say. But this is all that matters: she is wearing six-inch zebra striped heels, and I'm in Converse. I'm gone before she's halfway to the door.

Chapter Eight

Here's the thing about angry mothers: they are more dangerous than gang members. Get them mad enough, and they will spill your blood. They could be June Cleaver. They could be Carol Brady. They could be Maria Von Trapp. Doesn't matter. A pissed off mom is a whip waiting to crack. So when I pick up my messages and hear Xinran's voice, the first thing I do is count the dogs to make sure one of their heads isn't bleeding into my pillow. She says, "Why would you tell your mean daughter that Pei gets sick every morning before school? Now Pei suffers more than before. You are a very bad mother."

Despite the rising fear in my throat, I push play and listen again. And this time I feel like I'm sampling a new wine. Ah, yes, behind her robust words I sense a bouquet of murderous thoughts and arsonist impulses. Wait! Aren't there also hints of arsenic and oak? What an impressive vintage of maternal rage.

Grace Claire, who is young after all, doe not quite appreciate the complexity of what she's hearing. She just hears the word mean. "I am not mean. I didn't do anything. Why are they picking on me?"

From the living room comes the sound of growling and a crash of glass. "We're not done," I say to Grace Claire as I rush to investigate. The boys are staring at Buster, which is what we've named the Newfoundland. He's twice the size of all of them and yet he's flopped on his back as if to say, "I am a mere puppy of a dog. You can't possibly be worried about me." Next to Buster lies a shattered vase, and behind the shattered vase stands Pablo. He's got his teeth out. It's a warning: You next Newfoundland. "Go!" I say. "Out!" The dogs line up behind Pablo and slink away.

It's a very nice vase that the dogs have shattered. Waterford. Owen gave it to me on our first anniversary. You'd think I'd feel sentimental about the vase. I should feel sentimental about the vase. So why is it that all I can do is feel grateful for a diversion, a minute to think about what Xinran said?

Grace Claire is lying. I think. She is lying and being mean. Maybe. My daughter! Mine! Me of read-all-the-parenting-books! I've spent the last thirteen years telling Grace Claire to be nice, to be kind, to think of others before herself and to make good choices. I've spent the last thirteen years teaching her to be fricking me but without a crappy mother, and now I think, it's possible, that's she's turned into one of those reality show devil girls. But…but…but…what if she's not? What if she's just afraid and inse- cure and scarred by Owen's leaving? What if this Pei character is a dement- ed lying little witch? What if Grace Claire only accidentally told people that Pei has diarrhea every morning, because that could happen, right?

All this, right now, is exactly why I teach toddlers. With toddlers, the an- swers are easy. If a three year old starts to eat dirt, you stop him. If two three year olds fight over a tricycle, you find another tricycle. Once they're older, the answers to all the parenting questions seem so fraught. Grace Claire comes home with a D in math. Do I ground her or hire a tutor? Grace Claire forgets her homework. Do I drop it off at school so she'll get a decent grade or do I not drop it off and let her live with the consequences, even if the consequences mean letting her get cut from cheerleading—which she loves and which makes her happy—or denied access to the college of her choice? You see, no easy answers. Now there are only imperfect answers, which is why it is only possible to be an imperfect mother, although some mothers are more imperfect than others.

"Hello, dear," says Georgie, who calls at this perfect moment to tell me that she's just spoken with William. She says, "How can I play Cupid to your Venus if you send this fellow William packing every time I ask him to try and help you."

"I knew you were trying to set us up."

"Of course, darling. Tamara told me how he showed up right after your reading, and then when he called, well, I'd have to have been fucking brain dead not to put two and two together."

"There are no two and two to put together. He has a girlfriend. I'm not even divorced."

"Yet."

"Yet."

"I just want you to be happy. I'm only helping Venus along."

"That's exactly—shit. Mom I've got to go," I say hanging up and staring down at my shoe, which has just landed on an arrowhead shaped piece of glass from that fucking vase. "Shit. Oh my God." One more millimeter and I'd be calling 911 right now. "Shit. Shit. Shit."

"We don't talk like that in our family." Grace Claire is slumped against the doorframe.

Maybe it's the mocking singsong of her voice. Maybe it's the smirk that she just can't swallow. Whatever it is whacks me hard against the head and makes every little jigsaw puzzle piece come together. Xinran. Pei. Grace Claire's Moses-like ability to divide seas of people whenever she and her friends walk down a hall. Eight years of reports cards saying "Citizenship needs improvement." Flog a fucking duck. Xinran is right. My daughter is the nightmare of every social misfit at Charlotte Perkins Gilman Middle School. She is mean and sneaky and—worst of all—she is proud of it.

"You!" I say. "You are in big trouble. You may think I am stupid, but I know what I know, and I know mean. You told people about Pei on purpose. You did it to puff yourself up and make yourself look special. You did it because you're pretty and popular and because you could and because you weren't thinking about anybody but yourself."

Grace Claire looks at me like she is trying hard not to laugh, but then something happens, something changes, and Grace Claire takes a step back. She opens her mouth to speak, but instead of saying anything she starts to shrink. Her head falls into her chest, her arms wrap around her torso, her knees buckle and her feet turn inward. It's like she's a rejected orange or tangerine, all dried up, all skin and pores. The dogs are behind her, crouched low, eyes on the floor. And I am suddenly Joan Crawford—who my mother actually knew and who apparently really did have the maternal warmth of a glacier. I am towering over my thirteen-year-old mean daughter, barking. "I didn't devote myself to your upbringing so that you could become a plotting Pomeranian. I didn't spend the last thirteen years cooking your meals and wiping your tears so that you could treat people like crappy little Happy Meal toys.

"Do you know what it's like to suffer at the hands of someone like you? Do you? Do you know what it's like to eat every lunch by yourself because no one will talk to you, or to walk by a room and hear people laughing at you, or to never be invited to play dates or sleepovers or birthday parties? It hurts, Grace Claire. You feel like the world is a dangerous place, an unpredictable and scary place, where, no matter what you do, no matter how hard you try, you're at the mercy of the devil. The devil decides if you thrive, if you suffer, or if you just get to lie low and be ignored.

"And you know who you are right now, Grace Claire? You're the devil. *You* are the devil. Satan. Lord of hell. See? That's name calling. It doesn't feel very good, does it?"

Grace Claire unfolds herself. She straightens her back and juts out her chin. "It sounds better than 'fat.'"

"Oh, my God. Oh, my effing Lord. You are so fucking mean. You are the queen of fucking mean. You must be the meanest girl I've ever fucking met. You little bitch."

There are times, as a mother, when your heart and mind are in total sync and you know, you know down to your very toes, that you are a bad parent, that, really, there should have been a test for prospective parents so that you could have failed it and known how completely unsuited you were for parenthood. This is one of those times.

It turns out that there's really no place left to go when you have called your own child a bitch. You've pretty much closed the conversation. You've pretty much closed every conversation. You're pretty much as estranged as you can be without actually kicking someone out of your house or getting a restraining order, which is why Grace Claire has gone to Georgie's for a few—four—days, or maybe a week. We're calling it a "cooling off" period. Actually, the therapist is calling it a "cooling off" period. I am calling it Grandparent's week, at least that's what I'm telling the school, which doesn't seem to find that a compelling excuse and is now asking me to pony up the almost $50 a day the school would get from the state if Grace Claire were actually there.

Let's not get bogged down in that. Let's focus on the point. This is what I tell Nancy at work. "Let's focus on the point, and the point is this: I am fortunate. Grace Claire could have run away. She could have tried to drown her humiliation in Benadryl or wine—some thirteen year olds do that. She did not. She just refused to talk to me for two days, and when I proposed the therapist's 'cooling off' idea she went and packed her suitcase and allowed me to drop her off at Georgie's. And I'm lucky I have Georgie, right? I mean, Georgie is unreliable and unpredictable, but she's not evil. She'll rise to the occasion. She loves Grace Claire. And she's feeling very maternal right now. She's thinking about installing solar panels. They'll bond, and that's good. Every girl wants to be close to her grandmother. So, you see, it really could not have worked out any better."

"And this is all because you called Grace Claire a bitch?"

"Yes."

"But wasn't she being a bitch?"

"Who's to say? Probably. Yes. But I'm the grown up. I should not have lost my temper."

"Everyone loses their temper sometimes."

"I'm the mom. I'm the nurturer. I'm the safe harbor in the storm. I'm not supposed to be the judger."

"It seems to me that if you can't be the judger, then you're less a safe harbor in a storm and more a safe harbor where pirates get to hang out, in which case you're letting Grace Claire turn into Long John Silver."

Shit. "You think?"

She puts her arm around my shoulder. "Of course, that's not to say that a cooling off period is bad."

"Oh no," I answer. "It's not bad. It's great. It's fantastic. I have lots of me time, which is awesome. I'm reading Dickens. *A Tale of Two*—ouch!" Perfect. Now I've been beaned by a sippy cup. It's like I'm suddenly at war with common household vessels.

"Mallory!" I say crossing the room to a toddler who clearly dislikes her snack. "Cups aren't for throwing. I feel sad when I see you throwing cups."

"You know," says Nancy later. "Since you have so much 'me' time, why don't you come out with the rest of us tonight. We're doing Happy Hour. It'll be fun."

"Oh. Gee. That does sound fun, but tonight's no good. A new dog showed up, a Chihuahua. I found him in the backyard with the other dogs yesterday. He'll be counting on me, he and the boys and Lucy." I pull my purse up to my shoulder and back out the door. "Thanks though. Maybe another time."

Chapter Nine

Me time.

Free time.

Free me from my me time.

Oh, my God. I've never been so bored in my life. I hate me time. I hate it when Owen's visitations force it upon me, and I hate it more when my daughter who won't speak to me forces it upon me. And you know what I really hate? Dickens. I mean, have you read Dickens? How many words can one man put in a book?

You know what I've spent the last three nights doing? Cleaning grout. Why? Because there's nothing else to do. If I have to clean one more inch of grout I'm going to bang my forehead against the tile until I pass out.

At least that's what I think I'll do until I find myself driving down to Target to get a new grout brush. I walk into the store, and who do I see? Xinran and Pei. There they are, all cozy and functional-family looking, drinking tea at the Starbucks. Pei has her hand on her mother's thigh and she is laughing as Xinran reads aloud from some magazine. Gag me already. That's all I need. I turn round and head back to the car. There's another Target in Alhambra. I'll get my grout brush there. They probably have better grout brushes anyway. I hope they don't have a stinking Starbucks. Stupid Starbucks. It may seem like parents and children can sit there and bond and talk and laugh, but, really, it's just a place that tries to hook you on caffeine. There's nothing good about that. Nothing good at all. Really, a good mom would know better than to take to her socially awkward child to such a hang out. If you think about it, it's almost cruel.

Shit. Where is that Alhambra Target?

Double, double piss, shit. I don't even think I'm in Alhambra. Where the hell am I?

If I had an iPhone or a Blackberry or some other smart phone or even a car with a built-in GPS system, I would not be freaking out. I would be pushing an elegantly designed little button, and I would be saying something like, "Ah! I'm heading east when I need to go west. Silly me." Or, "Duarte? No problem, I'll just listen to this little talking robot voice and it will lead me straight home." But I do not have those technologies. I do not have them because, once upon a time, I was assured by my devoted husband that I did not need anything so *complicated*, that devices with so many *options* would just rattle my so easily distracted brain.

Well. Let me tell you this, my *Devoted Husband*, my fricking, distracted brain would sure appreciate a smart robot voice telling me what the fuck to do.

Damn. Shit is that the 710?

Where the hell does the 710 go? Isn't that the freeway that has all those truck accidents? Well, I'm not getting on there. That's road a deathtrap.

Wait. Is that the 10? I can work with that. The 10 intersects the 110. That I know, and the 110 East ends up in Pasadena, and if I can find my way back to Pasadena then, for sure, I can get back to Altadena. Right?

Right. So that's what I'll do. I'll the take the 10 to the 110.

Right.

Ok.

I'm feeling a little better now.

Shit. How the fuck did I get on the 101? Damn. Damn. Damn. Damn. Damn. Damn.

Well, I'm not going back to goddamn Hollywood.

I take the first exit—Vermont—and turn…shit: who the hell knows what direction I turn? I go toward the skyscrapers in downtown LA because if I can get to the skyscrapers I can get to the 110 East, and that will take me home. I think.

Miracle of miracles: I find my way over to Staples Center and hook a left onto Figueroa, which makes my tightly squeezed gut very happy because—hooray—Figueroa dead ends into the 110.

Something about half a block up on Olympic catches my eye: It's a flashing green and pink neon sign. It's shaped like a sailboat, and running down the mast—in yellow neon—are the words: "Dashed Sails." Dashed Sails! It's the club the one-eyed woman mentioned, the club where Rosa works.

Well, if this doesn't feel a little bit like destiny I don't know what does. I pull into a parking lot and head over to the entrance when—wham, smash, crash—a Mini Cooper bashes into the back of a PT Cruiser, which lurches forward into the back of a Lexus. The drivers get out and shake their heads.

They circle round the cars, their faces lined with confusion. "I don't know what happened," says the dazed driver of the Mini Cooper. "I'm such a good driver." Then he shrugs at the other drivers. "Oh well, how about I buy you guys a drink and we sort this all out?" The other drivers sort of nod and they all head over to the club.

Hmmmm.

I cross over myself and end up at the back of a long line of club goers waiting to get in. They're a respectable bunch. The men wear suits; the women wear high heels. Most of them look like they've come here straight from the office buildings downtown. They all look very polished. Actually, I've never been much of a clubber, so I might be wrong here, but it seems to me that this group looks a little too polished. Business suits? Really? And it's not even nine o'clock at night. Who parties this early?

Also, no one is really talking. People are standing quietly in line, like they're waiting to check out library books. They are doing something, though. They are listening. They are listening to speakers set up along the perimeter of the club. From the speakers, comes the voice of a growly jazz singer singing a sad song about lost love and a broken heart. Swear to God: the guy in front of me is crying into his Brooks Brothers tie. He's all very discreet about it, but I see tears.

By the time it's my turn to enter, the music has stopped, and the crowd outside the door has grown. The bouncer takes one look at my sweats and tennis shoes and shakes his head. "Sorry," he says. "We have a strict dress code."

"Please," I say. "I'm just looking for someone who works here. Rosa Luna. Do you know her?"

"If I let in every loser who knows Rosa, I'd be out of a job."

"It's really important, and I'll only be a minute."

From inside the dark entranceway, a voice hollers, "Hey! Hey! She's ok! She's with us."

The bouncer leans in. He mumbles, "She's wearing sweats."

A full-length, sky blue satin evening coat sails across the threshold. The bouncer reaches up and catches it. Handing it to me, he says, "Welcome to Dashed Sails."

The coat is a little tight, and a little short, but it camouflages me well enough, especially since the inside of Dashed Sails is pretty dark. Still, it's not so dark that I can't make out my fairy godmothers, both of them, sitting at the bar in pastel-colored chiffon dresses, drinking Kir Royales, and, in fact, holding one out to me.

"What a surprise!" says Bast.

"We didn't expect to see you here," says Uzume.

"I wasn't planning on coming. What are you doing here? Would Tamara approve? I see a lot of electronica."

"It's just the tent that has to be electronica-free. But it's nice of you to ask," says Uzume. She hands me a Kir Royale.

I look around the room. It's not a big space. A bar in the back, a small dance floor surrounded by maybe a dozen tables and a stage, empty but for a wooden swing suspended from the ceiling by sturdy metal cords. It hangs about three feet from the ground and is painted gold.

"It's Bast who brought us here," Uzume adds. She leans into Bast. "You know her, she's the playful one."

"You guys love it," laughs Bast.

"Well, that's true," replies Uzume.

"This is our first time here, though. Pretty cool, huh?"

"It is pretty cool," I say. "But it's kind of different, too. Isn't it? I mean, some of the people seem kind of different."

"Hmmm," says Uzume. "I don't know. Everybody looks like they want to have a good time."

"Penne!" I turn to see Freyja waving and walking toward me. She's wearing a yellow chiffon dress and is being followed by two short men.

"Oh, no," whispers Uzume. "Again?"

"What?" I say.

"Freyja—the actual goddess—once slept with four dwarves in order to get this golden necklace that she totally lusted after, and now, wherever we go, short guys try and pick up our Freyja."

"Ten bucks says they gave her their watches," says Bast.

Sure enough, Freyja steps up to the bar with two metal-banded watches dangling from her small wrist. The two men stand behind her, smiling dumbly.

"Thanks guys," says Freyja.

They nod.

"We can dance later."

They nod some more and then, after a sort of dazed look at one another, shuffle away.

"Penne," Freyja says. "How awesome that you're here. You have to sit with us. You have to."

She grabs my hand and pulls me across the dance floor to a dark table near the stage. Uzume and Bast follow suit, and soon we're all sitting with our Kir Royales. The band takes their place on the stage. The singer, a doughy guy whose bad boy air stirs up the suspicious-mom in me, starts singing about cruel, cruel love. His eyes brood and then, in a flash, they seem sarcastic and mean. My companions look enraptured. Me? If I want to get pissed on I'll stand too close to my dogs.

"Where's your necklace?" Uzume asks. She's giving the singer a moody look and fingering her goddess necklace. It's similar to mine, but with jade beads, instead of pearls, and a small moss-colored pendant affixed to the middle. Bast has one too, but with yellow beads and an onyx pendant.

I pull down the collar of the coat and show them my necklace. Like I said, I kind of like it now.

"And how's your goddess?" she asks.

"To be honest, I haven't really been thinking about goddesses. I have a lot of family things going on."

"Oh, but your goddess can help you with that," says Bast. "Just look at Uzume here. She used to be totally depressed. She would only wear black and read, like, dead Russian guys."

Uzume puts her hand on mine, "No. Also astrophysics."

"Astrophysics?" I say.

"Sure. That's what we study at Cal Tech."

My jaw drops. "You're Cal Tech students?"

"That's how we met," says Freyja.

"Then why do you work at The Goddess Lounge?"

"One, we need money. I mean who doesn't?" says Bast.

"Two, it's totally fun. We love The Goddess Lounge," says Freyja.

"Gods and goddesses made the constellations," says Uzume. "It was how they made sure that heroes would always be remembered. So it's also sort of related to our profession."

"You're telling me that three young, intelligent Cal Tech astrophysicists actually believe in goddesses?" I say.

"Why not?" says Bast. "The goddesses change lives. Like I said, Uzume used to be all depressed. She was always crying because of the destruction of the rain forest and for dying pandas and stuff."

"There are not a lot of pandas left in the wild."

"I know, Uzume. We all know, but you were, like, stuck there. You were caught in this sad, sad groove. You could only see the bad and never the good."

"So what happened?" I ask.

"I got Uzume," says Uzume.

"What does that mean?"

"Uzume is the Shinto goddess of laughter," says Bast. "One time, this storm god guy pissed off the sun. The sun got so mad that she hid in a cave and plunged the world into darkness."

"It was really bad," says Uzume, "because all the chaos gods totally took over and the world was a mess."

"So Uzume started dancing in front of the sun goddess's cave. She was all, 'Cry if you want, but there's joy in this world if you only look.' Uzume got so carried away with her dancing that she threw off her clothes, and the other gods just started laughing, but not in a mean way, more in a check out Uzume, she is so awesome way. The sun goddess heard all this laughter and she got so curious that she finally looked out the cave and even she had to laugh, and when she laughed light returned to the world."

"Get it?" asks Uzume. "When I handed myself over to Uzume, I handed myself over to joy. I realized that I didn't always have to look at the bad side of things. I could see the good things too."

"She's way more relaxed now," adds Bast.

I take another sip of my Kir Royale. Then, with appalling tactlessness that I can only blame on three nights devoted to cleaning grout, I blurt out, "No offense, but couldn't you have just learned that from Oprah?"

Uzume and Bast burst into laughter. "Oh, Penne," says Bast.

"You are so funny, and believe me I know funny," says Uzume. "You must get that from your mom."

"No. Really. I've seen a lot of Oprah. I read her magazine. I think that's the basic Oprah message."

Freyja returns with a tray full of drinks and Bast regales her by recounting our discussion. "Oh Penne," says Freyja, "Oprah would never dance naked in front of a cave."

The band takes a break and I see my chance. "Excuse me for a minute," I say before getting up and following the band members through a black curtain near the bar. "Hey!" I holler as the singer opens a door marked "Performers Only." "You guys got a minute?"

The singer turns to me. "Finally!" he says walking toward me, an exasperated sigh escaping his wide lips. "You were supposed to be here over an hour ago. We can't cover for you all night. Get inside."

I follow them into a small dressing room with a big mirror and bright fluorescent lights. The musicians sit on a pink vinyl couch in the back of the room. One of them pulls a Sudoku book out of his jacket and starts working on a puzzle. The other two lean back and close their eyes. The singer has lost his bad boy attitude and is now all very Ricky Gervais. His plump lips have become dental floss, his eyebrows little accent marks. He walks over to a locker and pulls out a very short, very transparent, white dress. It is quite possibly made out of wet rice noodles. "Here's your dress," he says. "You can change back there. We won't look."

"Oh, I'm not a performer."

"You're not the trapeze artist?" He looks at the men on the couch. "She says she's not the trapeze artist." His hands crossed across his belly, he says to me, "Where the hell is the trapeze artist then?"

"I don't know. I'm looking for Rosa Luna. Is she here tonight?"

He looks back again at his musicians, who don't even react. Then he looks back at me. "Is Rosa here? No. No. She quit three weeks ago, didn't she? That's why the agency has been sending us trapeze artists to fill in until we cast another one.

"You look flexible. Here's your big chance. Put on the dress. It's not that hard. You just twirl around on the swing. Every once in a while, make sure the audience can see your underwear; they like that."

Now, the fact is, I actually have experience on the trapeze. I spent six weeks at Circus Camp. I was ten, very round, very un-athletic, and very prone to sweating. Georgie thought it would help me discover the "fun" in exercise. It did not. Having failed at the trapeze, acrobatics, unicycle riding, cross-country clowning and pie throwing, I spent the end-of-camp "performance" dressed as a bear and sitting in a cage. So I know what I'm talking about when I say, "Really, I think you'd all be disappointed."

"People will be disappointed if you're not a trapeze artist. They're expecting a trapeze artist. Come on. Help us out here. We'll pay you two hundred. That's more than we were going to pay the temp."

"I don't see it happening."

"Come on. It'll be fun."

"Look. I came here to talk to Rosa. If she's not here, I think I should be going."

The singer circles round me while the musicians remain entirely unengaged, although they might secretly be with me on this one. Maybe it's my fat ankles. "Rosa. What a weasel. What do you want her for anyway?"

"Actually, I'm looking for my husband—or my almost-ex-husband. He lives with Rosa and he's sort of fallen off the map. I thought he might be with her."

"Blond guy? Tonka Truck body?"

"You know him?"

He motions to the musicians. "She wants to know if we know him. Oswald, Owego, Orlando. Something like that."

"Owen."

"Owen. Of course we know Owen," he sniggers and wiggles a little breakfast link finger at me. "We know all about Owen. In fact, we know exactly where he is…on the map."

"Where?"

Again he looks over at the musicians. All three of them look asleep; one has his Sudoku book folded open on his face. "Well, boys," he says, "you thinking what I'm thinking? Thought so. Tell you what, Miss Won't-be-an-acrobat. Seems like we both have something to bargain with."

I look at the singer. I look at the dress he's dangling in front of me. "Sorry, guys. Owen will just have to stay off the map for a little longer."

"Don't be like that. Come on. Let's make a deal."

"You come on. Be a nice guy. What does it cost you to just tell me where he is? Do the right thing. It will make you feel good."

Apparently, some people are saturated with a bottom line mentality. Sad really.

"Here," I say, handing Uzume the blue silk coat.

"What? Are you going? You just got here."

"Yeah, well, I'm crazy busy these days. It's just by accident that I came here anyway."

"Too bad," says Bast.

"It is too bad," says Freyja. "And several of my new friends had wanted to dance with you. They said so."

"Yeah," says Uzume. "Well, Penne does light up the room. I guess our table will be less 'popular' now. It will just seem a little dimmer."

Bast and Freyja nod.

Hmmm. I think I love these girls. They're big liars, but I love them.

Message from Georgie when I get home: "Just checking in. Grace Claire is fantastic. My agent put her up for a Disney Channel show and she got the part! Now, I know you've never wanted that for Grace Claire. I know you think celebrity kids are psychotic, and I know you'll never forgive me for sending you to summer camp with that horrible *Beverly Hills 90210* girl, who wasn't even famous then so I don't know why you always bring that up, but—listen—Grace Claire is really excited about this. This might be just the thing to turn you into a nice mom again. I'll messenger over the paperwork when it's ready. And don't worry about school. She's got one of the studio teachers working with her. Isn't that great! And you don't need to thank me, but you should thank Ishtar. I really feel her moving in me right now."

Hmmm. The grocery store should still be open. I wonder if it sells grout brushes. Best go check.

Good news. It's taken me five days, but I've finished the grout. I've moved on to caulking.

Chapter Ten

It turns out that caulking should be left to professionals, like the one currently re-caulking my ruined shower. But you know what is really relaxing? Baking. Baking is the best, especially when you know that it is appreciated, which is why I am now perfecting my recipe for dog biscuits!

The dogs love them. They can't get enough of them. And unlike certain daughters, they really seem to understand that baking is something you do out of love. It's something you do to show love.

I'm pushing the dough through little bone shaped cookie cutters when guess what? Owen calls. I think. It's hard to tell because of the death-like rattle in his voice and the moans that escape at the end of each breath.

"Penne. I think I really messed up." He starts sobbing. Hacking, spastic wails erupt from my phone.

I sit down. "Owen, where are you? Are you ok?"

"Listen, I need you to do something for me. Can you do something for me?"

"Owen, where are you?"

"I need you to withdraw $10,000 from the Fidelity Account. It's important, Penne. You need to trust me."

"Owen, what's going on? Are you in trouble? Is it the pansy eaters? Are you doing drugs?"

"Shit. I've gotta go. Just get me the money. Lives depend on it. Ok? I'll call in a few days."

He does not call in a few days. The weekend passes. He does not call. Monday, I call William. He hasn't heard a word from Owen. No one at the office has. I gather every last ounce of gumption and head back to the loft. This time it's empty. The furniture has been gutted. Upholstery stuffing is everywhere. Tables are overturned. Plants knocked over. Dirt scattered all around. Colored pansy petals lie faded, wilted, on the floor.

What choice do I have? I return to Dashed Sails, the one place where someone seems to know something about Owen. But the people there are as close-mouthed as before, and—to my own disbelief—I soon find myself dressed like an opalescent Japanese noodle, pumping my arms and legs on a not-very-regulation-looking-acrobatic bar. It's more a swing, actually, which is good because I can sit on it and not dangle there in a pathetic display of upper-arm weakness. In all honesty, I kind of like swinging. I often swing with my preschoolers. We see how high we can go, how far we can lean back, how curved we can make our spines, and that's pretty much what I do now. The only difference is that the swing is pretty high, (I had to climb on the piano to reach it), and people can look up my dress, but even that's not too different. I once taught a girl named Ruby. She used to invite all the boys to lie on the ground and try and catch a peek at her Wiggles panties as she swung forward and backward. So I guess the lesson here is that if you give adults enough alcohol they will devolve into four year olds and even find matronly women in see-through dresses and white bras and undies an awe-inspiring sight of delicious decadence. It's ridiculous: people gasp when my skirt hikes up to my panty line. They audibly sigh when I over extend my back to reveal the nether regions of my cleavage. I can only believe that they are lit up like Christmas trees or they have grown up in pop-culture-scorning-right-of-Mormon cults.

The only problem—besides the obvious one that I'm trading glimpses of cleavage for information about Owen—is that Ellard, that's the singer, turns out to be a much bigger dillweed than I'd imagined. He owns this place, and everyone is beholden to him one way or another. The bartender, the servers, the janitors and the band members won't talk to me. I ask them if they know anything about Rosa or if they've ever seen Owen and they just shake their heads and point at Ellard, and he's just teasing me along like a fish. He not so much as gives me details as sprinkles them at the top of my bowl.

Night one he tells me, "Rosa left Owen weeks ago, and your Mr. Lovesick Puppy is a mess. He's gone completely to seed. A couple weeks back, he came in looking like he hadn't shaved in days, like he'd been sleeping in his clothes."

"But did he seem like he might be in trouble or some sort of danger?"

"You got to earn it, peach."

"Oh, come on. I did what you asked."

He surveys his club. He surveys his workers. He surveys me. "Do you like it when I sing, Penne?"

I shrug. The truth is, the guy is amazing. When he sings, he's all danger and seduction, a mind-bending mix of chocolate and chipotle chilies. People get dizzy just listening to him. They can barely keep from spilling their drinks. In fact, they can't stop from spilling their drinks. Every few minutes there's a clatter and clash and a server soaking up martinis. Not that anyone seems to notice. Their eyes are fixed on Ellard. His voice hypnotizes them, even outside. Even the people listening to piped-out music lose themselves, give themselves, to Ellard. I swear, I think even the cars, boxes of metal, grease, and plastic that they are, give themselves to Ellard.

"Um-hum," he says. "I'll see you tomorrow."

Tomorrow comes. My preschoolers squeal and cry and rule their little worlds, oblivious to everything but their own cravings. A messenger brings me an inch-high stack of papers and asks me to sign my daughter over to the Disney Channel, which I fricking do. God forgive me. Nighttime roles around, and I'm up on the swing. Tired, but strangely free, soaring in rhythm to Ellard's gravelly, beautiful voice.

"Did you like my singing tonight," he asks me.

"I've heard worse."

A mean little smile lifts one corner of his mouth. "Rosa moved north with her new beau, Mr. Rich Rancher Pants. That's why she quit her job here," says Ellard. "Pisses me off. She was nothing before me. Nothing. Lucky for you, though."

"I'm not so much interested in Rosa as Owen."

"Same thing," he says. "Owen paid me $500 for her new address."

"You think he went after her? But that doesn't explain why—"

"Why what?"

Well, I'm not telling Ellard anything. I'm the one earning the information. "Nothing. What's the address?"

He waits a long moment. "That's all you're getting tonight, plum."

"You're killing me. Owen could be dead. Don't you even care?"

He puts an arm on my shoulder. "No. I don't care. Neither should you. He's a douche."

"He's…messed up, and he's…." I don't even finish. I don't know what he is. I don't know why I'm doing this, why I care. I don't know why my daughter is mean, and why my mother is driving me crazy, and why I'm wearing this goddess necklace, or why my life has fallen to ruins in the span of heartbeat. I don't know anything anymore. I'm running on fumes.

Another tomorrow comes. More preschoolers squeal and cry and rule their little worlds. My daughter does not take my calls. "It's not you," says my mother, "it's just that she's getting a Brazilian Blow Out and meeting with a personal trainer."

Night four I show up and tell Ellard that this is it. Tonight he gives me everything he knows or else. Or else what? I have no idea! I have no cards to play! All I know is that my daughter is now co-starring in a show about a teenage medium/pop star/crime fighter. My husband has gone down a road I can't even imagine. My life is quickly devolving into some horrible Lifetime movie, and all I can do is balance on a fricking swing for a bunch of fricking drunks. And I am so tired. I've barely slept in days. All I want is to sleep and to wake up and find my people in their proper beds.

But then I'm up on that swing, and Ellard is singing, and I'm thinking, this isn't so bad. This swing. This music. It sort of sucks you in. It sort of takes over and everything else sort of fades into the background. It makes you feel so light. I swing higher than ever before. My naked toes feel the heat of the klieg lights whenever I swing past. When I lean back, I start letting go with one hand and letting my fingers drift over Ellard's head. I manage to pull myself up to standing and go for a Degas-ballerina look. I fold over leaving a wake in my cleavage that makes a man in front of me perspire. I do a few Arabesques and then point my toes and stretch one leg behind me so that the man in front can look straight up my dress at my incredibly unsexy Hanes underwear. What do I care? I don't know him. He's nothing to me. He's just more background. I sit back on the swing and lean all the way back, elongating my neck so that it continues the arch of my spine.

And then the background zooms to the front. I see William. He's sitting in the middle of the room. His jaw is practically on his chest and his eyes have gone a disbelieving—yet mischievous—shade of gray. I pull myself up, but I pull too hard, too fast, and I somersault off the swing and land straight on Ellard who collapses to the ground. The band stops. The audience gasps, and about a hundred glasses seems to fall to the ground all at once.

William is there, pulling me off Ellard. He leads me to a table. "Are you ok?" My eyes stay on Ellard. The band members have helped him up. He is opening and closing his mouth, his eyes are wide, and he's fingering a lime-size bump on the side of his head. He mumbles something and the band members walk him to the dressing room.

"I didn't expect to see you," I say pulling down on my dress and trying to ignore the gawking faces staring at us.

He narrows his eyes, and as he does so soft lines etch into his forehead. He takes off his jacket and rests it on my shoulders. I lean into the dark material and let it cover me up. It smells a little like Kit Kats. He brings his face close to mine. "What are you doing here, Penne?"

"It's complicated."

"You know, you're all over YouTube."

"What?"

He pulls out his phone, hits a few buttons, and there I am, in all my rice-noodle-dress glory, swinging on the trapeze, for the entire world to see. How can I not have foreseen this? People post videos of their cats playing with dust bunnies on YouTube. Why wouldn't someone post something as ridiculous as a grown woman in what could double as a baby-doll nighty wobbling around on a swing? I'm the freak show. That's why I'm here.

"I've gotta go," I say handing William back his jacket and making my way to the dressing room.

Ellard's there. He's sitting on the couch while the piano player presses an ice pack to his head.

"Good work," Ellard says. "I can't sing now. Not tonight, at least. You've humiliated me. You've ruined everything. I'm not telling you anything now."

"What?"

"You were supposed to earn it, pineapple. That was the deal. And don't think you can come back tomorrow. You're hazardous, that's what you are."

I shake my head. "No. No. You said—"

"Doesn't matter. Go. Get out of here."

I look at the band members. They're looking down at the floor. The drummer's picking at some fuzz on his wool blazer. I slide past him into a little closet that doubles as a dressing room and start to change. I picture William. I picture the YouTube video, and the swing and the man in the front, and the gawking stares, and the stack of papers selling Grace Claire's soul, and my dogs barking at doorbells, and Owen, dead, beaten, drowned. And I'm tired. I'm so tired. And Ellard promised. And it wasn't my fault. No. It wasn't my fault. I tried. I did what I was told to do.

I walk out of the dressing room. "I did what I was supposed to do." I'm barely whispering.

"Get out."

My eyes stare down at Ellard's feet. "No. I did what I was supposed to do. You said. You promised. I need that address. You promised."

The drummer says, "Come on, Ellard, just give her the address."

"No. Get her out of here."

The bassist steps forward. I step back. "No." My voice rises. "You promised. Give me the address."

The drummer says, "Shit, it's no big deal. Just give it to her."

"She ruined my show."

"It was the last number. They'll be back tomorrow. You know they will. They love you."

Ellard sits back. He purses his mean white lips. "Do you like my singing, Penne?"

"I love your singing Ellard. You're the best."

"You mean that, don't you?"

"Absolutely."

He stands looking at me, waiting.

"You are so wonderful, Ellard. It's amazing. There is no one like you, and it's shocking to me that you aren't on television all the time or that more people haven't heard about you, although I'm sure one day they will. One day, this place won't be big enough to hold all your fans. Then, I'll tell everyone that I knew you, that I knew you at the beginning. That I always knew what a big star you'd become."

He looks me up and down. "You weren't horrible up there, Penne." He pulls a card out of his pocket. "Here you go."

"Thank you."

"Good luck finding your husband. He's an asshole. You know that."

"Yeah," I say. "I know."

William is waiting for me outside.

"I don't know what to tell you," I say. "I'm just…I'm still trying to find Owen, ok? The guys here said they could give me some information. We made a trade."

"Wait. You traded *that*—he points to the swing—for information about Owen? That seems…crazy."

My arms flap up and down. I don't even think I consciously make them do it. They just flap, willfully and without permission. "I know. I know. It's crazy, and I'm so tired. I've barely slept in days, and my daughter won't talk to me, and I don't know what I think I'm doing. I just…I want everyone to be happy. I want everyone to be where they are supposed to be. I want them to do what they are supposed to do. Is that asking too much?"

William scans my face with his eyes and then brushes what looks like glitter from my coat, and I can tell that I have yet again revealed too much drama. So I'm a little surprised when William, his voice kind but barely above a whisper, says, "And where exactly is Owen supposed to be?"

Where is he supposed to be? His loft? Our house? I don't know. I really don't know. I shrug, and for lack of anything else to say I ask him how he knew I was on YouTube.

He says, "Our receptionist stumbled across it. She showed me."

I nod. "She's kind of a bitch, you know."

He smiles a little. "No. I don't see that."

I shrug again.

"Can I ask you a favor?" he says, still smiling. "Can you drive me home? Someone smashed into my car when I was parking."

How can I refuse? He directs me toward Montrose. He asks about Grace Claire. I ask about Ashley. We both fall silent. I'm tired and embarrassed, and for reasons I can't explain, it hurts me that William of all people saw me looking so stupid on that swing. Still, as we make our way up the surface streets toward the foothills of the city, my foot starts to lighten up on the gas pedal. And as I pull onto his street an achy knot starts to tighten in my stomach, and when I stop the car in front of his house, a numbing melancholy wraps itself around me.

"Thanks for the ride," he says.

"No problem."

"Penne, I didn't mean to embarrass you back there, and you have every right to do whatever you want to find Owen, if that's important to you."

"It's ok."

"No. It's not. It's just…it surprised me. You surprised me. You're very… determined."

Oh, God. That's just what every woman wants to hear. I look down at my lap.

"So what are you going to do? About Owen, I mean."

"I guess I'm going to find him. I guess I have to."

"Did you find the information you needed?"

I pull the card Ellard gave me from my coat pocket. "Maybe. I might look in Los Olivos. Rosa moved there. Ellard thinks he followed her."

"That's up north of Santa Barbara. Wine country."

"I know where it is. Doesn't seem very Rosa though. I see her as more high-end urban."

"There are some pretty nice spots up there. You'd be surprised."

"I guess."

"Well, good luck." He gets out of the car. He's closing the door when, all of the sudden, he pulls it wide again and looks over at me. "You were good up there, Penne. On the swing. You looked very…free."

I feel my face begin to flush. "You're a bad liar, William, but you're a nice guy."

His eyes light up with an unfamiliar twinkle. "Not always," he says. "But enough of the time to count."

With that, he's gone. As I watch him walk away, my hand slides up to my necklace, and my fingertips linger over the pearls. His front door opens, and from the streetlamp I can see two good-sized pit bulls jump up on him. In one swift movement, he moves to close the door and welcome the dogs. For just a second, it almost seems like the pearls grow hot under my touch, but the sensation passes almost as soon as I notice it. I put the car in gear and head home.

Chapter Eleven

I'm map questing my route when the dogs go crazy. They know it's Grace Claire even before the bell rings. No hackles. Just spit, scrambling paws, and spastic tails. They've missed her.

First words out of Grace Claire's mouth: "Who's that?" She's pointing at the Chihuahua.

"Butterbean."

"What kind of a name is Butterbean?"

I smile. "Well, you weren't here to name him."

"Obviously." She brushes through the dogs and heads toward her room. "This won't take me long."

Her arm draped over my shoulder, Georgie says, "Doesn't she look great? Don't you like her hair?"

I follow Georgie to Grace Claire's room. "I'd like it better if she were moving back and not just picking up more clothes. You said signing the contract would make her forgive me."

Georgie sighs, "You forget that artists are very sensitive. Give her time."

"Grace Claire," I say. "How about a brownie? I made your favorites."

"No, thank you," she says all suffering-Cinderella like.

"I made sugar cookies too. Would you like one of those?"

She won't even look me in the eye. "I've given up sugar."

"Sugar is shit for your body. I'm very proud of you," beams Georgie.

"Wow. Given up sugar. That must be hard."

Grace Claire just empties a drawer into a bag.

"Grace Claire, sweetheart," I say. "Come on. I've said I'm sorry—so sorry. We can work this out. Talk to me. What—are you going to live with your grandmother forever?"

"Penne, I know this is hard for you. The sense I get from Ishtar is that you two still love each other very much," says Georgie. "But the thing is, Grace Claire has a wardrobe fitting in an hour." She glances down at her new Ishtar watch. "Crap. I mean twenty minutes."

Grace Claire lifts a duffle bag to her shoulder and heads for the door. Then she stops and turns around. Gazing at the base of my neck, she says. "You're wearing your goddess necklace?"

I pull it out and show her.

"Good."

Wham. She's out the door.

"Don't worry," says Georgie. "I feel very good about this. Everything will be fine. I'll call you tomorrow."

"Actually," I say, checking to make sure Grace Claire isn't looking. "I won't be here tomorrow. I'm driving up to Los Olivos. I think Owen might be there. I think he's in trouble."

My mother rolls her eyes, "Of course he's in trouble. He's on Venus's shit list. Divine retribution, baby. He's gonna fucking pay for what he did to you."

"That's not it." I explain about Owen's desperate call for money. "But don't tell Grace Claire," I say looking at the hunched down leaf of a body in Georgie's car. "I don't want her to worry."

"Penne, darling," she says. "This is the stupidest thing I've ever heard. Owen's not a lost dog. You don't need to save him. If bad things are happening to him, maybe he deserves them to happen. He's a fucking shithead."

"Goodbye, Mom."

"Seriously. Bad karma breeds bad karma. Don't do this."

"I'm going to do this."

"Fine, fine, but at least talk to Tamara first."

"No."

"Yes."

"Goodbye."

Around midnight the dogs let loose. Barking, whining, running. At first, I think maybe another dog has shown up, which is, frankly, exhausting to contemplate. Then the doorbell rings.

No way. It's Georgie, and she's not alone. She's got Uzume, Bast, and Freyja with her. The minute they're inside, Uzume grabs a pile of dog treats from her pocket and throws them down the hall. The dogs turn as one and run toward the kitchen, where Uzume barricades them so effectively that all I can hear from them are low pathetic whines.

The women are all wearing togas. Did I mention that? Uzume, Bast, and Freyja are wearing flowing togas of raw white silk. The material falls from their shoulders in loose folds. Naturally, that's a little too modest for Georgie, who is dressed in diaphanous chiffon that swaths her body like a cocoon. Even by Georgie standards, she looks dazzling. Her face is pink with reckless excitement. "Ha!" she says. "Don't try and resist. We're fucking kidnapping you." Bast and Freyja grab my arms while Uzume huddles with Georgie and then runs up to my room.

I try to free myself, but, despite their china doll size and appearance, Bast and Freyja are surprisingly strong. They squeeze my arms and smile.

"It's for your own good," says Georgie.

Uzume runs downstairs. "I couldn't find socks. Will these work?" she says dangling a pair of flip-flops.

Georgie nods. "Put these on," she tells me. "It's cold outside."

I step toward Georgie. "Where is Grace Claire? Did you leave her alone?"

"She's asleep. She's fine."

"This is ridiculous. I'm not going anywhere."

"Actually, Penne," says Bast. "We're kind of late already so it would really help if you could just go with the program."

"We're late?" asks Georgie. "How did that happen?"

"I'm sorry my mother dragged you into this," I say to the girls. "But I'm not going anywhere."

Georgie shakes her head. "Her father was just like this. Very stubborn." Her eyes glisten and she blinks back on-demand tears. "He died, you know."

Uzume gives Georgie a hug. "I'm sorry."

"Yes, well…" sighs Georgie.

"It was decades ago. They'd been divorced for years," I say.

"You never really get over someone you've had a child with." The tears are falling now. I might as well be talking to ferns. You see! This is what Georgie does! She gets all weepy and moony and gets whatever she wants. Every time! Bast and Freyja frown in determination and, suddenly, I'm racing down the Pasadena Freeway in the back of Georgie's new hybrid.

Gone are Georgie's tears. Gone are her sighs. She says, "Don't be mad, baby. This'll be fun."

But fun is not what I'm thinking of when she pulls up near The Goddess Lounge. I shiver as I hoist myself from the backseat. Wind bites at my toes and runs through my pajamas. For a split second, I consider making a run for it, but—let's be real—where would I go? I have no cell phone, no wallet. I'm wearing pajamas and flip-flops. The street lies practically deserted. It's the dead of night. In winter. There are no tourists strolling by. There are no theatergoers. There aren't even any protesters. There are only prostitutes and scary people shrouded in cardboard fortresses, so I pull myself together. I will get through this, like always. This is one night of my life. "Soldier on," I tell myself. "Soldier on."

Georgie looks over at me. "Oh, it's not as bad as all that, babe."

But one look inside The Goddess Lounge and I know my mother is wrong. It is worse—much worse—than "all that."

The Goddess Lounge has changed. Drastically. The curtains separating the café and the tent: gone. The round wooden tables: gone. The chairs: gone. The shelves full of knitting supplies: gone. The crimson menstrual tent itself: gone. Only the long wooden bar, still topped with its industrial strength cappuccino machine, remains of the building's daytime function. Everything else has been transformed into nothing less than a Greek temple. There are Doric columns. Fricking Doric columns. They are nine feet high, and they're arranged in a circle around the room. There are palms, ferns, white gladiolas, camellias and azaleas. There are miniature orange trees covered in white blossoms and pots of sweet-smelling star jasmine. There are luminaria and hundreds of small, twinkling gas-lit lanterns. And there are women, lots of women, lots of barefoot, toga-clad women holding long white tapers. Erect and solemn, they look expectantly at us. Most of them seem to be in their sixties, and it strikes me now that for a whole segment of the population the Hippie era never really ended. It just moved underground into afterhours coffee houses and knitting salons.

A lot of the women seem familiar. Finally, I realize why. They are celebrities—faded celebrities. Mothers from old sitcoms, forgotten nighttime soap vixens, once sexy pinups with bigger than ever breasts and red, sausagy lips. I see a once-funny TV waitress and a path-breaking news anchor who now occasionally shows up on late night infomercials.

I see younger women, too. I see women in their twenties and desperately-trying-to-look twenties. These women are not celebrities, at least I don't think so, but who can tell these days? They all look vaguely identical with their long straight hair, deep tans, hipless bodies and perfect, made-to-order little noses. My whole life I've known women like these. They want to be celebrities. They want it very much. A few have probably done commercials. One or two may have been on reality shows. They probably all have their own YouTube channels. They're not here for spiritual enrichment. You can see it in their hungry eyes. They're here for contacts, for social climbing. Ten bucks say they're hedging their bets with similar visits to the Scientology center on Sunset and the progressive Episcopal Church in Pasadena.

Still, you never know. A few of the younger women could be true believers. Uzume, Bast, and Freyja aren't faking it. They believe, all right. In the very back of the room I spy Ashley, and she's looking as devoted as a nun. Her long golden hair is braided and wrapped like a crown around her head. Helen of Troy has nothing on her. She smiles and gives me a little wink.

A woman who played the attractive but not beautiful sidekick on a 1970s sitcom hands a long-white candle to Georgie, who nudges me. "Take a candle," she whispers.

"It's ok," says the sidekick. "She doesn't need one."

From the back of the room comes the beating of drums, which grow louder as two sober-faced women with small snare drums slowly approach the platform. Between the drummers walks Tamara in a loose-fitting toga and a flowing, sheer white veil that covers her head and shoulders. She swings a smoking incense pot that smells of burnt sage, cloves and orange. One whiff and my eyes sting. My stomach churns and curdles. I sway dizzily to the left, and, then, Bast and Freyja are right beside me, holding me steady.

"Penne," whispers Bast. "You need to go to the circle now. This is fun. Relax."

"Take off your shoes," adds Freyja. "Trust your goddess. You'll be all right."

I slip off my flip-flops and walk, slowly, queasily to the center of the circle. I am soldiering on. I am soldiering on.

The drummers and Tamara—still swinging her incense pot—weave around the people and plants for what seems like a nauseatingly long time until, finally, they stop directly across from me.

"Welcome sisters," says Tamara. "Welcome to this sacred circle of the feminine, this place where we embrace the call of the ancient goddesses. May we hear our goddesses in our dreams."

"May we hear our goddesses," chant the women.

"May we hear our goddesses in times of bliss and rage, sorrow and fear."

"May we hear our goddesses."

Tamara pauses. "Fear not the divine within you."

"We will not fear it."

Tamara looks from woman to woman. "Sisters," she says. "Tonight, we ask the goddesses to bless one of our own as she embarks on a quest. There is nothing greater than a quest. Quests make us heroes, and heroes get as close to the immortal ones as is possible in this life." She looks directly at me. "Penne, you are the one embarking on a quest, yes?"

I glance at Georgie. "I guess."

"And in this quest you will seek your husband, even though he has left you and caused you nothing but grief. Yes?"

"I guess."

"You do this for your daughter's sake?"

Sure. Why not? That sounds as good as anything I've come up with. I nod.

"We will confer."

A small group of women, including Georgie and Uzume, huddle around Tamara and whisper. Soon, Uzume heads over to the coffee counter and rummages through a gold-colored box.

Tamara steps away from her advisors. "Wise women, you have heard about the quest. Now share your hard-earned wisdom with our heroine."

The sidekick steps forward. She tilts her head to the left and opens and shuts her mouth before speaking. "I would say that…you might want to think about this. It's all very good to do things for children. But remember: They really don't appreciate much. They take maternal sacrifice for granted. So, whether you stay or go, you shouldn't assume your daughter will thank you…because she probably won't. Ever."

A double-chinned woman with penciled-in eyebrows takes her turn. In the contours of her now round face, I recognize the mother from an old family-friendly drama who, in real life, was dumped by a powerful studio executive in favor of her adopted daughter. "Kids…parasites, really. They suck us dry, like vampires. And then, when they've used up every bit of us, when there is nothing left, they look at us like we're these repulsive creatures, like we're a stray bit of mucus or a maggoty carcass—something old and unpleasant. Your heart will be broken no matter what you do. So what's the use? Your husband sounds like an asshole. Leave him be. He deserves whatever hell he's fallen into."

A few of the younger women eye each other uncomfortably. They know that a woman this bitter will never open doors for them.

Ashley steps forward. "I totally disagree. Kids want their parents to be happy and successful, and even independent. Growing up, you want to see that it's OK to live your own life and have your own interests, and not be… you know…everybody's doormat. The real problem is that most women have small imaginations. The world is full of amazing opportunities and possibilities if women just claim them. Really, demand them. Really, insist on having what they want. Instead, most women do what people expect of them. They play the nice wife, the nice mother, the nice daughter, the nice worker. Fuck nice. Be the woman you need to be. If you need to find this loser, find him."

"I agree," adds a woman with short, violet hair. "Fuck nice. Embrace your bitch. Cut off this asshole's balls and whip 'em in a milkshake."

"Oh my," says the sidekick, who looks very alarmed. "I hope you won't do that. No, no, no. In my experience, nice is good. Nice keeps the coffee sweet. It makes everything go down easier—and it can curry you a lot of favors. By all means, be nice if you can."

Georgie slices her hands through the air. "I think this all boils down to most men being shitheads. I've known a lot of men. Whatever you do, do not apologize. Do not explain yourself. Do not justify yourself. A man is lucky if you glance at him. He is blessed if you speak to him. Owen is a fucking piece of dried up dog shit. He thinks he can fucking make you invisible and just do what he fucking wants. Well, fuck, fuck, fuck him. You are a fucking goddess! And goddesses cannot be treated like crap. Whatever you do, remember that."

The room falls quiet, and I feel myself blush. It's too much, what Georgie said. It's too ridiculous, too obviously the mark of maternal blindness. "Mom," I mumble. "That's enough."

"Oh, sister," says the sidekick. "Don't be embarrassed. You are a fucking goddess. We all are."

Ashley sticks out her perky chest. "Penne Armour: You are a fucking goddess."

The violet-haired woman says, "You are a fucking goddess."

And then Bast, Freyja, and all the women, one by one, look at me with steely eyes and determined jaws and say, "You are a fucking goddess."

And, sure, it's cheesy. And, sure, it's insane and stupid and ridiculous and dumb. But, despite myself, I think I sort of begin to glow. No doubt about it: Georgie is vain, irresponsible and three kinds of crazy, but this time maybe she got things right. These women, young and old: they don't know me, but they believe in me.

Uzume returns to the circle and hands Tamara the golden box. Tamara steps forward and nods at me. "Penne, take these boons, these gifts. Use them wisely and with cunning." She pulls a dark green bottle from the box. "Sobriety—the eternal enemy of Venus—will seek to stop you. This wine will combat its dull rationality, but so will any wine. So don't hoard it."

"Be intemperate," says Uzume.

"Be reckless," says Bast.

"Have fun," says Freyja.

I take the bottle of wine.

Tamara continues, "Venus was married to Vulcan, a gifted craftsman. He gave his wife a golden girdle covered in jewels and that inspired desire in all men. Obviously, Vulcan wasn't the smartest god, but some men like nothing more than to be envied, and, luckily, Venus liked nothing more than to be desired. For you, we have this much more practical girdle." Tamara hands me a gold coin purse. It's the size of a large fist and made of shiny gold satin. It's the kind of thing a very old—very flashy—grandmother might use to tip her hairdresser. Still, it's a sweet gift, and I'm grateful that no one expects me to strap it round my stomach.

"Vulcan also gave Venus jewelry, such as that necklace you're wearing now," says Tamara. She walks over and pulls the necklace from underneath my pajama top. Then she walks me to the middle of the circle and turns me round so that everyone can see the necklace. "Pearls and sapphires were Venus's favorites. They look pretty on you. When you hide your necklace, you slight your goddess and yourself. You can't slight yourself and succeed in a quest. Heroines must be bold and confident. After all, they're goddesses in training. The greatest heroes became gods. So wear your necklace proudly. Show your glory."

Tamara raises her hands. "To the quest," she says. "May you find what you need, even if it is not what you are looking for."

The other women raise their hands. "To the quest," they reply. The ceremony over, they fall in around me and shove golden Sacagawea dollars into the coin purse.

"Good luck," they say. "Find what you need."

I squeeze their hands and thank them in turn. Such kindness. I did not expect such kindness.

Over the sound of the crowd, Georgie shouts, "Sweetie, I wonder if you can get someone else to take you home?" She waves a hand toward Uzume, Bast, and Freyja. "The girls and I are going for a nightcap. Take care." With the hint of a wave, she turns round and heads for the door.

"Wait! Mom, wait."

The women huddle closer. "You're a fucking goddess," they tell me. But, here's the thing, in LA, even a fucking goddess is nothing without her car. I try to break through the crowd of well wishers, but they hover round me like I'm birthday cake.

"Mom!"

"I can take you home," says Ashley. She has her hand in mine and she's leading me through the crowd. "Where do you live?"

"Altadena."

"It's practically on my way."

Practically turns out to be a mere thirty minutes (one way, no traffic) out of Ashley's path, but, as she giggles upon making this discovery, "I have no sense of direction." She barrels down the Hollywood Freeway in her banana-colored Hummer, a boat of a car that flies along the deserted early-morning streets, a regular conquering warrior. Proud. Unafraid. Young.

Ashley turns on the car radio and speeds past a series of commercials until she settles on a hip-hop station. She rolls her neck and begins to tap her bright pink fingers against the steering wheel in rhythm with the beat. "We used to dance to this song," she says.

"You and William?" I say, finding it hard to picture William Browning grooving to just about any hip-hop song.

Ashley laughs. "No. The Clipper Dancers—my cheer squad."

"Oh. How's that going?"

"You don't know? I stopped a long time ago. It was fun, but I needed a bigger challenge. I'm basically a Hera with strong Green Corn goddess tendencies. So I had to find a place where I could practice my intellectual gifts in a nurturing, leadership capacity. You understand, right? Cuz you're a Hera too."

"Venus."

"But your pendant is a star sapphire. That's Hera."

"I think it's just a regular sapphire. I don't know. This is what Tamara chose for me."

"So you're Venus? Wow. Housewife with a straying husband...for sure I thought Hera. I guess that explains why Tamara kept talking about Venus."

"I guess so." Hmmm. That seems a little obvious. "So," I say, "what do you do now?"

"I have a chain of Pilates studios. Well, three. One in Silverlake, one in West Hollywood, and one in Echo Park. But I'm looking to expand."

"That's amazing." Really. It is amazing. Ashley, the cheerleader, has three Pilates studios. "You mean you work at three studios?"

"No. They're totally mine. I've had the one in Silverlake for, like, over a year. The others are newer. It's great. You should come. You do Pilates?"

"No."

"It's awesome." Ashley waggles her finger at me. "But you must do something right? To be Venus you probably have to be pretty hot underneath those pajamas. Or—what—is it like a sex secret thing?"

"Do you like owning your own business?"

"Ahhh...you don't want to talk about it. Must be the sex thing. That's cool. You and your goddess need your secrets. I get it. My goddess and I have secrets too."

A new song comes on and Ashley starts singing along. When it ends, she fingers her braids and says, "Hey, you know those times I ran into you at William's office? You didn't tell him you saw me, did you?"

"No."

"So…why do you keep going there, anyway?"

I look over at Ashley. An entire goddess ceremony has just been devoted to my "quest." Twenty to thirty people had to dress in togas and drive to Hollywood in the middle of the night so that they could hear how I'm looking for Owen.

She turns her face toward mine. "So?"

"Owen is missing."

"Oh, duh. Right. But what about William?"

"What do you mean?"

"Well, it seems like you've had to see him a lot. Like, really a lot."

"He's just been helping me out. I've appreciated it." He's a nice guy that William. I suddenly feel a little sad.

"That's all?"

Shit. He told her about my trapeze act. Bastard.

A CHP motorcycle pulls up next to the Hummer. Ashley waves and gives the officer a flirty smile. It's such a Georgie move. The cop gives Ashley a sheepish grin and taps a finger on his speedometer. Ashley's eyebrows pop up in mock surprise as she lets up on the gas pedal. Then, as soon as he exits the freeway in Chinatown, she floors it.

"It's just…he's been very helpful." I say.

She wraps her fingers tightly around her steering wheel. "Really? Well, he's a helpful guy. Lucky you."

"Yeah," I say thinking about Dashed Sails, Grace Claire, Owen, Georgie. "Lucky me."

Chapter Twelve

History tells of dogs that could sense earthquakes, tsunamis, even melanomas. My dogs sense desertion. And why not? They have lived through it many times. They know the signs: The packing of luggage, the double-checking of windows and doors. I try and spare my dogs anxiety by doing those things at the bitter end, but they always know when I'm leaving. They smell the guilt.

When I wake up, they're waiting for me, staring at me with accusatory eyes.

"I won't be long," I tell them. "You'll be ok."

They wait outside the shower for me and then follow me down the stairs. "Nancy's coming to feed you. You like Nancy. Nancy? From work? You like her. Remember? You'll have fun."

But we all know that's a lie. When it's time to go, I do what Uzume did. I throw a fistful of dog treats down the hall. The dogs run off in stupid bliss, and I escape out the front door. Almost immediately, the boys realize they've been scammed. They run through the doggy door to the side yard, howling in moony protest. Far behind limps my poor, sweet Lucy, her eyes portraits of broken trust.

Across the street, a car door slams. The dogs wag their tails. I turn to see William walking toward me.

"Hi," he says all matter of fact. "Funny thing. I was thinking about you last night, and I was thinking maybe you shouldn't go to Los Olivos alone. Maybe I should go with you."

"What?"

"You know, for safety's sake."

The dogs are moaning now. They're scratching at the fence, begging William to come to them.

"Do you even know where Los Olivos is? It's three hours from here. This isn't a picnic."

"I know. We could take my car." I follow his gaze as he motions to a black BMW, and then I look back at his face, which seems filled with genuine concern. And maybe something more? Maybe?

I swallow, and the pearls around my neck almost do a little jump. I hear myself say, "Ok."

We make our way to the 101 north and find that rare and beautiful thing, that one unpredictable gift that can always lift a person's spirits: an open road. And, lo, we make excellent time through Ventura, through Santa Barbara, all the way to Buellton, where we leave the freeway and stop for breakfast at a brown and orange coffee shop with glossy, leather-buttoned booths and waitresses in brown uniforms and pleated orange aprons.

For no other reason than to make polite conversation after two hours of almost complete silence, I say how lucky we were to avoid traffic.

"Yes," says William. "Very lucky."

Like a pair of synchronized swimmers, we sit there, in perfect rhythm, stirring our coffee. Clockwise: circle, circle, circle, circle. Counterclockwise, clockwise: circle, circle, circle, circle.

"So I guess Ashley told you I was leaving this morning. Nice of her to let you come."

William puts down his spoon. He looks down at his cup and then up at me. "Ashley and I broke up months ago."

I have to let that one sink in for a minute. "Does Ashley know?"

"That's something I want to talk to you about."

Just then my phone rings. I shove my hand down my purse and let my fingers wade until they find it. "It's Grace Claire," I say, looking down at the screen. "Hold on a second." I slide out of the booth and head for the privacy of the parking lot. "Hey, babe. You ok?"

Perhaps this is needless to say, but Grace Claire is not ok. As she so kindly reminds me, if she were ok, she would not be talking to me at all, but she has to talk to me because I did not initial something on the contract and now everyone is mad at her because they have to shoot around her until I do what I was supposed to do in the first place. "So you need to come to the studio right now and initial the stupid form," she says. "Ok? I told them you'd be here in, like, twenty minutes."

"First of all," I say. "I'm really glad you called. I really miss talking to you, but the thing is, I'm nowhere near the studio—"

"Ok. Thirty minutes."

"I'm sorry. I don't think I can do it today."

"What?"

"I'm too far away, and I'm in the middle of something, something important."

"Fine. Fine. Don't do it ever. I'll just go back to being a fat nobody. This is all because you hate me. You hate your own daughter." She hangs up.

Confession: She's right. At this moment, I do sort of hate her—no, not hate—but, my god, what a cow! How did I raise such a selfish drama queen? I don't get it. I know so much. I know about teaching kids to use their words and helping them understand the natural consequences of their actions. I know about developmental milestones and learning styles. I teach parents this shit. I practice patience, kindness, tolerance and acceptance. Goddamn it. I've done everything right. I'm supposed to have the good daughter, the nice daughter, not the mean, evil one. I'm a fricking good mother. I deserve a fricking good daughter. That should be the fricking natural consequence of every fricking action I've taken over the last thirteen years.

William walks up to me, "You ok?"

I head for the car. "I'm not hungry anymore."

"Your daughter ok?"

"I guess." And I can say that in all honesty because while she may be a venom-spitting, possessed demon-child whose head spins around while she channels Satan, she is healthy and alive and not homeless. Plus, she doesn't take drugs. Which is good perspective. Right?

Pretty soon we're on the base of a windy, hilly road that runs along an earthen field punctuated with ginger cows. They have jowly heads and sad eyes that remind me of Pei and every other girl I've known who eats lunch alone and holds her pee for six hours a stretch rather than risk humiliation in a middle school bathroom.

"Can mean girls turn nice?" I blurt it out. I don't even realize I've actually spoken until I hear William say, "About that…sometimes people aren't what they seem."

"Exactly."

"Sometimes you don't know who a person really is until you've known them a while, but that doesn't mean you've done anything…personally… in fact, maybe you've done everything you can think of to counteract what the other person has done."

"Yes, yes."

"Still, if you don't take responsibility, won't you somehow be to blame if something happens?"

"People would definitely blame you."

I look over at William. I see him trying to say more. His tongue rests on the back of his bottom teeth as if it's stuck behind a dam. But the dam holds, and the words don't come, and, after a while, we both just stare ahead.

I wonder. Is there a goddess of mean girls? A deity who looks after the cold hearted and cruel, who protects them from avenging mothers? If so, how skinny is she? How flawless are her skin and hair? What precious gemstone does she wear round her neck? And in exactly how many seconds would it take her to beat the shit out of the goddess of love? Probably about five, I think. Maybe less. Maybe just as long as it takes for the goddess of love to stupidly bend down and smell a daisy so that the goddess of mean can kick her in the stomach and tie her up like a roped calf. Goddess of love. How useless. How can love ever beat mean? Especially when what you love is what is mean.

Chapter Thirteen

Have you been in the mountains north of Santa Barbara? Do you know how curvy those roads get? It's Machu Picchu plopped down in the middle of California. Think steep. Think rural. Up, up, we go. Past pastures made green by the recent rains, fallow fields, and row after row of arthritic, bare-leaved and brown vineyards.

Every so often we drive by a bright sign announcing the award-winning zinfandel/chardonnay/pinot noir available for tasting at the very next turn off. "I've been there," William says by way of making conversation, and then he goes into some small detail about the wine's "terroir" or "fruiti-ness." Every once in a while, I glimpse for that sparkle in his eyes. The one I saw when I drove him home. But it's not there now. To be honest, I don't think these vineyards impress him. But it's not like he's snobby. It's more like he's disappointed. It's like he really wanted to like the wines, but that, despite his best hopes, he just couldn't commit.

I think he's trying to draw me out. He'd probably have better luck with a hibernating bear. I mean, damn it. My fucking mean daughter who hates me is such a fucking bitch that I don't even think I like her anymore. There. I've said it. I don't like her. She's horrible. And it's fucking my fault because it's always the mother's fault. People will tell you it's not, but everybody knows, deep down inside, that it fucking is. Now fuck. I sound just like fucking Georgie, who is also fucking pissing me off, by the way, what with her tak-ing Grace Claire in and getting her a job on a fucking Disney Channel show. And what can I do? What can I fucking do? Nothing. Grace Claire has chosen a path, and it's her path. This is what children do. They choose paths their mothers can't follow. I can't make Grace Claire nice. I can't make Grace Claire care about people she doesn't want to care about. I can't get Grace Claire to take out the trash. It's delusional to think I can have any impact on the person Grace Claire aims to be. And now Grace Claire is going to be on this stupid show, and she'll just get meaner and more self absorbed and she'll fucking self destruct because that's what celebrity children do. And I can't do anything about that either.

So there you go. I can't do anything. So why try? Why bother at all? Why not just forget?

Yes. Just forget. That sounds very…peaceful.

I turn to William. "So you must really like wine."

William's chin sort of shutters and he gives me a sidelong glance. Apparently, he'd forgotten I could speak. He offers a suspicious, "Yes."

"And you've been up here before. You like it. Yeah?" For the first time, I really look around. My God. It's beautiful. We're enveloped in oaks, pines, thick clumps of chaparral and silvery shrubs. It's amazing. It's so…green. I didn't even know places like this existed in Southern California. I've lived a lifetime here. How could I not know this? "You know what," I say. "I like it too."

And, like magic, we're off. We talk about wine, food, life in LA. Common things. Nothing earth shattering. But there's a kind of intimacy to it, a kind of secret sharing, like when I confide that I hate the Hollywood Bowl. "I know it's this great LA landmark, and everyone is supposed to love it," I say. "But that stacked parking! I've never gotten my car out of there in less than an hour. It's the worst!"

"I know," says William, the twinkle finally back in his eyes. "And if I want to listen to live music, do I really need to drive to Hollywood? I hate the 101."

"The only thing worse than the 101 is the 405."

"Just keep me clear of West LA. I hate the Westside."

"I don't hate anything as much as I hate the Westside."

And so we go gloriously on, bashing everything west of Downtown. Not once do we mention Grace Claire, Owen, Rosa, or Ashley. Not once do we mention The Goddess Lounge or Dashed Sails. It's awesome.

Or at least it's awesome until we reach a gravel turn-off marked "*Ranch degli Cinghialle.*"

"This is it," I say. "We turn here."

"Already?"

"Yeah." We sit there for a minute, and it's like we're waiting for the fog of doom to descend upon us, like we're waiting for this big shift to happen that will suck the fun right out of us. And you know what? It happens. It's like someone takes a vacuum to our personalities. We just sit there and deflate, and then we turn down the goddamn gravel road.

The road takes us even higher through thick forest until the hillside finally gives way to a wide plateau covered with olive trees. The trees stop at a ramshackle stone and brick barn and then start again, continuing until the end of a curved gravel road, which gives way to a paved, circular driveway that leads to a large house. Like the barn, the house is made mostly of stone and brick, but while the barn has seen better days, the house is impressive. It's three narrow stories high and has three balconies, each furnished with an iron patio set and a pair of bubble-shaped mini citrus trees.

As impressive as the house is, however, it's not what catches your attention. What captures your attention is the woman in a tight black leather coat, skirt, and boots standing at the front door. Hands planted on her meaty hips, she waits there with a curl of scorn on her lips. Oh, and did I mention she's surrounded by about a dozen enormous pigs? They're huge things—probably three hundred pounds. Their eyes are bitter little pinpricks. Their bristly hair stands sharp as darts.

"I don't think that's Rosa," I say.

"No," says William.

"She doesn't look happy, does she?"

"I'll take care of it," says William turning off the car, getting out, and assuming his Mr. Confident stance. The woman mutters something to the pigs and they run toward him.

"Ok," says William quickly sliding back into the car. "That's not going to work. You sure this is where we're supposed to be?"

"This is the address I got."

"Ok. Let's try this." He rolls down the window and sticks his head out. The pigs grunt. He smiles at the woman and says that we're looking for Rosa Luna, who, he promises, is not in any trouble, but who, he hopes, might be able to give us some information about a missing friend.

The woman sticks out a pair of fleshy red lips and makes a clucking sound with her tongue. The pigs trot obediently in front of her, amble round the car and head the opposite direction down the road. With a nod toward William, the woman sashays behind the animals. Each step is a hip-swaying hula.

"I think she wants us to follow her," says William.

"Do you think it's safe?"

"Probably. But let's stay in the car."

The woman leads us back to the old barn. There, surrounded by the pigs, she gestures for us to come inside.

"You stay," says William.

I look at the woman. She's not unattractive. Late fifties. She's got shoulder-length brown hair that's streaked with ribbons of silver and a curved, round body clearly designed for birthing. Most likely, she's somebody's mother. And now that I've survived the wrath of Xinran, I wonder how suspect most mothers could be, especially mothers of this girth, mothers whose very body size must have taught them compassion and empathy. The woman is standing tall and her arms are crossed, but it's not like she has any homicidal quivers or a maniacal smile. She looks displeased, maybe, but surely she's not dangerous. "It's ok," I say. "I think she's all right."

We get out of the car and follow the woman into the barn, which is cold—really cold—and, actually, pretty modern looking for such a ramshackle building. It's got two industrial-sized refrigerators, steel sinks and steel counters. The back wall has a giant magnetized band running across it. On the magnet hang dozens of meat cleavers, some the size of machetes, and the side walls are covered in wine racks, cupboards and assorted mechanical looking devices. In front of all of this are tall metal tables. The whole place has a spicy, smoky, Christmas ham smell that drifts down from the ceiling. I look up and see why. There's a bunch of dead pigs and pig body parts hanging from it. There are whole pigs, half pigs, headless pigs, pig heads, and pig shanks, lots of pig shanks, some with hooves still dangling, some still covered in their owners' bristly hair. Hams hang from the ceiling too. So do prosciutto and pancetta, and, most of all, long, thick salamis spotted with paper white flecks.

The living pigs lead the woman to one of the cupboards and stare with their beady piggy eyes as she removes something from inside. At first, I can't tell what they're looking at, but then I see it and my stomach begins to roil. In my whole life, I've never actually seen a real shotgun, but I've seen lots of movies and television shows, and the shotgun the woman holds looks exactly like the ones on Bonanza. Of course, for all I know, the shotgun might be as real as the ones on Bonanza, but the body parts dangling in the cool air above make me doubt it.

William must be thinking the same thing because his voice has lost its briskness. He stutters, "may- maybe we should—"

The woman silences him with a loud, "Eh." She points to a set of metal chairs next to one of the tables and motions for us to sit down and clasp our hands atop our heads. Georgie made a movie like this once. It did not end well for the people on the chairs.

"I know who you are," the woman says in a sandpapery voice. "Sons of bitches. Bastards. This is private property—my property. You have no business here. I'll tell you the same thing I told those whores on the telephone.

You want your money? You talk to Matteo. If you think for one tiny second that you can take my farm then I hope you're on good terms with all your family members because you won't be able to resolve any leftover, petty squabbles in hell."

William, his voice squeaky old leather, says, "Um." Honestly, as scared as I am, even I can tell that he sounds ridiculous. He could not sound more uncertain, and this seems to annoy the woman even more. She swings her arms wide so that the shotgun makes a jagged arc in the sky. She steps forward. The pigs follow. They bump each other along until they reach the table, where they greedily sniff our feet.

"What? Are you crazy?" asks the woman. "You think I won't do it? You think I won't kill for this? Are you sure?"

His face greenish gray, William replies, "No, no, no, no. You're mistaken—"

"Mistaken!" the woman hollers.

It is this exact moment when I realize that William—an intelligent man with fantastic hair who has attended Harvard, oversees the assets of a multi-million dollar financial corporation, and who definitely has an over-developed sense of responsibility—is making things worse.

"We don't want any money," I blurt. "We don't want your farm. We're looking for Rosa Luna. Actually, we're not looking for *her*. We're looking for my husband—Owen Armour—who..." I shake my head and make some lame floppy circles with my hands.

The embarrassment on my face must say enough. The woman lowers her gun a fraction. The pigs let out disappointed grunts and begin pacing the length of the table.

"You're not from the credit card company?" says the woman.

"No."

Tapping a finger on the stalk of the gun, she adds, "What's your name?"

"Penne Armour. And this is William Browning."

"Penne? That's a kind of pasta. Why are you named after pasta?"

"Hippie parents."

The woman lifts her eyes to the ceiling and considers this. "No," she says. "A hippie would have named you Strawberry or Starlight or Bougainvillea. Not Penne."

"Show business hippies, then. They conceived me over a plate of penne arrabiata. In Rome. So I'm told." I usually don't go into this much detail, but when my patent answer isn't enough and people are pointing guns in my general vicinity, I find it best to get to the facts.

The woman again sticks out her plump lips. "Show business hippies? Posers, more likely. All those show business types are posers."

"You're right. They were more posers than actual hippies." I sink into my seat a little and try and relax. "But, really, I think it's an occupational hazard. The constant need for reinvention."

"Maybe, but you're the one stuck named after a noodle."

"Hey, now," says William, his voice starting to come back to him.

The woman points the shotgun at him. "You: shut up." The shotgun still aimed at William, she says, "Tell me about Rosa."

"I haven't actually met her," I admit.

"No? She seems a very cheap kind of girl to me. No class," says the woman.

I shrug. I'm not so sure about cheap. That Silverlake loft was not inexpensive.

"Cheap. Vulgar. Trampy. All sex. Not a nice girl at all," adds the woman.

"So you know Rosa?" ventures William.

The woman shoots him an angry glance. "Matteo brought her. They're *engaged*." She practically spits out the last word.

"Matteo's your son?" I ask.

"Yes, I'm sorry to say." She drops the gun to her side and the pigs give a disgruntled squeal. "Outside," she commands. The pigs head for the door and the woman looks back at me. "Why would my future daughter-in-law know anything about your husband?"

"Ok." I take a deep breath.

"Don't bother," the woman says. "I can imagine. I hate that bitch." With a thud, the woman sinks in a chair and plops the shotgun onto her lap. She shakes her head. "Stupid, stupid Matteo."

"Maybe not so stupid," I say. If anything, Rosa seems a treasure chest of persuasive tools.

"No. Stupid. Always stupid. Brain of a melon." The woman gives a great sigh. "Still, what's a mother to do?"

I sigh too. Then I cautiously drop my hands to my lap. "It never ends, does it? The worry, the fear, the longing to protect them?"

The woman exhales an exasperated billow of air and rolls her eyes.

"Motherhood isn't like what you think it will be."

"No. Motherhood's the shits," says the woman. "You have boys?"

"A girl," I say. "Thirteen. I love her more than anything, but it's hard. That's the part no one tells you. You want so much for them, but it's so hard. You worry so much. And sometimes it feels like nothing you do is good enough. You try and help them make good choices, but…they're not like dogs."

The woman's eyes widen. "Yes," she says. "That's right. And now, what do I do? Credit card companies keep hounding me about Matteo's debts—I don't know anything about these debts—I didn't know he had credit cards! Now he brings home this twig"—she holds up her pinky—"and says he's going to marry her. What am I supposed to think? What am I supposed to do?"

And for no good reason except, perhaps, the fact that I have imagined such scenarios myself, the right words fly out of me. They fill me like a summer rainstorm fills a thirsty riverbed. "About the money, I don't know. I don't see how you could be held responsible for your son's debts. But as for Rosa, that seems very easy."

"Easy?"

"Test her. Give her tasks—tasks that prove if she loves Matteo or if she's using him, tasks that show her what being part of your family means, what being a daughter to you means."

The woman wets her lips. "Like Psyche, yes? Then we will see her true colors." Rubbing her fingers up and down her broad belly, she says, "You are a wise woman."

I smile. I might even blush, although, to be honest, I have no idea what she's talking about. I glance over at William and almost laugh. He's looking at me like I've performed some sort of dodgy miracle. His face is a mixed-up palette of relief, astonishment, perplexity and skepticism combined with just a tiny shade of terror.

The woman laughs too. "Poor fellow. They're all so stupid aren't they?" She gestures for him to put his hands down.

And there you go. Success. No longer are we captor and prisoner. Now we're collaborators. We're two tired, abused women against the whole wide world of stupid, ungrateful men. Slapping her thick hand on my knee like we're old friends, the woman says, "Tell me, why do you want to find this stupid husband of yours?"

Again, instinctively, I know what to do. "Ah. That story will require some assistance."

With the courage of a Marine, but the unthreatening ease of my pre-school-teacher self, I take the shotgun from the woman's lap and put it on the floor. That's right. Me. I do that. I take a fucking gun from the same lady who's just pointed it at my fucking head, and, like it's a fucking sticky cup of apple juice, I put it on the floor. Then, arm and arm, I take the woman out to William's car and I get the bottle of wine that Tamara gave me. I hand it to her and say, "Sustenance. My husband will make your son look like an altar boy."

When we go back in the barn, William is sitting as stiffly as ever, but the shotgun is gone, so he's not as useless as he looks, really. The woman brings over three glasses and, though it is not yet noon, we make quick business of the wine, or, I should say, the woman makes quick business of the wine, which she slugs down with happy sighs of satisfaction.

But, you know, I'm liking this wine too. The truth is, I'm not much of a drinker. A lifetime of observation has taught me that alcohol lessens self-restraint, and, for the life of me, I can never see why anyone would want less self-restraint when what most people really need is more. But this day, in this barn, the wine loosens my tongue in a good way. My story flows. I'm a different person. Basically, I'm Georgie, but with an appetite. For, as I regale the woman with the tale of Owen's disappearance, the woman pulls from the cupboards and ceiling an enormous feast. At first, William and I just eat with polite moderation because, after all, this gal could have more guns hidden around her barn.

But then, you know what? The moderation stops and we just dig in. The food is that good. Think briny, pungent prosciutto, buttery salami that almost melts the moment it touches your tongue, porcini mushrooms, black truffles, olives and bowls of shimmery olive oil, half a dozen hard cheeses sliced into paper-thin wedges, and more wine—always more wine—two bottles more. The meal is sin itself. It is hypnotic. It demands slow and steady gluttony. It inspires lust and sleepy eyes.

All the while I'm eating, I'm talking. I'm telling the woman everything. She listens with friendly attention but I can see she's not impressed. A missing spouse? Run-ins with drug-addicts? The slump of her shoulders tells me that she doesn't even consider that drama. So she begins her own saga. She introduces herself as Griselda Maggiore and explains that she has lived on this farm for over thirty years. She and her husband, Bill, moved here when it was nothing but chaparral and raccoons. Back then they even ate raccoon. Rabbit, if they could get it. Berries. She and Bill bought the property in the hopes of getting back to the land, she explains, back to nature. They wanted to commune with mother earth. What a joke. They didn't know a seed from a stem. They were urban kids, city dwellers, both from San Francisco. "But we had this dream, right? A dream," she says. "And you know how dangerous a dream can be."

Still, she and Bill loved it. They tilled soil. They plowed fields. Griselda read books and took agricultural classes at the university in San Luis Obispo, and most everything they tried failed. But then they grew olives because her father was Italian and said, in this climate, they should grow olives or wine, but Bill said, "Who's going to buy wine from Santa Barbara County?"

And then, much later, came Matteo, and that's when everything turned to shit. He was a beautiful baby. Gorgeous, Griselda explains. Everyone said he should be in commercials, until he started crying and his skin turned splotchy red and purple and his eyes bulged like they were boiled eggs about to pop out of his head. Then he wasn't so gorgeous. Then he was a nightmare. "Little Mosquito," Bill called Matteo because the boy sucked every thought, every feeling out of Griselda, leaving her numb and practically comatose.

Griselda's voice grows hard and tired as she recalls the constant tension the new baby brought to the farm. She and Bill fought constantly. They fought over the baby and whose turn it was to take care of the baby, and whose turn it was to go to town for supplies, and whose fault it was that Griselda now had the sex drive of a carpet slipper, and whose fault it was they ever bought this land that would never make them any money and that didn't even produce enough olives to trade for diapers. And the truth was, the truth that still turned Griselda's gravelly voice hollow with wonder, was that these weren't ordinary fights. These were knock down, hair pulling, blue-gray-green bruise raising brawls that left Bill with permanent bald spots and Griselda with a missing tooth that she couldn't afford to replace for seven years. And, through it all, there was Matteo. So stupid he had to repeat third grade. So needy she had to sing him to sleep until he was twelve. So splendidly gorgeous he lost his virginity at fourteen and had so many girls calling him that he couldn't get a damn piece of homework done and had to be sent to a military boarding school so that he wouldn't flunk another grade. It kept him out of trouble, until he got expelled for growing hydroponic pot in his dorm room.

While such trials might have driven other mothers to alcohol or prescription sedatives, they sent Griselda back to the land, which she discovered was a worthy substitute for children. The cool, fertile earth did not get thrown out of school. It did not alternately beg her attention and demand her exile. It did not bring home slutty girls and talk back to her. The land did not talk back at all. After years of steady wooing, it finally decided to take her nurturance and return it one hundred fold in the form of thriving olive trees that, with Griselda's forward-thinking turn toward organics, finally offered a modest living for her and Bill.

"But, of course," says Griselda, "the real moneymaker is the boar."

And this is where Griselda Maggiore's tale takes an unexpected turn, for it turns out that Griselda has a way with wild pigs. It started about a decade ago, soon after Matteo got expelled. To ease her worry, she began exploring the forest. She'd walk hours at a time until physical exhaustion helped her forget about her fights with Bill (which resumed the day Matteo returned from boarding school) and her struggles to get Matteo back into school and focused on the future. From the day they saw her, the pigs were smitten. They couldn't help following her. Bill said it was Griselda's scent, which was earthy and salty, the human equivalent of a truffle. Whatever the reason, the boars wouldn't leave her alone. Not content to lumber behind her in the forest, they followed her everywhere. Every morning she found them waiting outside the kitchen, in the mud, piled one on top of the other, studies in fruitless yearning.

Alas, this is an unreciprocated passion. Griselda explains that she accepts the boars like many people accept feral cats. She doesn't particularly like them, but they don't bother her. And how can she complain? They make her a small fortune. Griselda need only walk out her kitchen door, cozy one of the fat, lazy beasts over to the barn, and—wham—prosciutto, ham, salami, filetto, salsicce di cinghiale packed in the farm's own organic virgin olive oil.

It was the boars that killed Bill. A few years ago he went for his own walk in the woods. He brought a picnic lunch and a girl who worked at the Walgreens down in Buellton. Unfortunately, a new mother boar had had her litter right behind the tree where Bill and the girl set out their feast. The mother mauled Bill to death in the time it took the girl to run to the farm for help. At least that's what Griselda assumed when she found her husband's pants still wrapped round his ankles as he lay dead on the muddy, blood and flesh-splattered blanket. Still, Griselda says she might have been able to indulge in a respectable period of mourning if another lover of Bill's hadn't shown up at the funeral, crying, beating her breast, and lunging at the coffin, saying Bill was the best, most gentle man she'd ever known.

"But I'm sure, in your own way, your tragedy seems just as bad," says Griselda.

I'm speechless. Truly, Griselda has me beat. Domestic abuse, school expulsion, adultery, death by wild animals. Griselda has wrestled monsters and lived to tell the tale. How could a measly missing husband and some flower-eating potheads compare? All I can do is stare open-mouthed at Griselda, which is apparently the right response because my dazzled face seems to fill Griselda with an overflowing spirit of generosity. She offers William and me a gift. She says that, yes, Rosa had been at the farm and would be coming back, although she couldn't say when. Matteo had taken her to Laguna, or La Jolla or, some La La place like that. More than that, she thinks maybe, perhaps, quite possibly, she did see a blond sort of Big Foot lurking in the distance when Rosa was here. "He could easily have been your missing Owen," she says. "In the meantime, why don't you come up to the house? You can rifle through, mutilate, and/or take anything of Rosa's you can find."

She leads us back to the house and up a dark stairwell to the third floor. "This is Matteo's place," she says staring down at a silver doorknob at the top of the stairs. "I don't usually come up here. Matteo and I have an understanding. I ignore the stupid things he's wasting his life on, and he does whatever he wants." A reckless gleam shines in Griselda's eyes. "I shouldn't be doing this, but too bad. I'm sick of that boy's bubble-headedness."

She opens the door and the dank, heavy smell of dirty sheets and old tennis shoes fall upon us. We fall back, steel ourselves and step inside. A flick of the light reveals a large space covered in piles of dirty, wrinkled clothes, sweetly pungent, mildewing towels and socks. Somewhere, there must be a bed, but if there is it has been completely taken over by women's shoes. Hundreds of them. Lined up neatly, each with its pair. These, presumably, are Rosa's. Not to be outdone, the closet is filled with twice as many pairs that look like they belong to Matteo. On what turns out to be a beanbag chair stand stacks of sealed shopping bags from Barneys, Bloomingdales, Lucky Brand, Apple, Game Stop. On top of these rest unopened credit card bills and envelopes from serious sounding firms stamped with words like: "Final Notice," "Past Due," and "Legally Liable."

It takes us hours to search the room, but in the end we don't find anything more interesting than a pile of unopened stockings, a five-year supply of birth control pills, and photographs of Rosa wearing nothing but high heels.

"Too bad," says Griselda. "I really thought you'd find something. I know. Why don't you stay for dinner? I feel so bad about holding you at gunpoint. It's the least I can do."

Well, she's been so nice.

"Here's what I think," I tell William when we're alone. "Rosa has either found true love or she's really misread Matteo's prospects. Why else would she leave the comfort of Owen's bill paying for this toxic room?"

"I can't imagine her wanting to come back here too soon," says William, who is in top form as he rifles through a pile of mail and, every once in a while, peers intently out the window toward the barn. "Especially if she thinks Griselda's out to get her."

"No. You're right, but she'll want her things eventually."

"Yes, but as long as Matteo can keep at least one credit card going, she probably won't be back in a hurry."

I plop down on the beanbag chair. "So we came here for nothing."

William sits down on the monster-sized lump that may be Matteo's bed. "Why don't we call Matteo? If Rosa's with him, maybe she can tell you something."

We ask Griselda for his number at dinner. She's made Osso Buco. Apparently, it once made a vintner down the road cry in despair because he knew that in his whole life, he would never—could never—create anything that made him feel as close to God as one bite of her heavenly stew. We eat in Griselda's dining room, which has a large rustic table that overlooks the front yard and the circular driveway. William's car is still down by the barn. "We don't want to upset the boars," she explains, "they get very distressed when they see cars." Now the pigs line the driveway. The moonlight shades their hulky shadows dark blue and, occasionally, I catch a yellow flicker of the animals' lovelorn eyes.

The idea of calling Matteo makes Griselda laugh. "Goodness, no. I don't have his phone number."

"But you're his mother."

She shrugs. "Have some more of my homemade orrechiette. And did you try the merlot? It's locally grown."

I take a sip and melt. Everything is so good, which is why, for the second time, I cannot stop eating. I'm devouring everything in sight: the butter-soft meat, the sauce-drenched pasta, the salad, the green beans, the plate of fruit and soft white cheeses that Griselda puts before us after the meal.

My pants start to feel tight and I try to stop, but I can't. How can I? After the cheese and fruit she gives us each a salad-plate sized ramekin filled with the fluffiest, whitest, smoothest, most amazing honey-covered panna cotta. "My grandmother's recipe," she says. "Try it." I tuck in, eyelids heavy. I glance over at William. His skin has gone a dusty pink. He blinks and seems to almost fall asleep before my eyes.

"You look so tired, William. Maybe we should go." But I can't go. I may never have panna cotta like this again.

"Don't go," says Griselda. "Stay. I have an extra room."

"Oh, we're not together," I say.

"Even better. I have two extra rooms."

She shows us to our rooms, and for a while I just sit there on the bed. The wine must have really gone to my head. I'm so dizzy. But isn't there something? Something I'm supposed to do?

I know. I should call Grace Claire. Tell her I'll come by tomorrow to sign the—what was it?—the thing.

"Fuck it," I whisper. "I'm not calling anybody. I don't want to. So there."

Chapter Fourteen

I dream of a gooey river of honey knocking down a ramshackle barn and of angry boars gnawing the toes off naked couples, but when I awake I feel fantastic. And why not? This soft bed is like a cocoon, what with the cradling mattress and the warm flannel sheets that caress my skin. Yes, my skin! Cuz, you know what? I didn't feel like sleeping in my pajamas last night. I felt like sleeping in my pink camisole and cotton panties. Oh, and my necklace. I almost forgot about my goddess necklace, but here it is, lying warm and smooth against my neck, like a little hug from my crazy but sweet Goddess Lounge sisters.

Sigh.

The world is good.

But enough! What's that smell? I throw on some clothes and pad over to the kitchen, where Griselda stands frying thick slices of fragrant, apple-cured bacon as the lovesick boars look on from outside the window. On the table sits a golden frittata bursting with thin slices of potatoes, a stack of ricotta pancakes resting in a pool of melted butter and syrup, an enormous platter of blueberries, strawberries, cantaloupe, red grapes, raspberries, kiwi, honeydew melon, watermelon, and mango, and a bowl filled with small balls of fried dough—like donut holes but lighter and less cakey—covered in cinnamon and sugar.

"Good news!" Griselda exclaims. "Matteo called. He'll be home soon. All you need to do is wait. He said Rosa will be happy to talk to you. That she knows exactly where your Owen is." Leaving the bacon to sizzle in the pan, she pours me a cup of pudding-thick hot chocolate. "Try this. You'll like it."

"Umm. So good."

"Help yourself. I made all of this for you, oh, and your friend."

"Wonderful. Where is William?"

"Still sleeping, I guess."

"Sleeping!" Why is he still sleeping? I want to share this with him. I want to see his face as he tries the hot chocolate. I want to hear him gasp in ecstasy and smile at me like he's discovered nirvana. "I should get him," I say, but then I take a bite of one of the dough balls.

Heaven explodes in my mouth. Time, space, and memory are obliterated as the airy sweetness melts my whole body and sends my fingers reeling back for more.

"Let him sleep," says Griselda, finishing the last strips of bacon and putting them on a platter.

I take a bite of the frittata. Layers of creamy potatoes, translucent onions and Parmesan bonded together with golden eggs and a touch of olive oil dissolve in my mouth and send me fairly sliding off my chair.

"So," says Griselda, "Who is this William?"

"He's helping me. He's Owen's boss, or he used to be Owen's boss."

She looks out the window at the boars. "You're sure you can trust him? Because, I don't know. I get a funny feeling about him."

"William's great." When she gives me an unconvinced frown, I add, "He has rescue dogs, pit bulls."

As if on cue, William enters the room. He's showered but unshaven. His hair, still damp, curls up near the base of his neck and ears. It looks as slick and smooth as the hot chocolate Griselda hands him. I pick up my own cup of hot chocolate and inhale as I wonder if William's hair actually smells like this chocolate. I wonder if it tastes like it. Suddenly, it occurs to me that I could just plunge my tongue straight into his hair and find out. He wouldn't need to know. I could just, sort of, lean into him. I feel myself tilting to the left.

"Are you all right?" William's hands are on my sides. He's straightening me up. Alas, he smells like soap.

"I'm fine." I grab another dough ball and stick it in my mouth. "Griselda's heard from Matteo."

William says we should call him right away. He says we could use call return, but Griselda says, "Oh, no. My old phone can't do anything like that."

"Are you sure?" asks William. "Why don't you let me take a look?"

She drops a slice of bacon on William's plate. Then, wiping her hands on her apron, she hisses, "I am not so incompetent that I don't know what my phone can do." It seems a little over the top, but she's been cooking all morning. "Matteo will be here soon," she says more calmly. "In the meantime, relax. Go for a walk. Eat. I'm roasting a boar for dinner. Won't that be good? Crackling skin basted with a nice rosemary and balsamic emulsion. Delicious."

"I don't know if we can stay that late," says William looking at me. "Didn't you need to get back, Penne?"

"Yes," I answer in a vague, noncommittal sort of sigh. The image of Xinran saying "you gave birth to a mean girl" flashes through my mind. "But I'm sure I can stay a little longer…if you can?"

"Always with men, it's zoom, zoom, rush, rush. Are you here to help poor Penne or not?"

The frown lines on William's forehead deepen. He rubs his hand across the back of his neck and looks down at his watch. "Ok," he says at last. "Ok."

With little to do but wait, William and I follow Griselda's advice and explore the nearby woods, where the cold air bites my cheeks, and where the thought of mean Grace Claire waiting for her initialed contract and of Owen—of anything to do with the past—seem wonderfully fuzzier by the minute. Who can think of such annoyances when mule deer silently glide past and rabbits scamper across the forest floor, when the sun illuminates leaves and trees like movie stars, when the sky shines Cinderella blue, the scent of pine fills the air, and birds chirp and sing? In such Disneyfied heaven, more pleasant topics consume us. Like lunch, a simple picnic of cheese, prosciutto, bread and wine, spread out on a plaid wool blanket, in a clearing, carefully chosen for its distance from the possible lairs of boars.

You would think all this eating would weigh us down, but it's the opposite. It's as if with each bite we become lighter, as if each bite takes away another layer of our former lives.

I spread this fantastic, milky Humboldt Fog on a slice of bread and hand it to William. As he takes it, his thumb grazes mine.

I swallow. "This is the best cheese I've ever had."

"It's good, but once—when I was skiing in Argentina—I had this white cheese. It was toasted on these thin pieces of bread. It was unbelievable."

"Really? You ski?"

He takes a sip of wine. "Not as much anymore. You?"

"No. I tried. I nearly killed myself. But I like the idea of skiing."

William smiles, and that twinkle shines in his eyes, both secretive and playful. "Once," he says, "I was skiing in Montana, and I had this apple pie. Just apples, and maybe a little cinnamon, but you know what made it stand out? What you could really taste? Butter."

Oh my God. "Good butter is so underrated." I feel myself inching closer.

"So is pie."

"But not store bought pie. Homemade pie. Homemade pie is incredible."

He leans into me. "I make pie." I tilt my face toward his.

Something rustles, and we hear a squeal in the bushes. William gets up and scans the clearing. Finding nothing, he comes back and sits down. Our hips jut against one another. Then there is more squealing and, this time, loud, proprietary grunting.

William sighs. "Maybe we should head back." He stands and offers me his hand. Pulling me up, his lips close to mine, he whispers, "Nice necklace."

"Oh. Yeah. My mom gave it to me."

Then, even more grunting. Very determined grunting. As we head back, at least for a few seconds more, he keeps my hand.

When Matteo does not show up by dinnertime, frown lines again burrow into William's forehead. He looks at his watch.

Not wanting to seem too out of sync with William, I frown too. "Still not back?" I say. "Hmmm, that's a problem." HA! But it's not my problem! I'm in heaven. I don't want to go back. Although, I do feel bad about the dogs.

"I guess I'll be one more night," I say on my phone message to Grace Claire. HA! HA! Grace Claire doesn't even pick up! What icing on the cake is that! "Sorry about the contract."

The next morning arrives with no sign of Matteo. "Don't worry," Griselda tells us. "He'll be here. Any minute. Relax. I'm making pasta carbonara tonight—the best you've ever had."

"That's kind of you, Griselda," says William. "But if Matteo will be here any minute, we'll be gone long before dinner, which I'm sure will make your life a lot easier."

Griselda says, "Of course." Then, looking at me, she adds, "I'm glad *you* at least enjoy all I'm trying to do for you."

"We both enjoy your hospitality," says Williams. "But we do have things to do."

"You've been wonderful," I say between bites of quiche. "Oh my God," I say to William, "Have you tried these fried potatoes?"

After breakfast, I call Georgie and leave another message. "In for a penny, in for a pound," I tell the answering machine because Georgie's gone too! Hooray! "We've waited so long; we can't leave now."

Next, I call Nancy, who seems almost amused to hear my voice. "You sound different," she says. "Very relaxed."

"You think?"

"Don't worry," she tells me, "I can watch the dogs a while longer, and you know you have tons of vacation time. Any sign of Owen?"

"Not yet. But William and I are making progress."

"*William* and you?"

"Oh. He's a sort of friend of mine. He's helping me."

"I see. Well then, *William* and you better keep up the good work. And ask him if he has a friend for me."

"Nancy!" I look around, a little bit tickled in spite of myself. William is outside with the boars. Well, he's not with the boars. They're a good thirty feet to the side, but they're watching him. They stare at him with unimpressed eyes as he gazes toward the barn. He does that a lot, actually. He turns to see me watching him, and a flash of anxiety crosses his face. The corners of his mouth turn down and he looks away so that my eyes rest on his hair. "It's not like that," I say. "William's just a friend, more of an acquaintance really." Even as the words slip out, the aroma of dark, bitter chocolate seems to surround me and saliva fills my mouth. I wonder what's for lunch.

I find Griselda in the kitchen and she gives me a slice of the most amazing cake. Get this: it's made of olive oil. It's an olive oil cake. I didn't even know such a thing existed. To think of the decades wasted is almost tragic. Best take another bite.

"You're so fun to cook for," says Griselda.

I smile and stuff more cake in my mouth.

"But this William. I have to be honest with you. I don't trust him at all. There's something he's not telling you. I can feel it. Believe me, Penne. He's all wrong for you."

"We're just friends," I say, and as I say it I feel a little jolt in my stomach and I think about his chocolate hair.

She points a finger at me and says, "Be sure you keep it that way."

When William comes in he says, "Matteo's still not here, Penne. I think we should head back. We'll think of another way of finding Owen."

With a thud, Griselda puts down a bowl of whipped cream. "I said Matteo would be here. Are you saying that I'm lying to you? After all I've done? You are the one who is lying."

"Lying? What have I got to lie about?"

Hands on hips, she tilts her chin and says, "You tell me."

"Hold on," I say putting down my fork. "I hear a lot of tension here." I look at Griselda. "You've been wonderful. We can't thank you enough for all you've done." I look at William. This is the hard part. "You need to get back. Don't you?"

He looks down.

"You need to get back. I understand."

"He—" says Griselda.

I look back at her. "He needs to get back, but I know you're expecting Matteo. How about this? We wait until lunch. If he's not here by lunch, we leave."

They give each other grumpy looks and nod. "Ok," I say. "Great."

"Fine," says Griselda. She points at William. "But keep him out of my hair."

"Ok," I say. "We'll go for another hike."

And we do. This one is hard. We have to scale rocky terrain and ford a stream. Swear to God. We ford. But here's the part that leaves a hole in the center of my chest and that tightens my throat like a vice: The deeper into the forest we move, the softer becomes the roll of William's shoulders and the lines on his face. His lips become pink, his face ruddy plum. Now he's happy. Now that we're leaving.

At the top of a ridge we sit and look down at the valley.

"I'm sorry," I say.

"Why are you sorry?"

"You came here to help me, and I bullied you into staying. It's just, it's nice sometimes not to be the mom."

"You didn't bully me."

"You have your work. You have your dogs."

"Can I ask you something, Penne? Do you love Owen? Is that what this whole thing is about? Really?"

"I….No." I shake my head. "It's not that. I don't know what it is. But it's not that I love him. He's moved on, and so have I." A slight wind has started up. It sweeps William's hair forward. I take my hand and brush it back. He reaches up and laces his fingers through mine, and, what can I say, we kiss, and his kiss is deep and sweet and warm and wonderful. And I run my hand up his shirt and wrap my arms around his smooth back, and the hollow part in my chest? Gone. The vice on my throat? Gone. I am filled, instead, with champagne bubbles and cinnamon. Every delicious thing Griselda has made, every cake, every donut hole, every pasta dish, every glass of wine is nothing compared to this now, to this heaven, to this kiss.

He pulls back and puts his hands on my waist.

"This is why you stayed," I say.

He kisses me again, softer this time, as we slide our bodies onto each other and the ground.

"This is why I wanted you to stay," I say.

And for one perfect moment, everything is good. Fantastic.

But, let's be honest, we're lying on rocks. As warm as William's lips are, as smooth as his hands feel as they touch the skin under my shirt, these rocks are really cold. They're like ice cubes, sharp little frozen daggers that press against us. We wince and kiss and wince and finally we just look at each other and start laughing. With a sigh, he pulls me up and wraps me in his arms. "Let me take you home, Penne," he says, his lips brushing my ear.

"Take me home."

We walk hand in hand back to the ranch with hardly a word, both afraid, I think, to spoil the moment with something as banal as chitchat, or—worse—personal stories.

Griselda's has laid out a beautiful lunch. I barely see what's on the table. I look up to see William smiling at me. I smile back and then notice Griselda staring at me. Her eyes have gone small and black, like the pigs'.

"Any news of Matteo?" says William.

"Yes, as a matter of fact," she says. "He's here."

"Of course he's here. You said he'd be here," I say. "When can we talk to him?"

"He's in the barn. We can go now." She pauses as she looks from me to William. Then she adds, "Since you don't seem very hungry."

"Terrific," I say standing.

We head down to the barn. William's car is still standing out front, and new tire tracks crisscross near by. It almost looks like two sets of tracks, but there are no other cars, just William's. Griselda opens the door to the barn and leads us into the darkened room.

"Matteo's in here?" William says.

"Yes," Griselda answers. "He's with the rest of the pigs where he belongs. Just like you."

And thump, bang. My cheek hits the floor, and I hear myself moan.

Chapter Fifteen

"Penne? Penne? Wake up, dear." It's Griselda. She's leaning over me holding an ice pack to the back of my head. "I told you: you need to stay awake. You might have a concussion."

"What happened?" I look around. I'm in my bed at Griselda's house. "Where's William?"

"Shhh, take this." She hands me a couple of Tylenol and a glass of water.

"What happened?" I say again.

"It's just what I warned you about. It's William. He was lying to you."

"What?"

"Soon after you left for your walk a woman showed up. Very pretty. Fake boobs. She said she was William's girlfriend."

"Ashley? But William broke up with her. He told me."

"He lied to you."

"Ashley did this?" I put my hand up to a tender and lumpy welt at the back of my head.

Griselda nods. "Of course, I sent William packing after that," she says. "I knew you wouldn't want to see him after the way he used you. You did sleep with him, didn't you? I could tell when you came back from your hike. I could tell things were different. That bastard."

"We didn't sleep together. William wasn't lying. He wouldn't lie."

"But you would have slept with him. I could tell." She shakes her head. "You're not thinking straight. It's the concussion. All men lie. Men are pigs. You know that. Your husband taught you that. Now here: take the Tylenol and rest. I'll take care of you. I have the most wonderful meal planned."

I think I fall asleep again because, the next thing I know, I'm smelling rosemary and thyme. My head feels heavy and sore. It takes me a minute to remember what happened, to remember what Griselda told me. William lied. I can't believe that William lied and then just left.

Griselda's cooking again. I can smell pork chops and biscuits, but food won't help me. I know that now, and I know I need to get home.

I pile my things into my purse and go to the kitchen.

"Penne, darling. Sit. Eat. You've been through a lot."

"Thank you for everything, but I need to get back to my daughter. I've been a bad mother. Do you think Matteo might be able to take me back to town after I talk to him? That way I can rent a car and get back to reality."

Griselda tilts her head, thinks about this a minute and then laughs. "Don't be silly. Why bother with reality? Stay."

"Where is Matteo, anyway?"

She sets a plate of wonderful things in front of me, wonderful things the sight of which only make me nauseous. "In the barn. I did what you said."

I finger the welt on my head. "What did I say?"

"You remember. You said to test Rosa. You said it the day you arrived. You said to test her like Venus tested Psyche."

"Venus?"

"Of course."

I drop my hand down to my necklace. "I'm quite sure I never said anything about Venus."

"Remember? You said that I should test Rosa to see if she loved Matteo or was using him. And I said, 'like Psyche,' and you agreed."

I shake my head. "I really don't know what you're talking about."

Griselda sighs and puts down the frying pan in her hand. "Don't tell me you don't know this story?" She rolls her eyes and says in a singsong voice, "Once there was a princess named Psyche. She was so beautiful that Venus got jealous. Venus tried to embarrass Psyche by making Psyche fall in love with some loser, but, Venus's son Cupid fell in love with Psyche himself. He took her as his secret lover. Venus found out, and she did what any sane mother would do: she locked him up. When Venus realized that Cupid and Psyche really loved each other, she decided to screw over Psyche a different way. She told Psyche that she would let her be with Cupid if she did one little favor. Psyche had to go the underworld and bring back a jar of youthful beauty. Of course, as the goddess of beauty, Venus didn't need any jarred help. What she was really trying to do was kill Psyche since humans can only get to the underworld by dying. Anyway, Psyche couldn't very well say no to Venus, and so Psyche climbed to the top of a high tower and prepared to throw herself to her death, but the goddess Athena, who hated Venus, stopped Psyche and told her about a different way to enter—and escape, that's the tricky part—the underworld. Psyche literally went to hell and back to prove her love, and eventually—through the help of the gods—she was allowed to marry Cupid and become immortal herself."

I look out the window. It's beautiful outside. It's perfectly still, but for the gentle swaying of trees in the wind. It's a perfect contrast to the turmoil inside me. My head aches. I'm tired. William is gone. That bitch Venus has inserted her story into my life again. And Griselda makes no sense, no sense at all. I need to get back to Grace Claire. I need to get back to real life, to my dogs, to my...devoted pets.

"Griselda," I say. "Where are the boars?"

"The boars?"

"The boars. They're always outside of here. They're always waiting for you. Now they're not. Where are they?"

She shrugs her shoulders. "It's a nice day. Maybe..."

"Griselda, why is Matteo in the barn?"

"I told you," she says simply. "I'm following your advice."

I'm gone. I'm out of the kitchen. I'm running to the barn. Griselda is behind me. "It's for his own good," she says. "I'm helping him." Still, I'm running. I turn the bend and see the barn ahead of me. I see something else too. I see William's car. What I don't see are the boars. I run faster. I'm halfway there. "I did it for you," Griselda yells. "He lied to you."

Ten feet from the barn Griselda lets out a loud, "Sueeeeeeey."

Here come the pigs. They scramble from the barn and head toward me. I stop. They close in around me. They snort. I can feel their breath on my hands. Griselda is behind me, panting. Gray clouds appear from nowhere and tower over her, turning the whole sky dark. The air grows cold and damp. "I tried to help you, Penne," say Griselda. "I don't know why you couldn't see that." She clicks her tongue and the pigs snort and move in closer. One of them bangs my calf with its snout.

"What have you done, Griselda?"

Big, sloppy raindrops land on my shoulders and face.

"Done? I haven't done anything except shower you in kindness and hospitality. I've treated you like a goddess."

"I'm not a goddess."

"Men lie, Penne. They have to get what they deserve." Thunder rolls. The rain falls harder, faster.

"Your own son?"

"Matteo's fine. He just has to wait here until Rosa proves her worthiness."

The boars nudge me, sniff me. "How will she do that?"

"Simple. She has to get a job. All she has to do is show me a paycheck and she can have him. If not, well, he's better off. He'll know her true colors."

"And William?"

Griselda walks around the boars, her fingers lazily grazing one pig and then the next. "Now you've made that very difficult."

"Ashley never hit me, did she?"

"No. But she was here. She was very angry too. Why not? He lied to you, Penne, and we can't let men lie to good women. It makes them feel entitled." Griselda's voice turns hollow and cold. The boars wiggle with excitement. They root at the wet earth and snort. One comes in close. His beady eyes shine as he snaps his teeth at my pants.

"I was only thinking of you, Penne."

Slowly, I drop my hand into my purse. My fingers glide over the contents.

"What are you doing, Penne?"

"Nothing."

"Take your hand out of the bag, Penne. Slowly."

"Sure." My fingers find what they're looking for and wrap around the heavy coin purse full of Sacagawea dollars. I push the bag up my sleeve and withdraw my hand from the bag. I lift up my hand and feel the coin purse slide down to my elbow. "See?" I say. "Nothing."

"Good." Water drips from Griselda's nose and chin. She circles round the boars again, faster this time. The boars turn in unison with her. They copy her every step. "I really don't know what to do with you, Penne. You refuse to do what's best for you. How can I help you if you won't help yourself?"

My palm facing up, I drop my arm. The coin purse slides down to the bottom of my sleeve. With a swift flick of my wrist, it's in my hand. Griselda looks at the boars as she talks on. "Really, you're as helpless as Matteo."

I clutch the coin purse in my hand and, with all my might, hurl it at Griselda. It's the sound that catches her attention first. The coins clatter their way toward her, but it's too late. She's confused and frozen, and the bag lands squarely in her face. She reels backwards, slips on the fast-forming mud and falls to the ground. The boars race to her side and begin sniffing her, licking her.

Into the barn I run—and there's William, tied to a metal chair, a black gag in his mouth. Next to him sits a young man with shoulder-length black hair. Finally: Matteo. I untie William and, together, we free Matteo. "Hurry," I say.

We race outside. There's Griselda curled up in a ball, a muddy trifle being greedily foraged. The pigs nose her, beat against her, burrow into the crevices where her arms cling to her torso and her knees to her chest. The pigs moan. They sigh. Their beady eyes smile.

William ushers Matteo and me into his car. I take one last look as the car pulls away. One of the pigs rolls over onto Griselda and squeals, happy at last.

Chapter Sixteen

No need for niceties. No need for cordial introductions between our new friend Matteo and us. We are bound by shared freakish trauma. Our souls practically co-mingle, and so I have no qualms at getting straight to the point as we careen down the mountain toward Buellton.

"Your mother is fucking crazy," I say.

"Tell me something I don't know." He slinks low into the backseat.

"And you can slow down," I tell William. "Those pigs are going to keep Griselda busy for a while."

If anything, William drives faster.

I look out the window. Vineyards, trees whizz by in a water-colored blur. "Don't get any wrong ideas about why I helped you," I say to William. "It's not because of what happened on the hike. I would have helped anyone."

William doesn't even look at me. He stares straight ahead. He knows I know. He is so busted.

"You should have told me you were still with Ashley. Now you've made me as bad as Rosa."

"Rosa," sighs Matteo.

"And slow down," I say. "You're going to get us killed."

"No," says William. "I'm trying to prevent that."

"Griselda—"

"Not Griselda," he says. "Ashley."

"What?" I turn to face William and out of the corner of my eye I catch a glimpse of a yellow vehicle coming up to pass us. William steps on the gas, but the car keeps up with us. I look closer. It's Ashley's Hummer, and there, sitting in the driver's seat, her beautiful blond hair tousled and wild, is Ashley.

"She's been stalking me for months," says William. "She's convinced she's channeling the goddess Hera."

"Hera. That's her inner goddess. But why would that make her stalk you?"

"Hera was the goddess of marriage," chimes in Matteo. "She was married to Zeus, and Zeus totally cheated on her, like, constantly. Hera was always trying to catch him in the act."

"How does everyone know all of this but me?" I scream.

"She's convinced I'm sleeping with you," says William. "She's been convinced of it since Dashed Sails. She saw you drop me off. She left a letter at my house. Threatening you. That's why I wanted to come. I thought I should look out for you. I felt…responsible."

"That's why you came?"

William jerks the car to the right just in time to avoid colliding with Ashley. The road narrows and a car approaches from the opposite side. Its horn blasts. Ashley falls in close behind us. The rain falls harder and faster, the scale of water increasing with our speed, as if determined not to be outdone by our panic. We turn a corner and skim aimlessly on the wet road. William overcorrects and sends us careening toward the edge of the mountain road.

Ringing erupts in the car. It's my phone, but who cares about my phone. Ashley is staring me down from her Hummer. She points at me and then taps the side of her head. Only then do I realize she's wearing a shiny Bluetooth. "Shit," I say.

"Don't answer it," says William, but it's too late. I've already fished my phone out of my purse and picked up.

"You cow," she screams. "You are so dead."

"William says he broke up with you months ago."

"William didn't mean it."

"I think he did. Get a hold of yourself." Speaking a language I'm sure she'll understand, I add, "I can't believe Hera would want you to do this."

"No. Hera would want me to do *this*."

With the pounding sound of smashed metal, we lurch forward as Ashley rams her Hummer into the back of William's car. Matteo grabs my phone and throws it out the window. "What are you doing?" he says. "You're making things worse."

The road levels out. Farms pop up. Soon we see gas stations and a few strip malls, and now, I think, yes, safety. There is no way Ashley's beast of a machine will be able to match William's nimble chariot on flat, open road, and I'm right. We make for the freeway and watch her yellow Hummer get smaller and smaller. And—Hallelujah—we are free! We are delivered! We are on the 101 and we are flying south. We pass Solvang. We pass Goleta. And then we stop. We find ourselves in the worst traffic nightmare I have even seen. Every single car, in every single lane, has ground to a halt. People are getting out of their cars. They are holding umbrellas and straining their necks and eyes to see what is going on. William pulls out his smart phone and tries to figure out what has happened, but a KNX traffic report beats him to it.

Dammit piss shit. A massive mudslide just south of us has closed the entire northbound freeway, and now emergency crews have commandeered the southbound freeway—our freeway. Southbound drivers are being rerouted, via one slow, meandering lane, to some fake freeway called the 192. What 192? I've never even heard of it, but William's smart-alecky car assures me that it exists anyway. I am so glad I don't own a GPS.

"It does exist," says Matteo. "It takes you North, through Santa Paula."

Yeah. Like that's even a real town.

"The point is, we don't have a choice," says William.

"But do you think Ashley will be able to catch up to us?"

"How could she?" says William. "Look."

Behind us is a thick sea of cars, all locked in place, just like us. I scan the cars. No banana Hummers.

So we relax a bit. How can we not? We can't run on adrenaline forever. We've got to crash to earth eventually, and we do. We're like zombies. We're too brain dead and hungry to do more than stare ahead as we move forward at glacial speed.

After a while Matteo says, "So who are you guys anyway? Why were you at my mom's?"

We tell him about Owen. He says he knows Owen, but only by reputation, only by what Rosa has told him. Still, what he knows is enough. Owen did follow Rosa and Matteo to Griselda's. They'd both seen him hiding out by the barn. It was soon after they got there. What a joke, they'd thought. What a loser.

"He's got some issues," I say.

"He's a loser," says Matteo.

"But at least he knows what he wants. Right? At least he's not afraid of that. At least he owns that. And, to be honest, when you're what is wanted, it's not always so bad. He's not always so bad."

I glance at William who looks back with a questioning sort of hurt in his eyes. "The point is," I say, "What really matters is that Owen wasn't injured, right? He wasn't in danger? He was just following Rosa?"

Matteo stretches out and flops back in his seat. "He wants her back. He's desperate. He's like a puppy. But he's not crazy like the Hummer babe. He's just pathetic, all pale and blobby."

"I still don't see why he would need money."

"I don't know," says Matteo.

We fall quiet, and then, after we move forward a few more inches, the rain begins to let up. Twenty minutes later it's like it had never started. By now it's night, and the sky is a cloudless midnight blue dotted with stars and a giant yellow moon. I say, "Tell me about Rosa."

"Rosa," he sighs. "I think I really fucked that up." Then his sad story spills out. They met at Dashed Sails. It was after the show. He bought her a drink. They had sex in his car, and then she went home to Owen. One night and Matteo knew it was over; he was her slave for life. He began waiting for her after the show. He'd buy her a drink. They'd have sex in his car. It was perfect. But every night she stole more of his soul until he was an empty vessel. He went crazy. He couldn't stop thinking about her, wanting her. And, oh, how he hated Owen. Owen, who got to wake up and smell Rosa's hair. Owen, who got to touch her in the sunlight. Owen, who was old and fat and who Rosa only tolerated because he paid the bills. Owen. What a putz.

So Matteo made a plan. What he needed, he realized, was money. But, as he told me in a still awed and shocked voice, "You're totally screwed if you don't have a job and you haven't paid your credit cards in a while. It's like no one even respects you."

"Hard to believe," says William.

"Tell me about it," says Matteo.

But, like I said, Matteo had a plan. One night, at Dashed Sails, Rosa and Matteo ran into these old groupies of Rosa's. They were these totally rich stoner kids from the Valley who were desperate for her to try on the latest Ojos shoe collection. They'd brought her four-dozen Milk's bon bons in the hopes of luring her to the store one last time.

Rosa took the bon bons.

"You'll come with us then?" they asked.

"No," she said, and then she went to change in the dressing room.

Matteo and the stoners got to talking. It turned out they had a lot in common. They were all community college students. They all thought Rosa was hot. And they were all really into pot. When the stoners learned that Matteo had once grown hydroponic pot, and was, therefore, sort of an expert on pot, they about fell over in excitement because, more than anything, the stoners hoped that Matteo could shed light on one of the most legendary highs of all time.

"Dude," one of the stoners had said to Matteo. "Have you ever done Lotus?"

"Lotus?" said Matteo.

"Dude," the stoner went on. "Dude, you've got to know Lotus. It's like this mythic thing. It's like this stuff that's totally organic and natural so it's good for you and it's like, God even gave it to man, so we're, like, supposed to take it. It's supposed to give the most awesome buzz. It's like so awesome that you don't even remember who you fucking are."

"Lotus?" Matteo said again.

"Yeah," the stoner said. "Lotus. It's some kind of flower."

"And you smoke it?"

"No, man. You eat it. That's the best part. It's edible so it won't give you lung cancer."

It was at that moment, right when the stoner said, "eat it," that Matteo knew what to do. "Ahhhhh," he said nodding his head. "Lotus. Sure. My guys call it 'Flower Power.' It will blow your fucking mind. It literally takes you to another dimension—another dimension, man—a dimension where you're just, like, chill."

The stoner grabbed Matteo's arm and the other stoners leaned in closer so that they could breathe in the essence of someone who had actually done Lotus. "Dude," the stoner said. "You gotta get us some. You got to."

"I don't know," Matteo told them. "It's hard to come by, and it's really expensive. It's private-jet expensive."

The stoners huddled together and whispered. One of them said, "How expensive is private-jet expensive?"

Matteo looked down. He pressed the tip of his shoe into a little puddle of beer on the floor and smeared the liquid around. "I don't know," he shrugged. "For all of you?"

They nodded.

"Maybe 25K."

The stoners huddled. "We can do that," one of them said.

A week later, Matteo went down to the flower mart and bought a truckload of pansies, the kind he'd seen Griselda sprinkle on salads and cupcakes. He brought it to the stoners and said, "Here you go. The best high you'll ever have."

"We just have to eat 'em?"

"You just have to eat them. But if you eat them when you're already high, it's way epic."

The stoners grinned. Way epic was what they'd always dreamed of.

Twenty-five-thousand dollars richer, Matteo went to Rosa. "Now you can dump the old geezer," he told her. "Now I can take care of you."

She looked at the cash. She looked at Matteo. She looked at the cash. She said, "Ok."

Bliss. Heaven. Whatever you want to call it, Matteo and Rosa had it. For about a month. First at Griselda's, where Matteo and Rosa went to drop off the pilfered booty of her relationships and jobs and then in Santa Barbara, where they stayed at the best hotel in town, and, where, also, they saw Owen a second time.

"This was maybe a week ago," says Matteo.

"How did he know where you were?" I ask.

"No idea, but he looked wild, real wild, and he was stressing out. He was screaming for Rosa wherever we went, begging her to talk to him, said their lives depended on it. Finally, she just had to beat the shit out of him."

"What?"

"Beat the shit out of him. Well, not really. She just had to jujitsu-him-up a little, so he'd leave us the hell alone. It was the only way we could chill again and, you know, live large, at least for a little while longer. The thing is that 25K isn't really that much. You'd be surprised how fast you can burn through it."

"Is that why you went back to Griselda's?" asks William.

Matteo runs his hands through his long black hair. "I guess that wasn't such a good idea."

"Didn't you know your mother would flip out?" I say.

"Oh, no," he says. "I knew she'd flip out—maybe not as much as she did, but she's crazy, I knew she'd flip out some. I just didn't know Rosa would give up on us so easily."

"But Griselda didn't give her much choice," I say.

Matteo shakes his head. "She had a choice," he sighs. "And she chose to leave. She wasn't coming back. I could see it in her eyes. She was never coming back. You know, I don't think she ever loved me. I think she only loved the money. She probably went back to the geezer. She's probably with him right now."

I look back at Matteo sprawled out in the backseat. He's got his hands wrapped around his skull like he's trying to squeeze his brains out or press his tears in. Of course she only loved the money, I want to tell him. Of course, she was never coming back. But there is such a thing as too much truth, and there's such a thing as knowing when to keep your mouth shut. And he's just a boy.

Sometime around midnight, we drop Matteo off at some divey apartment in Koreatown. "You're wrong about Rosa, you know?" he says getting out of the car.

"How so?" I say.

"You think she uses people. You think she's selfish. She's not. She's just more."

"More?"

"It's like we're down there," he says waving his hands in front of his waist. "And she's up here." He raises his hands high above his head. "It's like we're not even the same species. She's more." He shrugs his shoulders. "So she deserves more."

We head back to the freeway. Without Matteo as a buffer, an awkward silence envelops us. I glance over at William. "You could have told me," I say at last. "About Ashley."

"I should have told you. But the thing is, it wasn't just because of Ashley that I came. You know that right?" He puts his hand on mine.

I did not know that, but it's pretty nice to hear. Actually, it's really nice to hear.

"Can I take you home now?" he says.

I look at William, all shadowed and blue in the dim light of the car. His face is haggard, his hair a mess. I swear, I could gobble him up whole right now. "Can we do one more thing?"

"Sure."

We go to Silverlake. We pass the damn Venus banners and Gelson's. We make our way to Owen's loft. The door is closed but unlocked, and it only takes about two seconds to realize that no one is here. The whole place has been cleaned up and straightened. The pictures of Rosa have been removed from the walls. The vanity table with all her nail polishes is gone. So are most of the plants. An ugly orange and brown sheet that I recognize as once belonging to Owen's parents is draped over the couch. Also, the television is playing.

"Owen's been here." I say.

"Not with Rosa."

"No. It looks like she didn't want the geezer after all."

William slides his arm around me. "So what do we do?"

I lean into him. "We go home. It doesn't matter anymore."

"Ok," he says. "Let's go home."

The house is dark and quiet when we park William's car on the driveway. Actually, it's really quiet, which seems a little weird, but there's no banana Hummer around, and I have William with me, and I have six protective dogs capable of keeping jealous goddesses away, and all I really want to do is cuddle up next to William's long, lean body and smell his yummy hair and go to sleep until noon, after which all I want is all manner of bliss, so I probably don't read as much into the quiet as I should.

"Shh," I say as we make our way to the door. "We don't want to wake the dogs." Without a sound, I open and close the door. William reaches for a light switch. "No," I whisper. "The dogs."

I take William's hand in mine, and with my other hand I feel for the wall. We cross the entryway. We go up the stairs. I open my bedroom door and pull William to the bed. We kick off our shoes and begin to undress. I feel on the bed for Lucy. "Sorry, girl," I whisper, "You'll have to go."

My hand brushes across a form on the bed—in the bed. It's not Lucy. I jump back. "Who?"

The bedside light goes on. "Welcome home, Penne. Where the hell have you been?" Oh for godsake, it's Owen.

Chapter Seventeen

"Owen," I stammer. It's like the two hemispheres of my brain have been wrenched apart. Everything is dizziness. I stumble backward into William's arms.

"What is *he* doing here?" Owen says pointing to William.

I feel my brain trying to knit itself back together. Owen: Here. William: Here. Owen, here. William, here. Owen and William here. Oh…shit. But then the swirling colors in my head turn: Why, oh shit? This is my house. This is my life. "William is with me," I say. "Which, by the way, is none of your business, and where the hell have you been? I've been worried sick—"

"So that's the way it is, is it?" says Owen looking from me to William. "Fine. Well, since you've been off *having fun*, I've been here helping our daughter recover from the trauma you and your crazy mother have instilled upon her with your bullshit goddesses and your whatever crazy other things you expose her too. Really, Penne, if I knew you were going to lose it completely when I left I would have rethought the whole plan."

"What are you talking about?"

"What am I talking about? What am I talking about? Where have you been? I'm talking about this." William points us downstairs and we follow him over to the TV. He turns it on and quickly switches from channel to channel until he lands on CNN.

Above a banner reading, "filmed yesterday," we see footage of dark clouds and rain mingling with thick black smoke. The smoke is rising from a storefront on Hollywood Boulevard, in front of which a mob of people is rioting.

"Oh my God," I say. "That's The Goddess Lounge."

The camera pans in to show the crowd. There are probably a hundred people. Most are unrecognizable, but then I see Uzume, Bast, and Freyja, dripping in their saris. They're wielding long knitting needles in an effort to protect The Goddess Lounge entrance. Three burly men with crew cuts throw a garbage can into the window. Uzume, Bast, and Freyja cower, and one-minute later, their rain-soaked outfits are covered in blood.

The scene switches to a thick group of women being shoved into a police van. That's when I practically cough my entire heart up. There, in the crowd, looking panic stricken and feeble, stands Tamara, stooped and frail, afraid, not one ounce of goddess moxie left to straighten her spine, and right behind her: Georgie and Grace Claire.

"What happened?" I stammer.

"What happened? Your mother happened."

"What?"

"Some church in Orange County shipped in a bus load of protesters to your goddess hangout. Then some news crew showed up and—no surprise—your mother wasn't far behind. Right in the camera she says some crap about divine fucking womanhood and how all people should learn to embrace the 'great goddess of the universe.' Then what do you think happened? The protesters got pissed off and started destroying everything. You're lucky your daughter wasn't killed, Penne."

"But why were they even there?"

"Ha! That's another thing! Grace Claire started her period, Penne. And you weren't here. I had to buy feminine products. I did. Me."

"But what—"

"It was your mother. 'Wouldn't it be fun,' thought your mother, to make Grace Claire just as much of a freak as her. 'Let's celebrate your womanhood by getting you a goddess,' she told Grace Claire. 'Celebrate your womanhood.' Jesus, Penne, I can't even believe I have to say this shit."

I fall onto the couch. "My God. My God." William sits next to me.

"Luckily, I saw the whole thing going down on TV," says Owen. I was able to get an attorney, get Grace Claire—and even get your mother, thank you very much." Owen points a finger at me. "You owe me for that one, Penne."

"Shit. Shit." I'm rocking back and forth now. "I'm such a bad mother. I'm such a bad mother."

William pulls me close. "This wasn't your fault."

Owen turns off the TV. "Well, it sort of was. You don't have to beat yourself up about it though. I fixed it. Grace Claire is fine now. She's sleeping. Georgie's fine too. I took her home."

"Thank you, Owen. Thank you so much. I can't believe I let this happen."

"You didn't do this, Penne," says William.

"Yes. I did." I stand up. "I'm the mom. I should have been here. It's all my fault."

William stands up.

"You should probably go," says Owen to William while inserting himself between the two of us. "Grace Claire could wake up. She shouldn't see you."

William balks. "Why's that? She's seen your girlfriend a thousand times. Before Rosa left you, that is."

Owen's ears go pink. He folds his arms in front of him. "Grace Claire needs her family right now. That's all I'm saying."

William looks at me.

"You should probably go," I say.

William takes a deep breath and pulls himself taller. He cradles my face in his smooth hands. "Penne."

I slide away. I reach my hand up to my necklace, which suddenly feels tight. Too tight. "I'll call you."

"Yeah. She'll call you," says Owen opening the door. "But knowing Penne as well as I do, she'll probably focus on taking care of Grace Claire for a while. She tries hard to be a good mother, you know."

I sleep in the office/extra bedroom. It's closer to Grace Claire's room, and it seems highly likely that an experience like the one she's endured could provoke post-traumatic stress-induced nightmares. I should be nearby just in case. It's the least I can do, considering. The futon's a little short for sleeping, but it doesn't really matter. I plan on torturing myself for about the next 50 million years anyway. Might as well let the furniture in on the fun.

When I see Grace Claire in the morning, we are full of tears and hugs, but, naturally, I have more of both. I apologize. A thousand times I apologize. For everything. For accusing her of being mean, for driving her out of the house, for not initialing the contract, for letting her get arrested, for traumatizing her forever, for ruining her life.

"It's ok," she tells me. "I wasn't arrested, just held for questioning. And about the contract, the Disney show wasn't working out anyway."

"What? Did they let you go? Because of this?"

Grace Claire shrugs. "It's complicated. I'm just glad to be home."

And here I go again. Crying buckets of gratitude, rivers of guilt.

"I'll make you your favorite breakfast," I tell her. "I'll take you shopping. We'll talk. We'll make sense of this whole mess."

"Actually, I think I should go to school," she says. "I don't want to fall behind."

"Yes," I say. "That's a great idea. Get back to routine, predictability. That will be good."

So we shower, we put on our happy faces and off we go. I drop her off just before the bell rings, just in time to see Xinran kiss Pei goodbye. Xinran sees me and points a stubby finger at Grace Claire. She smiles a ghoulish smile at me. "Damn it," I whisper as goose bumps pop up on my skin. "Damn it, damn it, damn it."

Owen is waiting for me at the house. He's sitting there at the kitchen table reading the paper and drinking coffee. It's like he never left, except it's not like he's never left. It's more like a really bad dream. When he sees me he stands up and says, "I think we should talk."

"I know. I know. I messed up. I'm sorry. It will never happen again. Never."

"Forget about it."

"I'm just so glad you were there for Grace Claire. I can't imagine how terrified she must have been."

He puts his hand on my arm and guides me over to the table. "Let me get you some coffee. You're tired."

"I just, I'll never forgive myself. Do you think she's emotionally scarred? I should call her therapist."

Owen puts the cup of coffee in front of me and sits down. "Enough, Penne. Enough. She'll be fine. You always get so worked up about things."

"I know, I know. I shouldn't do that."

"You need to relax."

"I know."

"I want to talk to you about something."

Oh, God. He's going to sue for full custody, and he'll win because I am the most irresponsible mother ever. I look up at him. My mouth dry, I say, "Shoot."

He looks down at the table. There is a little pile of spilt sugar on it. He takes his finger and pushes the grains into a swirled pattern. "We're good at this, aren't we?"

"What?"

"This. One of us messes up. The other one fixes it. We're good at that. We've always been."

This time it's my turn to look down at the table. I straighten the newspapers.

"Do you remember when we met? In college? You were so much fun, Penne. You laughed all the time."

"Yeah. Where did that girl go?"

"I want to come home, Penne."

Even the house must be listening. Not a sound. Just the thumping of my heart. I whisper, "I don't think so."

He grabs my hands. "Come on. It'll be great. I'm ready now. I'm ready to be the husband you need. Can't you see that? I'm done with Rosa—"

"You mean she's done with you."

He throws his hands in the air. "Whatever. The point is, she's out of my system. We've both moved on. I want to come home. I'm ready to come home."

Owen rubs the top of my hands with his. I pull them away. I can't think. It's too quiet. It's too still and dead in here. It's so....Wait. Why is it so quiet? I look around the room. "Owen, where are the dogs?"

"Oh." He takes a sip of coffee. "They're in the garage."

"But...there's no doggy door in the garage. And it's cold in there, and there's no place soft to sit."

"I had no choice. Those dogs are crazy; they kept biting at me."

"There's no food in the garage either. Have you fed them? Do they have water?"

"I was going to."

"You," I say, "are bad."

I rush to the garage and open the door. Out come my babies. Poor things. They crowd round me and whine in relief. They're so hungry they lick every speck of salt off of me. They whack their tails into each other and push each other in eager attempts to lick my ankles. Poor Lucy walks stiff-legged over to me, her tail wagging, her bark hoarse. "Let me feed you," I say. "Come, come. Mama's home now. Mama will take care of you."

We go to the kitchen, where I fill their bone-dry water bowls and scoop piles of kibble in their food dishes. Tails wagging, they eat like they're starving prisoners of war and then circle round their empty bowls and lick them some more.

I hear Owen watching TV in the living room. "You are bad, Owen. You are so bad."

"Uh, Penne," he hollers. "You better come here."

"Why?"

"Just come."

I stomp over to Owen. "Go. Get out."

He points to the TV. "Just...look."

There, on a white couch, next to a small-headed announcer in a too-tight sweater, sit my mother and some tanned, bleach-toothed guy whose bulging eyes contrast with his calm, measured voice. "And while we shouldn't condone the violence of these men," I hear him say, "let's not lose sight of the larger issue: This is about the right of individuals to express their opinions about a lifestyle so far afield from accepted standards of decency, so anathema to mainstream beliefs, that it threatens the very values that most parents—most Americans—hold dear."

"What values are you talking about?" says Georgie. "The right to destroy property? The right to terrify innocent people?"

The man cocks his head. "I don't think there is anything innocent about the people visiting the Goddess Lounge—a debased and sexist institution that holds men, that holds families, that holds God, in contempt."

"Oh, for Chrissake," says Georgie.

"Exactly," glowers the man.

He looks at the TV announcer, who furrows her brow. "The real question," he says to her, "isn't what ignited this time-bomb in our midst. The real question is why the good American husbands and fathers—the Moses' Disciples—who tried to shed light on this disgraceful lifestyle are in jail, while the women who advocate evil are free to corrupt our children."

With a nod at the camera, the announcer wraps up the interview and the screen switches to a Carl's Jr. commercial where a girl in a bikini top sucks the ketchup off a French fry and then looks at the camera and licks her lips.

"You know what this means?" says Owen. "This isn't over. This whole Goddess Lounge nightmare has just begun. It's a good thing I'm back."

Chapter Eighteen

The Venuses on the banners are not happy. They frown at me wherever I go. From buses and bus stops they furrow their marble brows. They harden their marble eyes. "Say Goodbye," they taunt. "For the Very Last Time." Mostly, they judge me as I explain. Over and over.

To my mother, who is very hard to get a hold of because she is barnstorming the country speaking to media outlets and college students on the importance of religious tolerance/women's spiritually and, also, in her free time, is writing a prison memoir: "No. I did not take Owen back," I say. "I'm just letting him stay with us until this whole Goddess Lounge thing dies down. Grace Claire is traumatized. She needs her father. He's been a rock. That's one thing about Owen. He's always a rock."

To Nancy, who, as a childcare professional, seems strangely obtuse about this: "The thing is," I tell her. "I can't date my husband's ex-boss—or anyone—if my husband is actually living in my house. You see how that would be weird, right? What would Grace Claire think? And what would those Moses' Disciples people say if they found out? It's bad enough people at school call Grace Claire a godless heathen—they say that. You want them to think her mother is some sexually loose high priestess? No way. We're not going there."

To Bast, Freyja, and Uzume, who lay bandaged in their off-campus Cal Tech apartment, and who—at least in public—now go by Ann, Alexandria, and Teresa: "Besides," I say. "Owen really isn't that bad. All that stuff before? It was a misunderstanding. These crazy potheads were threatening Owen, demanding money because they thought he was involved with this guy who convinced them they could get high on pansies. So he called me for the money, and then he went to try and warn Rosa—who he'd already broken up with but wanted to help—to watch out for the potheads. But then Rosa actually, finally, just went off with the potheads because it turns out they really didn't need the money because they are all totally rich and they just want her to try on shoes. So, crazy, right?"

To the dogs, who seem the most skeptical of all: I say, "He did mean to feed you, but the nipping bothers him. It always has. You could help there."

So many explanations. So many clarifications. And always, those damn Venuses look down on me in disapproval. Like they think I had another choice. Like they think I could have run off with William and left Grace Claire to crumble like an old Girl Scout cookie. I don't see why this is so hard to understand. After being thrown in the back of a police van with rioting zealots, after being tossed into the center of an honest-to-god culture war, Grace Claire needs her father. He saved her. He's her hero.

You know what Georgie said when I told her this? Exact words: "But, honey, why would anyone want a hero when they could have a fucking goddess?"

This is what I'm up against. Me. The voice of reason and good mothering. I am the counter-cultural one.

William, by the way, actually gets it.

"Your daughter has to come first," he says when I call him.

"Exactly. Maybe later—"

"You know, I think this is for the best anyway. Our moment was great—"

"It was wonderful—"

"But…"

"But?"

"But…well, there's Ashley, isn't there? It's a relief to know that she won't try to hurt you now. I'll make sure she knows about Owen—"

"Owen is just staying—"

"I'll make sure she knows we're not together. That it was always about Owen. It will be such a relief to not have to worry about what she might do, where she might turn up…"

"Owen and I aren't—"

"I can't tell you what a relief it will be."

"Owen and I….Sure. I understand completely. That will be a real relief for you. I'm so glad."

Honestly, what more could those damn Venuses want? William is relieved. William is so relieved that he almost sounds like he is floating when I hang up the phone. William has peace of mind. That's a valuable commodity, believe me. Only someone who's lived a life of omnipotence would think otherwise. Besides, I'm not channeling goddesses anymore so I'm not even their problem these days. I took the necklace off. I threw it in my purse when some professor interviewed on NPR compared the Goddess Lounge incident to Tiananmen Square. My personal is not political. I am not red. I am not blue. I'm purple, and I am just Penne Armour. I am just me. And I did what I had to do to have a happy daughter. I'm not sorry about that. Any good mother would do exactly what I did, and any good mother would be as happy as I am because, guess what, I do have a happy daughter. Yeah. Happy. And get this: she's not mean. She's dropped cheerleading so that she can work twice a week after school at a food bank. That's right. A food bank. She unloads trucks of stale groceries so that they can be distributed to the poor. And when she comes home she does her homework and asks if I need help with laundry. Those Venuses would be so lucky to have such a happy daughter.

True. The Disney show is definitely off, and, also, many of Grace Claire's friends don't call anymore. It turns out that even in celebratedly-diverse middle schools a lot of people can be intolerant little bigots. I hate them all—especially that horrible Pei—the new president of Charlotte Perkins Gilman's Middle School's Moses' Disciples Club, which people should remember is not an official school organization—being, as it is, a single-minded forum for fostering hatemongering. Likewise, it is not sanctioned by school officials (although I am sure that Grace Claire's creation-spouting science teacher is letting them meet in his room. I knew he never appreciated Grace Claire. She deserved way better than a C on that Science Fair project that took me two months to complete.)

But let us not dwell.

In the scheme of things, Grace Claire is great. Sometimes she seems a little fragile, which is only normal. But she smiles. She does laundry. She plays Uno with her dad, which is unbelievably adorable. I can barely watch them without tearing up. Them on the couch. Me, with the dogs, in the suddenly smallish-seeming armchair.

True, there is some tension between Owen and the dogs. The fact is, the dogs don't like Owen. The old ones remember. They remember how he blamed them for driving him away and how he made me cry. The new ones don't know any of that, but they're true pack members and they know where their loyalties lay. I keep catching the Chihuahua nipping at Owen's heels. And, I swear, Buster is purposefully knocking Owen's beer bottles over. It's happened five times already. Also, Lucy keeps peeing on his bed. So, this isn't so good.

On the bright side, however, Owen is totally manning it up. One time, at the beginning, I did see him try and kick at the Chihuahua after being nipped, but I told him, I said, "Owen, these dogs are part of the family. You want to be part of this family? You make nice with the dogs."

He said, "But it nipped me."

I shoved my index finger in Owen's chest and said, "You make nice."

Now, he makes nice. How great is that?

So really, all in all, we are really awesome. We are really fantastic. We are all so fantastic and happy.

In fact, all this happiness is making it hard for me to sleep nights. I'm just so giddy. Plus, I see now why we never have return overnight visitors. This futon is Guantanamo bad. It's hard and cold, like the rest of this prison cell of a room. There's no carpet. The windows are covered in these cheap, almost transparent, blinds. It's right on the street so you hear every car or truck that goes by. You hear the sprinklers. You hear wildlife. I wouldn't let my dogs sleep in this stereophonic nightmare. Except, that, of course, they are sleeping in here. With me. On the futon. Which is surprisingly smaller than it looks.

The sleeping arrangements have also required some explaining. "Owen gets the bedroom." Georgie just about fell off her high heels with that one, although, I swear, I've told her a thousand times what a bad back Owen has.

Besides, it's not like I'd be slumbering much better upstairs, what with all my giddiness. And, you know, there's lots you can do nights when you can't sleep. You can clean. You can make slow cooker oatmeal. You can watch video of your daughter being manhandled by police on YouTube. You can organize your tax forms. You can go for a drive.

The other night, for example, I drove over to Dashed Sails. I don't know why, really. I think I just wanted to hear Ellard sing about cruel, cruel love. He really has something magical going there. I thought it might un-giddy me a little, and it did. It un-giddied me so much that I started crying into my Kir Royale. Ellard saw me and came over during the band break.

"Looky who's here," he said. "I never thought I'd see you again."

"Yeah, well," I said sniffing back my tears, "look's like you found a replacement." I pointed over to a dark-haired girl wearing my old rice noodle dress. "She's good." She is too. She can do handstands while swinging.

"She's ok. So what? You come to hear me sing?"

"I did."

"Do I discombobulate you? Do I unsettle you with my charming voice? It's a gift, you know. Not everyone has what I have. I don't think you ever appreciated that."

"I appreciated it, Ellard. You're the best singer ever."

He tossed back a shot of something golden. "Liar. You ever find your husband?"

"I did. He's back. It's great."

His eyes opened a little wider and he turned to face the dance floor. "That's obvious, isn't it? Well, my little kiwi, you can always work here, if you need to. This new girl is good, but she's not quite as fearless as you, not quite as sparkly."

Then I really started to cry. Poor Ellard looked like he was about to have a panic attack, so I decided I should probably head home. Naturally, when I pulled up to the first stoplight I got rear-ended by a black BMW. My heart leapt and then froze and then almost exploded. I thought maybe it was William, but it wasn't. Thank goodness. It was just some man. He took one look at my puffy eyes and my worn out skin and he wrote me a check for $2,000. Said he hoped it covered the damage and gave me his card just in case it didn't. $2,000! So bonus. Insomnia does have its benefits.

Of course, it doesn't have a lot of benefits. There are some things you shouldn't do when you can't sleep. You shouldn't go for a walk. Even with a pack of dogs, it's scary walking alone at night. You shouldn't garden. Neighbors will think you're a prowler and call the police, which is embarrassing. But, most of all, you shouldn't dwell on the past. I know. Blah, blah, blah, blah, blah, blah. It's all been said before. "Be in the moment." "Live in the now." Very Buddhist. But I think the Buddha got it from dogs. Dogs don't dwell. They don't hold grudges. Leave them alone for a few days and they're just happy when you come back. Deprive them of someone really great, someone who treated them well and who had fantastic hair, and they just wag their tongues and move on.

It's true.

Buster the Newfoundland is gone. His owners tracked him down and came for him when I was at work. They saw one of my signs. They told Owen Buster's real name was Baby. Baby! And now there is no more Buster. Just like that. No goodbyes. No nothing. And the dogs don't even care. They've just expanded into the space on the futon where Buster used to sprawl out. The dogs, you see, have moved on. They're out of the whole dwelling zone. They're in the "this is how things are zone," the "this is what happens, deal with it, just accept it and be happy in the fucking moment zone." One look at them on the couch and you see: Total relaxation, total overcooked fettuccine. If they were any more present they'd be dead.

You know who else is good at not dwelling? Surprisingly, Owen. I've never seen Owen more *not dwelling* in my whole life. It's like Rosa never existed. It's like he never moved out. He doesn't mention the loft. He doesn't mention the past. He is all present and future.

"We should remodel this kitchen," he says. "What do you think about marble countertops? They're all over the Home and Garden Network."

"We should," says happy Grace Claire.

"We should go to Hawaii this summer. Stay someplace really nice, like the Mauna Kea."

"We should," says happy Grace Claire.

"We should think about private high school for Grace Claire—someplace with zero tolerance for meanness. Don't take this the wrong way, but, really Penne, how could you send her to that place? What were you thinking?"

At work, as Nancy and I watch over a group of kids playing outside, I say to Nancy, "I notice he says 'we' a lot."

"Is that bad?"

"No. I notice he talks a lot about spending money that he isn't making."

"I guess he means when he gets a job."

"He's not looking for a job."

"What's he doing?"

"Oh, good dad stuff." This week alone he has taken Grace Claire for a bike ride so they could buy gelato. He has helped her with her math. Gone with her to buy new prints for her wall. Promised to repaint her room. He has said things to her like, "Just be strong, baby girl." "Don't let those jerks get you down." "You're better than all of those losers put together." "One day you're going to look back at those Moses' Disciples cretins and laugh. Yeah. You'll be driving your kid through some drive-through window and some greasy-haired kid who made fun of you will be giving you your change. Then you'll know who the real winner is."

"That's good. That must make you happy to see Owen manning it up like that," says Nancy.

"I couldn't be happier. No. I couldn't be happier. Like this morning. Owen comes up to me and says, 'I'm worried about Grace Claire. You know that whole Disney disaster? The producers told her they were going to let her go even before the police thing. They said she was too fat. Grace Claire told him that. That's how close they are. That's what a great dad he's become. She didn't even tell me that. Isn't that…great?"

"Wait. They said Grace Claire was too fat? She's a tooth pick," says Nancy.

"I know; it's crazy, but the point is: apparently, there are some things you can tell your father that you can't tell your mother. So, of course, I'm grateful…I'm so happy now. I'm giddy."

A pair of boys calls us to come and push them on the swings. "Coming," I holler. We cross over a sandpit and some abandoned Tonka trucks. Nancy says, "She probably didn't want you to feel bad. Or maybe Owen was just in the right place at the right time."

I push the back of the swing. "No. It's ok," I tell her. "I'm glad they've gotten so close. I'm glad he's her hero."

"Did the producers really say you were too fat?" I ask Grace Claire later. We're brushing our teeth in the downstairs bath. The Guantanamo room has no bathroom of its own, so Grace Claire and I are now sharing. Super good to do that, by the way. There are no secrets in a bathroom. We are opening up to each other in a healthy mother-daughter way. Grace Claire rinses her mouth and dries it with a washcloth. She starts to brush her hair, which is such a Georgie thing to do. Why brush hair you're just going to sleep on?

"They didn't say I was fat. They said I looked fatter on TV, and that if I wanted to lose some weight they had some people who could help me."

"But you're so thin already."

"The wardrobe people were the ones who said I was fat. They said it would be hard to find me things that didn't make my thighs look like turkey drumsticks."

"That's so mean."

"It's all right. They didn't know I could hear them. The kids—the other actors—were the mean ones. They said I only got hired because I had big boobs and that, since I had big boobs, I must be a total skank. Then, this one girl asked me if I'd had an abortion yet since I was such a big skank."

"I can't believe that." My hand is on my heart. My face is eggshell. "How can anyone be so cruel?"

Grace Claire looks at me, and it's like it's the first time she's ever seen me in her life. Suddenly, I'm not her mother anymore. If anything, she is the mother. She blinks, and her eyes go soft and glossy. She reaches out her hand and pats my own. "It's just words," she says. "Besides, those kids were all hopped up on diet pills. I don't want to be like them. Ever."

"No. Why would you? Why would you want to be like them? They're awful. They're pathetic."

She shrugs. "I don't think acting is for me. I think maybe I want to work with old people. I like old people." Then she lifts her hand to her throat and pulls out a small pearl choker with a small pearl pendant. I've never seen it before. Somehow, it has remained hidden, but I know what it is. She rubs the pearl pendant with her thumb and forefinger. "Like Tamara. I like Tamara. She's nice."

"Tamara gave you that necklace?" I try to keep my voice low.

Grace Claire nods. "It's for my goddess, Quan Yin. She helps me so much. I just love her. It's so great having a goddess. It's the best thing in the world. Don't you think?"

I smile. Damn. Just when I thought we were done with goddesses. Here they come again.

Chapter Nineteen

Quan Yin. Chinese goddess of compassion. She is a Buddhist bodhisattva, which means she could be sitting around Nirvana slurping up sangria but she feels so much compassion for humanity's pain that she waits outside the gates. She will wait until all people can enter with her, like on those days when all of Southern California shows up at Disneyland and we all pass through those little turnstiles at the same time. Yeah, cause that's fun times, all right. Everybody entering all at once. That's Nirvana right there.

Grace Claire says, "Quan Yin protects women and children. She protects them. Get it? She's the reason nothing bad happened to me at The Goddess Lounge. She took care of me."

We're sitting on her bed, wrapped in a blanket, all-confidential like, which is what comes from sharing bathrooms. Lucy lay on the bed with us, her head on my lap. The other dogs lie on the floor and blink at us.

"Quan Yin was born from a ray of light. And right after The Goddess Lounge burned down the weather turned really sunny. Have you noticed? Isn't that amazing?

"Quan Yin says we need to stop clinging, like you shouldn't be so obsessed with having the right jeans or worrying if some guy likes you, and she says we shouldn't be afraid either, because then we just get all Anakin Skywalker and turn all evil. And it's so true because, I think, those Disney girls were just jealous of my boobs and that's why they were so mean. They were jealous. Don't you think? But I don't even care because now I'm all, 'Hey, your jealousy only makes *you* suffer.' Just be happy with the boobs you have, right?

"Also, those mean kids at school. They all tell me I'm going to hell, but the joke is on them because I'm going to be reincarnated, and since Quan Yin is my goddess now, and I'm so into compassion and stuff, I'm totally going to be reincarnated as someone really cool—like maybe a lama—and they're all going to come back as bugs or rats. It's all about Karma, Mom. It's all about Karma." She snuggles in close to me.

"Wow. That's great. That's really great." And it is. The fact is, if a daughter must have a goddess, I'm all for it being a Buddhist one. Buddhism is California mainstream. Everyone loves the Dalai Lama. Even the Pope likes the Dalai Lama. In fact, Buddhism is so mainstream that I have a great idea. I say to Grace Claire, "Hey, why not tell the kids at school that you're a Buddhist. No one would be mean to you if they thought you were a Buddhist. You could tell them that the Pope is even friends with the Dalai Lama. Friends."

Grace Claire stiffens a little and shifts her weight away from me. She smoothes out the blanket and says, "Oh, no. I couldn't do that. That wouldn't be fair to my other goddesses. That would be like denying them; they would feel dissed."

"I see." And I do see. I see further evidence that nothing in this life is easy, and that even the best of people will go out of their ways to make things difficult. "And who were the other ones?"

Grace Claire looks up at the ceiling as if expecting her many goddesses to suddenly appear. She bites her lip. "There was the Corn Woman—who wants me to know I'm not fat, and Athena, who wants me to study hard, and some other ones too, but I'd have to look it up."

"Those are good goddesses."

"Yeah. Tamara says they would help me through The Pain."

"The pain?" Oh, jeez. What the hell is that? Is that another menstrual thing? Or just some weird goddess initiation rite I never got to because of my phone?

"The Pain. She says of all the planets in the solar system only ours has life because only ours was willing to accept The Pain. She said, 'pain and life are like two sides of the same coin. But even the world can't hold all The Pain. It's too heavy. So every living creature has to take some. That's the deal. You can't get around it, but the goddesses will help you through it.'"

I sit back against Grace Claire's headboard. "I never heard that story."

"Yeah, well, I guess that's not the story your goddesses wanted you to know."

Owen would like to talk to me. He tells me this at breakfast, his eyes heavy with concern, his hands steepled as if to pray. "We need a talk," he says.

"Really? Is this about Grace Claire's goddess?" HA! I've been waiting two full days to do this.

He pauses. "No."

"But you know about that, right?"

He rubs his hands together and looks off in the distance. "Possibly."

With more zeal than is probably appropriate, I fill Owen in about Quan Yin. Mostly, he just sits there blank faced because that's the only kind of face you can make when you know you've been shut out of the mother-daughter bond, which is always, in the end, deeper than the father-daughter bond. That's biology, baby.

I finish by saying, "But don't you see? Tamara must have done it on purpose. What other goddesses would a girl like Grace Claire need? What other stories would a girl like Grace Claire need to hear: Don't worry about your weight; study hard; be kind. It's sweet, actually."

Owen rolls his neck and exhales a long stream of coffee-breath. "Oh. Quan Yin. Yeah. Grace Claire already told me."

"You knew?" Damn. "Why didn't you tell me?"

"Grace Claire's therapist and I didn't want you to worry." My mouth drops open and he rushes on. "We think Grace Claire is clinging to this Quan Yin delusion to avoid the difficult feelings she's experiencing because of the police thing. We think it's important not to buy into this fantasy. That would just enable her and make it more difficult for her to process her emotions."

"But...if this is helping her—she's nicer too."

"It's only helping her in the way a crutch helps you when you've broken your leg. It is not curing an injury; it is just helping her limp along. Maybe we should have brought you in on this from the beginning, so that you would understand. But you've seemed so tired and distracted lately. Plus, you are working and I am not. I didn't want to give you anything more to worry about. I wanted to take care of this for you. Besides, the social/emotional dynamics are kind of complicated."

I think about this for a minute. "I'm not stupid. I understand things."

He reaches over and puts his hand on mine. "I didn't mean you were, babe. You're being a little sensitive there."

I pull my hand back. "No. I am not."

He sits back and splays his legs wide. Typical Owen pose. Typical 'don't even think you can rile me; I'm Mr. Reasonable.' Like he's asking some waiter about the special of the day, he says, "You're telling me you're happy that your daughter has gone delusional?"

I hate this. I can never do this. I can never be the unflustered one. I am always the hand-waving, tongue-lolling, mental patient one. And Owen is always so unfazed, so calm, which I used to love, which I used to count on, especially when things got crazy, like when Georgie hijacked my college graduation by signing autographs while I crossed the proscenium to get my diploma, or when Grace Claire broke her leg falling off a play structure when she was three. I used to love knowing that when chaos erupted, Owen would not succumb to the siren call of the drama queen, even when I was the drama queen. But now it irks me. Now his cool bristles like one of Griselda's boars.

I say, "Who's to say Grace Claire is delusional? Lots of people believe in, pray to, Quan Yin. Lots of people believe in all kinds of goddesses—people in India for example. Lots of people believe in God. Who's to say that only one story can be true?"

"Uh...God does."

I feel my face turning red. I feel my brain spinning. I stand up and walk to the sink, get myself a drink of water. "I'm just saying—"

"That you believe in Zeus and Venus." His voice crackles with sarcasm.

"I don't believe in Venus."

"Then what do you believe?"

I look at the water glass. I look at the baby ripples crossing the water surface caused by my shaking hand. I put the glass down. "I believe my daughter has the right to believe in miracles if that makes her happy."

I pick up my purse and slide the strap up to my shoulder. "I gotta go to work."

From the living room comes a rumble of rushing dogs. They moon after me as I make my way to the garage. Owen trails behind them. "I never got to tell you what I needed to tell you," he says. "It's about the dogs."

I open the garage door. Eyes straight ahead, I say. "I'm listening."

"Some of the neighbors have been complaining. About the noise."

I turn to face him. "My dogs don't make noise."

"I'm just telling you what I heard."

"From who?"

He shrugs. "I see people. They tell me things."

I look at my dogs with their sad, miss-you-love-you eyes. I drop my hand and brush it through Lucy's fur. Jealously, the other dogs crowd in and jostle each other until they've each received a love. Then I head off to work, my stomach tight with guilt. On so many levels, there is always so much darn guilt.

And there are those damn Venuses on the buses again.

And there they are when I go to pick up Grace Claire from school.

While I'm waiting on the curb a fist smacks against my car window. It's Xinran again. She's smiling that same ghoulish smile from before. My stomach turns a little. I roll down the window.

"Not so easy when your daughter is the outcast, is it?" she says.

I get out of the car and go over to Xinran. "Really, Xinran, can't we find a way to help the girls get along? All this conflict. I know Grace Claire doesn't like it. It must be upsetting to Pei too."

"Pei's very happy now. She's found her friends, thanks to your mean girl being also so wicked."

"Are you talking about those followers of Moses' Disciples? That science teacher's letting them meet in his classroom, isn't he? He could get in a lot of trouble, you know."

She lifts up her hands. "Oh, now you are Miss Rule Follower. HA! Besides, this is all your own fault."

I give her a blank stare.

She says, "I told you to fix things. I told you to make things right. You did nothing, so God helped me. God made all this happen so your daughter would suffer for being so mean."

She shoves an orange flyer in my hand. It's for a car wash benefitting Moses' Disciples. "This is at our church on Saturday. My husband is the pastor, so there. We have special influence. You should have stopped your mean girl. I warned you. God hates mean girls, and He hates their weak mothers even more. Bring your car. Maybe I'll pray for you."

Grace Claire waits about ten feet away. She's swinging her backpack and staring down at the ground.

I hold an arm out to her. She tiptoes over and, keeping a wide berth of Xinran, slinks into the car.

"Can't we all just...get along?" I say to Xinran.

Xinran shrugs. "This is God's doing, not mine. Good thing for you. He'll forgive you; I won't."

In the car, it is clear that Grace Claire does not want to talk about Xinran, or Pei or anything to do with Moses' Disciples. She puts a paper on my lap. "You need to sign this permission slip and chaperone form."

"Where are we going?"

"To the Antiquities Museum. To see Venus. Remember? You promised you'd come so that I can get extra credit."

I do remember. Every god in this fricking galaxy must be out to get me.

We're not home long when the doorbell rings. Like always, the dogs leap to their feet and run barking to the door. Then something kind of weird happens. From the end of the hall, I watch the dogs take one collective sniff and stiffen. They spring round, run back down the hall and into my room. Poor old Lucy hobbles behind them, whining.

From upstairs, Owen hollers, "Will you get that?"

You know how on TV the doorbell will ring, and some spooky music will come on, and you'll know—you'll know because you'll have seen it a thousand times—that something freaky bad is about to happen. And you know how you want to say, "Don't answer that door. Nothing good is behind that door." Well, except for the music, this is exactly what happens. The hallway actually begins to feel colder. Goosebumps pop up along my arms, and this little warning voice goes off inside. "Stay away," it says. "This is bad," it says. But it turns out that when you're in that position, you actually act just as stupidly as those TV characters. Even though you know you should grab the phone and dial 911, you feel yourself pulled to the door. You walk to it. You open it.

And, of course, you're fucked.

A heavy-set man in tan pants cinched high on his hips and a brown shirt and baseball cap with an extra-long brown visor stands on my front step. He chews a big wad of gum. Between smacks he says, "You the owner of the house?"

When I nod he says, "We got a call saying you have five dogs."

"Yes."

"Yeah, well you can't have five dogs. Two's the limit. City law."

"I've never heard that."

Owen joins me on the doorstep. "What's going on?" He hasn't shaven in several days and dark blond bristles cover his chin.

"He says we can only have two dogs."

"That's crazy," says Owen. "Who says?"

"You can try and get an exemption from the town council," the animal control officer shrugs. "But we've had a complaint so..."

"A complaint? From who?"

"You can't just come in here and take my wife's dogs. She rescued these dogs. She takes good care of them."

"I'm sure she does." The animal control officer shifts his weight. A guilt-inducing shroud seems to settle over him, making him smaller, squatter. He begins to fiddle with a pad of paper in his hands. He pulls out his pen and starts writing. "Listen, I'm sorry, but the law says two dogs so that's all you can have. I can give you a couple of days. That's the best I can do."

"These dogs need me," I say.

"Did you hear that?" says Owen. "They need her."

"I'm sorry." The animal control officer hands me a citation. Not only does he want to take my babies, but also he wants me to cough up $200 for the pleasure. "I'll be back Friday. Good luck."

"Don't worry," says Owen as we watch the officer walk away. "I'm sure that guy's wrong. Two dogs. That's insane. Half the people on this street have three dogs. I'm going to figure this out." He puts a hand on my shoulder. For a minute, I think he might try and hug me. Reflexively, my back stiffens. My lips pinch tight. Owen hesitates and then pulls back and gives my shoulder a little pat. "You can count on me. I'm on top of this." He steps back. "Although," he adds, "I did warn you. People. They don't really like the dogs."

Seventy-two hours later, Casanova, Jude, and the little Chihuahua are gone, delivered to a rescue society Owen found on the Internet. "Damn laws," Owen says to me. "So unfair. But the rescue society will find them good homes. Isn't that what matters most?"

No use telling him that that is not what matters most. No use telling him that my grief and guilt and disappointment in losing my poor little babies mean a hell of a lot to me. It's like somebody's kicked in my teeth, stomped on my spine and shoved my mouth full of dirt. It's absolute shit.

My poor little lambs.

My poor little orphans.

With their little clattering nails.

With their happy little waggy tails.

Let down, abandoned, once again.

"I let them down," I tell Grace Claire. "You should have seen them. They knew. I broke their little hearts."

"You seem so sad, Mom."

"It's just that...it's an awful power. Choosing who stays and who goes. But what could I do? Lucy's so old and Pablo—you know how prejudiced people are against pit bulls."

"You did the right thing. It was the only thing you could do."

"But Casanova has a heart murmur, and Jude...well, you know Jude. He's very needy. And the little Chihuahua—what was his name, Butterbean—had just found a home. He'd just come to us. All three of them must be so scared. They must be wondering where I am, when I'm coming back."

"It's ok, Mom."

But it's not ok. It's awful.

A week later, nothing has changed. Owen says to me, "For your own good, you have to let this go."

"It's not so easy," I say.

Not unkindly, he says, "No. But the alternative is worse." He blinks back a flicker of shame, and it occurs to me that maybe Owen does have some experience here. "Rosa wanted to leave," I tell him. "The dogs didn't."

His face turns a little pink. He swallows. "I'm just trying to be nice."

Grace Claire walks by. She whispers, "Quan Yin says channel compassion."

She's right, and he's right. Everybody's right. I know. But no one else looks at the only two dogs I have left with my eyes. Lucy and Pablo are traumatized by the removal of their friends. They barely leave my side. They walk eyes down, heads low. They quiver at the gate when I leave for work, and when I come home, there they are, in the exact same place, as if they haven't moved all day. It's like part of them left with the other dogs. It's like they think they'll be next.

And then, a week later, they are next. I come home to find the gate ajar and the dogs gone. "Pablo," I yell. "Lucy." I run in the house. Owen is sprawled on the couch watching European basketball. "Have you seen Lucy and Pablo?"

"I saw them earlier, when I put out the trash cans."

"Trash cans? Since when do you put out the trash cans?"

"I was trying to help...I suppose...you don't think..."

"You left the gate open!"

"I don't think so. I didn't mean to."

I run outside. "Pablo! Lucy!"

Owen follows, spitting apologies. "Penne, I'm sorry. I thought...I don't know what happened."

"They couldn't have gone far, especially Lucy."

In fact, Lucy hasn't gone far at all. Grace Claire finds her hiding under the futon. She won't come out for anything, not until bedtime, when she finally crawls out and cuddles up next to me, a handful of whimpers in the darkness.

As for Pablo, he's history. I put up signs. I leave a picture with the animal shelter and local vets. No one has seen him. No one knows anything about him. Lucy and I spend our time scanning the front yard, hoping he'll turn up, but hope won't buy you breakfast, and after a while Lucy doesn't even sniff the air for him. Even the remnants of his scent have faded away.

"He missed his buddies," Owen says one day. "He probably went to find them, but he's doing ok."

"Maybe."

He reaches a hand around my shoulder. And sure he betrayed me, and sure he pisses me off sometimes, but I remember now that Owen can be decent. We have been through a lot over the years, and there were many times Owen came through for me. He's not so bad. At least he cares.

Unlike some people. Unlike Georgie, who, home after her cross-continental religious freedom crusade, is still operating on Eastern Standard Time and calls at five in the morning. "Such bad luck, such horrible luck, and such a nice dog," she trills with absolutely unconvincing pity when I tell her about Pablo. "Did you see me in today's *The New York Times*?"

"I haven't even seen my face in the mirror yet."

"An op-ed piece. It calls me—let me see, it's right here—'An unofficial spokesperson for not merely The Goddess Lounge, but for all Americans angered by the bullying tactics of religious conservatives.' Can you fucking believe it? It's fuck-a-duck-fantastic. And I told you that next week I'm going to Washington-fucking-D.C. to testify before a fucking-congressional subcommittee looking into faith-based hate crimes. Right?

"And did I tell you, my agent called? Four directors offering me work. I'm talking A-list directors making fucking Oscar-worthy films. Plus, my agent has me lined up to advertise Boniva and Gap. That fire's the best thing that ever happened to me."

"I'm so glad the traumatic event undermining my daughter's entire psyche is working out well for you."

"Grace Claire is fine. You're coming to tonight's Goddess Lounge reopening, right?"

"Oh, Mom. I promise you. I am most definitely not."

Still, no escaping the damn thing. It's right there on *Extra*. Grace Claire is so excited she even relapses into Mean Girl when Owen tries to put on ESPN. "Can't you see I'm watching this?" she yells. "Are you blind? My goddess wants me to see this. Jeez. It's like you don't know me at all."

Then: Ta-da! There in sparkling living color: the ornate doors of The Goddess Lounge. In front of them stand my mother—William Penn incarnate—and beside her, of course, Tamara, her apricot lips wrapped in the smug smile of victory.

"I'm just happy to be here celebrating the re-opening of this beacon for women's spirituality. As a public figure, I think it is important to stand up for what's right, and there is nothing more right than tolerance and religious freedom," I hear Georgie say.

"You sound like you're running for office," says a reporter. "Tell us, is it true you're considering a run for governor?"

Georgie looks demurely into the distance, "I have no comment on that."

"What do you think, Tamara?" says the reporter, "Any chance of our viewers seeing the Red Tent tonight?"

Tamara smiles. "They'll have to come on down for that," she says. "But, I can assure you, we won't let hate stop women from exploring the divine feminine, and now they can go directly online—www.goddesslounge.com—for a virtual goddess reading. The goddesses are not bound by time or space, why should we be?"

"That's epic," says Grace Claire. "Quan Yin is totally impressed."

"What bullshit," says Owen. "Georgie. Governor. Don't make me laugh."

Grace Claire gets up to go. "Quan Yin is trying to feel compassion for your narrow mind," she says to her father. "But she is finding it very hard."

Chapter Twenty

It is my experience that there is a basic buoyancy to people's personalities. Like the surf, we may have high tides and low tides, but most of us, most of the time, swim at just about the same depth of emotion or mood.

Take me, for example. I am basically happy. That's just my disposition, despite what Georgie may say. Actually, let me amend that. I am basically as happy as Grace Claire is. That is, if Grace Claire is sunshine and roses, I am sunshine and roses. If Grace Claire is heavy showers and limp Swiss cheese, I am heavy showers and limp Swiss cheese. All the moms I know are this way. I blame evolution and La Leche League, but that's beside the point. The point is, and this is a real mystery, where is my buoyancy? That is the question I ask myself as I lie on my lumpy futon and listen to Owen's wheezy snoring as it drifts downstairs.

"What happened to my giddy?" I whisper to the ceiling. "Why am I so… stuck?"

Lucy gives me a flick of a lick and then turns her head the other way so as to better block out my nighttime lamentations. "Why?" I say again. "What's wrong with me?"

And then I do what practical women do best: I make a list. It's a mental list because—obviously—it's the middle of the night, and I will not be so pathetic as to actually scribble all Sylvia Plath-like under some glaring fluorescent bulb. I title my list:

Perspective on why this is actually the best time of my life:
Grace Claire is healthy.
Grace Claire is nice.
I have Lucy.
I am healthy.
I have a secure job that I like and friendly co-workers.

I have health insurance.

I am not homeless.

I do not live in one of those places that will be submerged in water as a result of global warming.

My mother does not show signs of dementia or osteoporosis, as demonstrated by her new position as Boniva spokesperson.

Owen can help Grace Claire with her math homework.

The list is actually much longer than this, but at some point, I think around three A.M., I decide that I *am* pathetic enough to scribble all Sylvia Plath-like under a fluorescent bulb, but I am not pathetic enough to include things of the following nature on my written list: I do not have cancer (that I know of). I do not have a flesh-eating disease or early-onset Alzheimer's. I have good teeth. I don't have to worry about William worrying about my safety.

William. Don't get me started.

I saw him. It was the night before last. I couldn't sleep—no surprise—so I went for a drive so that I could catch up on this audiotape Grace Claire wants me to hear. It's called *The Impermanence of Every Fucking Good Thing in Your Life*, or something like that. Anyway, I was driving and listening and crying about my dogs and meditating on how Buddhists are so fucking wise, and I just happened to find myself over by Dashed Sails and thought I might pop in and listen to Ellard. And I was driving and avoiding colliding with all the other cars in the vicinity when I looked out my window and saw William. He was coming out of Dashed Sails, and his chocolaty hair kind of shone in the neon glow. It made me hungry just to see him. I pulled over real fast and for a split second I thought about getting out of the car and going over to say hi, but before I even got my fingers on the door handle another person walked out behind him. It was Ashley. She had on this short, flouncy pink dress and a pair of the Ojos strappy high heels that almost killed me. She put her hand on William's arm and smiled right up at him, and he smiled back. Yup. He smiled back.

So I pulled into the street and plowed right into this old Volkswagen bus. Luckily, there wasn't a lot of damage to either of us, but the driver got out, and then I had to get out, and we had to exchange insurance information, and, needless to say, the whole crashing together of cars was loud, so William and Ashley saw everything, and they both ran over to me.

"Penne? What are you doing here?" said William. "Are you are all right?"

"You look awful," said Ashley.

It was humiliating. I'm still not exactly sure what I even said. I think I stammered something about running errands. I may also have said, "How nice to see that you two have worked things out. You always were such a cute couple." But I'm not sure about that part. It's all rather foggy, and that might have been the moment when I imagined a knife slicing right through the middle of my heart and started crying again. All I know for sure is that William and Ashley wore his and her frowns and looked slightly turquoise as I escaped in my battered Volvo.

But, it's all right, it's all good. Like I wrote on the list: this is actually the best time of my life, and it is so good that William and Ashley are back together because now, for sure, she won't kill me and that means William can have so much fucking peace of mind that he'll practically have a platter of mind, a mountain of mind—all peaceful.

Still, the question remains, what with this being the actual best time of my life, why do I feel like the heel of a week-old loaf of bread sinking to the bottom of the sea?

"What do you think? What's my problem?" I ask Freyja, Bast and Uzume, who are completely recovered, by the way, and are happy to be back balancing astrophysics homework and Goddess Lounge duty. We're sitting in their apartment talking while I wait for Grace Claire to finish working at the food bank. Bast puts out a plate of the most fantastic baklava. It's all honey and paper-thin layers of phyllo bread and nuts. Bast makes it herself. Apparently, she worked as a pastry chef before pursuing astrophysics. Girls today. They do everything.

Uzume, Bast and Freyja think about my question in the sweet little way that they have. They open their mouths and crinkle their foreheads. They sip their coffee and nibble on the baklava. "We feel your pain," says Uzume, and something about her tone makes me think they've been rehearsing this.

"We really do," says Bast.

"But your problem is that you've forsaken your goddesses," says Freyja.

"Really?" I say. "Because I thought it might be that William is back together with the psychopath who tried to kill us."

"Ah," says Uzume. "Jealousy. Venus can do jealousy. Maybe she's punishing you for neglecting her."

The girls nod. Uzume gives my shoulder a supportive squeeze.

I look at these smart young women. I think about the grades and test scores they must have had to get into Cal Tech. I think about the hours they must have spent studying and the sheer brainpower it takes to get into this exclusive school. I decide to take a risk. I decide to treat them like the intelligent individuals they must be.

"Do you really believe what you're saying?" I ask.

A new look passes over the girls' faces, and it's a look far too old for women as young as these. It's a careworn look. It's a look of ancient dust and faded linen and little babes nursed and grieved for. "Do you think there's even one lesson about life we can't learn from the stories of the goddesses?" asks Bast. "Do you think there's even one trial that you've encountered that an ancient goddess didn't encounter first?"

"Do you know what goddesses are made of?" asks Freyja.

I shrug my shoulders. "Legend."

"The Norse believed gods and goddesses started just like everything else: with the meeting of fire and ice. One drop of steam started everything. It started humanity. It started divinity. It started the beginning, and it started the inevitable ending. Fire and ice: That's the cosmos. That's what we're made of, and so that's what we must endure. For most people, it's too much. Ice shatters them. Fire consumes them. They end up frozen shells or walking clouds of ash. But not goddesses. Ice brightens them. Fire burnishes them. Goddesses become unrefracted light.

"The only question that matters is this," she says reaching across the table and taking another piece of baklava, "Do you choose to be destroyed by the cosmos, or do you choose to be illuminated by it, strengthened by it?"

"Isn't there another choice?" I ask. "Isn't there a choice that involves doing the right thing and, by doing that, knowing that the right things will happen to you in return?"

"No," says Freyja. "Everyday we balance on a precipice between a glacier and a volcano. It's destruction or illumination. That's it."

"Well, that sucks," I say.

Freyja points a finger at me. "That," she says, "is life."

I think about this as Grace Claire and I drive home. Is this true, I wonder? Are those really my only choices? I mean, how grueling is that? It's like high school all over again. It's like every experience in life is contributing to your overall GPA, except that, unlike high school, there's no four years of drunken college revelries ahead. There's only nursing homes and adult diapers.

Grace Claire turns on the audio and on comes more of *We're All Fucked so Why Cling*, or whatever it is. It's suddenly seeming very Norse. Grace Claire nods every few seconds.

"Buddhists are really deep," she says. She looks out the window and then adds, "You know how the Buddha says everything is impermanent?"

"Yeah."

"If that's true does that mean Quan Yin is impermanent?"

"Maybe. I don't really know."

She sighs and shakes her head. "What if she is? What if even goddesses don't last forever? I mean, why is there even a world if nothing lasts? Why would anyone invent a world that's so crap? That just breaks down like some fucking old car? What's the fucking use of that?"

"I have no fucking idea," I tell her.

She gives me a sidelong glance and then looks out the window again. "The potty mouth doesn't really work for you. It's not very mom like."

I look over at her. Her arms lay straight in her lap. Her legs are crossed neatly at the ankles. "You're right. I'll try not to do it again." And for some reason that I cannot explain, I feel different. I wouldn't say I'm floating, but I don't feel so sinking.

We get home to find Owen standing in the kitchen, his hands elbow deep in a plastic bowl. In front of him, lay an open cookbook and around him a jumbled pile of onionskins, breadcrumbs, bits of parsley, and eggshells.

"Surprise! I'm making dinner. Spaghetti and meatballs," he says.

Now Owen has many special gifts and talents. He is a good accountant. He is, clearly, good at crises involving police and religious zealots. He is— unbeknownst to many—an expert sailor, and he can play a mean game of pickup basketball. Not once in our married life, however, have I ever seen Owen cook anything more complicated than toast. The man doesn't even barbecue. So I am not trying to be contrary when I say, "Do you know how to make spaghetti and meatballs?" I am only trying to express my natural and honest curiosity, and, frankly, I think it's a little unfair when Owen and Grace Claire both look at me like I've just confessed to stealing money from little old ladies and orphaned kittens.

Owen plops his chin on his chest and goes all pigeon toed. "I just thought I'd try to help out."

"Think of this as a Quan Yin moment," Grace Claire whispers to me. "Thanks, Dad. Just pasta for me."

With a tska-tsk of claws against hard wood, Lucy ambles toward me, her tail wagging, her eyes tired but bright. She nudges her muzzle against my thigh, and I reach down to pet her.

"I even thought about old Lucy here," says Owen. "Look, I gave her a meatball." He points to a pink ball of meat in her food dish. "You know," he adds, "sometimes I think you want me to let you down."

"No," I stammer looking at Grace Claire. "Of course not. Thank you, Owen. I'm sure dinner will be delicious."

Still, I know it will be awful. We all know it will be awful. Before the pasta is even out of the pot, Grace Claire claims a sudden stomachache and asks if she can just have a bowl of oatmeal in her room. Even Lucy knows it will be awful, and she has no scruples at all. After downing her "special" meatball she parks herself next to me and won't even move when a handful of limp noodles fall to the ground.

That leaves Owen and me. I cut into the charred ball of meat on my plate. Pink juice runs from the bright red inside. I'm thinking e-coli. I'm thinking salmonella. I'm asking myself if this meatball—if this moment—is worth dying for. Owen looks at me, his eyes shining with expectation. "Good, isn't it?"

I smile. "Ummm. Wonderful."

He shoves a meatball in his mouth and nods happily at me as he chews. "The key is Saltine crackers. I saw it on the Food Network."

I nod back. "Good thinking." I swallow a forkful of overcooked pasta. "You know," I say, "maybe it was the car ride, but my stomach's a little upset too." I stand up. "I think I'll turn in."

Owen's face turns pink and his whole body begins to tremble. "They're horrible. They're the worst things you've ever eaten. I know. I'm sorry, Penne." He drops his fork on the table and cradles his face in his hand. "Oh," he sighs. "I can't seem to do anything right. I thought if I made dinner you'd see that I'd changed, but now I've blown that too."

"No," I say swallowing a mouthful of guilt. "That's not true. You do lots of things right. Look at all you've done for Grace Claire. Really, Owen, you saved her."

He slowly drops his hands to the table. "Do you mean that?"

I nod.

He reaches across the table and puts my hand in his two large palms. "I'm trying. You do know that, right? I am trying. And not just because of Grace Claire, but because of you. I love you, Penne. I think I've always loved you. And I think you love me too. Deep inside, I think you know it's true."

"What about Rosa?"

The sound of her name makes Owen wince, just a little. He tries to hide it. He sits a little taller; he cricks his neck and swallows. "That's over. You know that."

"Do you love her?"

He blinks. "What matters is that we—you and I—are together now. I love you, and I want to make this work."

Lucy shifts beneath me. She stands up and hobbles toward the guest room. "I gotta go," I tell Owen. "I'm really tired."

Really.

It's not just an excuse to avoid this conversation or those meatballs. Swear to God: I am tired. I'm exhausted. It's a lot to take in, after all. It's a lot to process. The brain, like the body, gets tired when it's overworked, and Owen's face, Owen's words, mingle in my mind with images of William and Ashley and the smell of sundried linen, and it's all I can do to keep my mind from switching off completely. It's all I can do to brush my teeth and crawl into bed next to Lucy, who's already snoring the minute I lie down. All these weeks. If only I'd known that indecisiveness and confusion were the cure to insomnia. I brush my hand against Lucy and breathe in her scent of wet dirt and old laundry, and I fall asleep.

Around midnight, I wake to find my bed shaking. My first thought is earthquake, but earthquakes are loud, and this shaking barely registers a sound. I switch on the light and almost throw up.

It's Lucy, my sweet Lucy. Her body is convulsing. Her tongue is slack and the whites of her eyes peek out from half-closed lids.

"Oh, my God," I whisper. "Oh, my God, Lucy." Trembling, I scoop her up and drive to the emergency vet hospital, where an aide whisks Lucy away and leaves me alone in the cold lobby. An hour later a tired-looking vet comes and sits down next to me.

"Do you keep any household cleaners where Lucy can get at them? Any snail repellant in your yard?" the doctor asks.

"No. Nothing."

"Are you sure? Lucy has ingested some kind of chemical toxin. Maybe mothballs? Rat poison?"

"No. She barely leaves my bedroom."

The doctor shakes her head. "Well, Lucy got into something." She stretches her back and stands. Rubbing the back of her neck, she adds, "She'll probably be OK after a few days here, but it would help if we knew what she swallowed."

"I…I can't imagine."

And I cannot imagine. I cannot imagine one thing that would have done harm to my darling girl. I have a very safe house. I never really recovered from the baby-proofing stage. Cupboards have latches. Cleaning supplies are kept high. It is inconceivable how Lucy could have found anything toxic in the house, and it really has to be the house since she barely goes outside but to pee.

We, all of us, are confounded.

"What could she possibly have eaten?" Grace Claire asks me.

"Are you sure there's nothing in the guest room?" wonders Owen. "Something secretly toxic? Some female thing used to keep shoes fresh, maybe?"

"Isn't that the one dog I like? Oh, poor thing," croons Georgie.

And then one of our assistant teachers calls in sick from salmonella poisoning and it comes to me: the meatball. Good Lord: It really did have e-coli/salmonella.

Driving home from work, I call the vet, "Lucy ate a raw meatball," I tell her. "It must be food poisoning."

"This is not food poisoning," the vet says. "This is chemical poisoning. Do you know anyone who might want to hurt your dog?"

"Some of the neighbors were complaining, but that was before all the other dogs…"

"Excuse me?"

"That was before all the other dogs….I only have the one dog now. I only have Lucy. Everyone loves Lucy except maybe…shit."

"I beg your pardon?"

"I…I'll call you." I pull off my Bluetooth and pull over. Cars whizz by. A homeless man pushing a rattling shopping cart walks past. I hear nothing. A bus with a placard promoting the damn Venus exhibit drives by. I see nothing. Click, click, click. Like a row of metal balls lining up in a pinball machine, everything falls in place. Everyone loves Lucy except Owen. He was glad to be rid of the dogs on the day he left, and he's glad to get rid of them now. I see it all now: The "neighbor" complaint. The gate. The meatball. My diminishing pack of dogs. Fuck a duck. This is Owen's doing.

How could I have been so blind?

Pablo knew. Every day he waited for me by the gate he tried to tell me. So Owen got rid of him. Lucy knew. She tried to tell me every time she crawled into bed, every time she tried to lick the scales off my dumb, blind eyes. And now Owen has tried to get rid of her too.

How I get home, I'll never know. But soon I'm on my doorstep. Soon I'm entering the house. Soon I'm staring at Owen and Grace Claire playing Uno. I'm watching them smile, laugh. They don't even see me, so caught up are they in their moment of togetherness. I look closer at Grace Claire. Her eyes twinkle—they goddamn twinkle.

Isn't that what matters?

Hearts can be heavy. My heart isn't heavy. It's just gone. My chest is a dark hollow. I lie down on the futon. I don't think anything. I just lie there. Numb. Practically, almost gratefully, dead. All I know is one thing: I'm clinging to the narrow space between a glacier and a volcano, and my arms are really tired.

Chapter Twenty-One

Shhh. I am hiding from Owen. He is in the kitchen eating breakfast, and I am hiding in the pantry because if I even look at him I may tear the skin off his face with my fingernails. I wish him a prolonged and miserable death. Maybe something involving wolves.

Wait.

I think…yes, he's getting up. I hear him putting his dishes in the sink, and he's not even rinsing them, the big jerk. He's padding out of the room.

Bastard.

The TV sounds from the living room. I tiptoe to the guest room and get ready for work.

"Oh, Penne."

Damn. Owen is standing at my door, the morning paper in his hands.

"Yes?"

"I was wondering if you could do some laundry today. I'm out of clean underwear."

I gaze at Owen. His skin is mottled. His head rests like a thumb on his shoulders. I don't know why I never noticed this before. Actually, he's entirely unattractive.

"I would do it myself," he says, "but, you know, I always turn everything pink." He laughs a little. I smile, and he heads back to the living room.

Georgie thinks I should kick Owen out. In fact, Georgie's ready to come and kick him out herself. She says that she will tie his balls to Lucy's leash and drag him behind her in her hybrid. She also says that she will find me wolves, let them loose in the house, and have them eat Owen as he watches European basketball on TV.

It's a generous offer, but Georgie doesn't understand. She doesn't have Grace Claire to worry about. This is what I tell the girls the next time I wait for Grace Claire to finish volunteering at the food bank.

"So you're just going to keep living with Owen and pretending everything is all right?" Uzume asks me as we eat our baklava.

"Yes," I say.

"You're going to ignore the fact that he tried to kill your dog?"

"No. I will always be fully aware that he tried to kill my dog. I will never, ever forget that."

"But you won't let him know that you know?"

"No."

"You're going to live your whole life like this?"

"No. When Grace Claire goes to college, I will reveal everything I know, and then I'll kick him out."

"And when is she going to college?"

"Five years and five months."

Uzume looks at Bast and Freyja. "Hmm," she says. "Hmmm."

"You don't understand," I tell them. "Grace Claire was mean. Grace Claire was troubled. Now she's kind and happy. For the most part. That's a good thing. That's worth preserving. That's what's important."

"She's kind and happy because of Quan Yin," says Freyja. The other girls nod.

"In part, yes," I say. "But, remember, Owen saved her. He's her hero. I can't take that away from her."

"So what'll you do about your dog?" says Bast.

"Ah! I have the perfect solution."

It is perfect, too. Here's my plan. Once I bring Lucy home, I never leave her alone with Owen. That's right. I'm going to get her one of those therapy dog aprons so that she can go into stores and restaurants and places. I do feel a little guilty about this because I really admire those therapy dogs. It takes a lot of work to become one—months, years of training—and I hate to take advantage of a system that does such good, but we're talking about saving Lucy's life here. We're talking about protecting an innocent dog. If that's not reason enough to bend the rules, what is? Besides, Lucy is practically a therapy dog already in the sense that she provides me with countless hours of therapy just by letting me cry into her dirty fur most nights.

Now, admittedly, work will be a problem. I could bring in a toothless, mute fifteen-year-old dog with no claws and no fur, and who can barely tremble himself across the floor and some parents would still think their kid was about to be eaten by Kudu. So, obviously, the therapy apron won't work here. But there's the staffroom, right? I could leave her there. She wouldn't be in anyone's way. Honestly, I don't even think most people would notice her. For a lab, she's surprisingly small. There is a chance that Nancy will say no, but she's co-director. It's not just up to her. I have a say here. And I say Lucy comes. Besides, Nancy likes Lucy. Everyone likes Lucy. It won't be a problem. I can't even imagine how it could be a problem.

I feel so good about this plan, so confident about this plan that, for the next few days, as Lucy recuperates at the vet and I look at downloadable therapy-dog apron patterns on the Internet, I feel a surprising degree of peace. Even Grace Claire notices. She says when I drive her to school one day, "Quan Yin would be very proud of you mom. You've been very good about dad lately."

"Thank you," I say. What I don't tell Grace Claire is that I've also managed to avoid being in the same room with him under the cover that I have some sort of virus and do not want to give it to anyone else. I've put away all my makeup to look convincingly pale.

Just then Pei and Xinran cross the street in front of us. Xinran's face is looking a bit fleshier, and when I see her eye Grace Claire in the car her cheeks glow pink. It's possible that hating Grace Claire has given Xinran the will to live. Xinran nudges Pei and says something to her. Pei swings her head toward us, locks her angry eyes on Grace Claire and holds up a large silver crucifix that hangs from her neck. She mouths something at Grace Claire and walks on.

"Well, that wasn't very nice," I say.

Grace Claire readjusts herself in her seat and exhales a long breath. "She is a bitter little girl, that Pei," she says. "I think even Quan Yin would want to slap her upside the head." She pauses for a minute and then adds, "That's not being un-compassionate, that's just being honest."

"So things still aren't so good with the Moses' Disciples? Pei and her groupies are still giving you a hard time?"

Grace Claire flips her hair behind her back and looks out the side window. "It's not like I want to be insensitive or anything," she says, "but can you just give it a rest. I totally have things under control."

"Of course. I understand." I pull over to the curb and look again at Pei, who has left her mother and joined up with some pasty-faced kids who are all staring at our car. Why are they always pasty-faced, these zealots? Why? It doesn't even matter what race they are. They're still pasty-faced. They look like zombies. They are zombies. Mindless, hateful zombies. "Just… take care of yourself then."

"Like I said," Grace Claire answers, "I have things totally under control."

Pei and her group watch Grace Claire get out and their heads turn as one as she walks past them, straight backed and poised. Then their eyes swing back to the car. Pei's face grows small as she squints her eyes and pushes out her lips. She holds up the crucifix for me to see. I pull into the street. Mindless, hateful zombies. No good can come from such narrow-mindedness. No good at all.

A cloud of evil zombie doom hangs over me when I pull into my driveway. But guess what? It vanishes. It is replaced by sunny, giddy, no-fucking-way surprise. Guess who is waiting for me? Pablo! My sweet-as-pie pit bull that I never thought I would ever see again in my life. He is standing on the grass wagging his tail and jumping up and down. I am so happy to see him that it takes me a second to realize that not six feet away from him stands William, who has Pablo on a long leather leash.

"Pablo," I yell getting out of the car. "Oh my God, you've found Pablo. Pablo where have you been?"

There's no stopping Pablo now. He lunges forward with such power that William lets go of the leash. I bend down and stretch out my arms, and Pablo runs to me and knocks me over and his tongue cannot get enough of my face—which is a little disgusting but totally understandable. Hovering over me, his eyes smiling, William says, "Need any help?"

"No, no." I sit up and Pablo wags his tail and calms down enough for me to scratch his belly. "How did you know? How did you find him?"

"One of my dogs escaped and got picked up by animal control. I had to go pick him up at a shelter in Sunland, and then I saw this guy, and I figured you might be missing him."

I lean over and rub foreheads with Pablo. "I was. I was missing him."

"That's a long journey he made. I wonder how he managed it?"

"I have some ideas."

With a quick flop, Pablo turns right side up and starts to sniff at the grass around us. He takes a few steps and begins to explore. William bends over to pick up the leash. "That's ok," I say. "He just wants to figure out what he's missed."

"You don't think he might bolt again?"

"I'm not too worried about that."

I stand up.

"It's nice to see you, Penne."

"You too."

He slips his hands in his pockets and looks over at Pablo, who is digging over at the azaleas. "So how's everything working out for you?"

I shrug. "Ok."

"How are the dogs? In fact, where are the dogs? I'm surprised they're not out here."

"Oh. Lucy is at the vet. And the boys, well, they've moved on to new homes, new families."

William's eyes grow narrow as he gives me a questioning gaze that weakens my knees.

"It's a long story," I add.

He nods.

My shoulders and spine soften just as I feel my throat and eyes grow tense. I don't know if I'm supposed to bask in gratitude or sorrow, joy or heartache. In my mind's eye I'm watching about five different movies, one where William grabs me in his arms and kisses me, one where I'm still watching William and Ashley coming out of Dashed Sails, one where William and I are back in Santa Barbara, one where I'm visiting Grace Claire in jail and I'm remembering that this moment, this moment right now, is what led her down the path of bad and imprisonable choices, and one where Owen is eaten alive by Pablo and a pack of wolves. Which is all a long way of saying that I don't even know what to say to William right now. I don't know what to say; I don't know what to do, but a part of me is just content to smile up at his face and watch him look all goofy and awkward over at Pablo.

Naturally, stupid Owen comes out and ruins everything. My God. How did I ever marry him? He marches out wearing pajama bottoms and a tee shirt. "William," he says glad-handing like he's running for office. "What a surprise. Come on in. It's nice to see you. I was wondering when you'd drop by."

"You were?" I say.

"It's only natural you'd have some questions about work. I left so abruptly. Boy, did I blow that." He shakes his head and laughs. "Oh well, no use regretting the past, and things haven't worked out all bad." He looks at me and smiles. Just then he gives a double take as Pablo walks slowly back behind me, head down, tail low. Pablo plants himself behind my legs. From the corner of my eye I see him peek out to look at Owen.

"Is that...that looks like..."

"Pablo," I say. "William found him and brought him home."

Goddamn it if Owen isn't one of the best liars I've ever seen. "Really?" he exclaims. "Fantastic." He looks from me to William and then back down at Pablo. "I guess I shouldn't ask how William knows your dogs so well," he jokes.

When William and I don't answer, Owen claps his hands together. "Doesn't matter. Pablo is home. Thank God. We were all so worried, weren't we Penne. We just love this guy." He waves a hand at Pablo. "Come here, boy. How you doing?"

Pablo lowers his forearms onto the ground and puts his head down between them.

William says, "Actually, Owen, I just came about Pablo, but I guess I should be going."

We exchange a long look. "I guess I do have to get ready for work," I say. And then it strikes me. Damn. Pablo. What am I going to do about Pablo? Pablo is not Lucy. Pablo will not rest quietly in the staffroom all day, and he will definitely not pass as a therapy dog. He humps grocery carts. He lunges at anything that moves. But I can't leave him with Owen. I definitely can't do that. William. Maybe William will take him. Pablo slides closer behind me and licks the back of my ankle. Shit. Piss, piss, piss. I can't do that either. It would break Pablo's heart to have to go off with William. Pablo's just come home. I can't send him away again.

"Ok then," says William. "I'll see you later." He takes a few steps toward the street and then turns to me. "Can I talk to you, Penne? For a minute?"

I walk over to him. Pablo keeps pace with me, bumping sideways into my legs every few paces. I look over at Owen, who has his body planted all Superman style in the grass; he waves and gives us a tight smile. William turns, and I walk with him toward his car.

"Penne," he says. "That night at Dashed Sails. I don't want you to think…. You didn't believe…me and Ashley? I mean, I just ran into her. I didn't even know she would be there."

"Oh. Of course. No. I mean, why would you? She's crazy. Beautiful, but crazy."

"Because you seemed—"

"I know. I really lost it, didn't I? It was Pablo. I was so worried about Pablo. But you brought him home. So that's great. So, I'm great. And you're great, right? You have peace of mind, and I know that's important to you."

William glances past me toward Owen. "And Owen?"

"Yeah," I sigh. "Owen. Owen is Grace Claire's hero."

"I see."

Pablo circles round us, tail wagging, and then lifts his head and gives William's hand a quick little lick.

"Thanks for bringing Pablo home," I say reaching over to Pablo and rubbing his muzzle.

"You're welcome," says William. He looks through my eyes, past my mixed-up brain, and into my broken soul. "Call me sometime, Penne."

"Yeah. Ok."

I watch William get into his car and pull away. Owen walks up behind me. "I always hated that bastard," he mutters. He sees me look at him and adds, "But it's great about the dog."

I point my finger at him. "It is," I say. "It is great news."

What can I do but call in sick? "Sudden migraine," I tell Nancy. "I'll see you tomorrow. Or maybe the next day. It feels like this might last a while."

"I hope you won't miss your daughter's field trip," she says.

"Fieldtrip?"

"Wow. You must feel bad. It's been on the calendar for months."

Right. Grace Claire's fieldtrip to the Antiquities Museum to say goodbye to that bitch Venus. I'm a stupid chaperone. "Oh, yeah," I say looking over at Pablo. "I hope I'll feel up for it."

The phone rings the minute I hang up. It's the Vet. Lucy is ready to come home. Dammit, shit, bang-my-head against a brick wall.

"You have to come on the field trip," Grace Claire says when she gets home. "I get extra-credit if you come."

"I want to come," I say, "but Pablo just got back and now I have Lucy to take care of. She's still very fragile."

"Dad can watch them," she says, expressing far less gratitude for the return of the dogs than a devotee of a goddess of compassion should.

"Or Dad could go on the field trip," I say.

Owen shakes his head. "Busses. Motion sickness."

"Well, he's not watching Pablo and Lucy."

"I don't mind watching the dogs," he says.

"No," I say.

"Come on, Mom," says Grace Claire. "Besides," she pauses for a minute before saying in a low voice, "besides, that girl Pei is on my bus." She twirls a thin section of hair around her finger and keeps her eyes roving across the floor. "You should be there if she's on the bus."

Which means, of course, the dogs are fucked.

Chapter Twenty-Two

When Grace Claire and I get in the car the next morning I see the dogs look at me with sad, resigned eyes, like they know this is it. This is the end. I say to Grace Claire, "You wait here," and then I head back to the house where I find Owen eating a piece of cake over the kitchen sink.

Like a woman possessed, these words tumble out: "If you touch my dogs, if you move my dogs, if you feed my dogs, if you do anything to my dogs, I will take your Lexus, and the first thing I will do is go to Taco Bell and order twenty assorted burritos and three extra-large Cokes. Then I will park your car in the Best Buy parking lot in the middle of the day and smear the burritos on every inch of your car's interior. I will let the sun bake the cheese, beans, chicken and beef into your leather seats. And when I am done, I will drive your car to the dog park on Orange Grove Boulevard, and I will leave every door open, and I will tell every woman I see how my husband tried to murder my dog, and then I will invite those women to let their dogs loose in your car for as long as they like. Only then, will I pour those three extra-large Cokes into your engine and head home, leaving your car—and your keys—to the elements and to any unsavory person who might happen upon it. Although, by then, I can't imagine that even the most hard-up criminal would want anything to do with that particular vehicle."

"What—"

I shove my index finger in his chest. "Don't 'what' me. I know what you did. You will be sorry."

Impressive. Yeah. I know. Really, I don't know how I thought of that. It just came to me, like a flash of lightening or something. It's like I wasn't even myself. It's like I was someone else, someone tough and vengeful, someone who really would do that to a Lexus, and I think Owen believes that too because he gives me a look I've never seen before. His mouth hangs open and his eyebrows rise up. His whole head seems to get longer, like some freakish parade balloon. And he is scared. He is scared and impressed. It's awesome. And I know then—I know like I know my own name—Lucy and Pablo will be just fine, at least today.

Let me tell you, it's pretty cool being the tough girl. It makes you feel all buoyant and powerful, so powerful, in fact, that when I see Pei seated near the front of the bus I sit right across from her and send Grace Claire to the back. Oh yeah, this Pei chick is not doing anything to my girl. I am in her mean little face. I am watching her. I use my big pink purse to block the seat next to me. This girl will feel my presence. My vibe alone will let her know how twisted I know she is.

Someone in the seat behind me taps my shoulder. It's the librarian, who I met when I volunteered at the school's book fair. "How's your daughter?" she asks. "She all right? That riot must have been scary."

"She's fine," I say loudly. "She is great. Very strong, resilient girl. Very unphased by peer pressure. Very compassionate also."

"That's nice. You know, I think it's awful what those bigots did. I mean, people have the right to their religion."

"It's not actually our religion, but yes, people do have that right. Some people should learn to be more tolerant."

"Yeah. You know, still, it was pretty amazing that day. I mean six inches of rain in one hour. Right there in Hollywood. I hear there wasn't even any structural damage to the building. The rain was that effective in dousing the fire. Is that true?"

"Yes. And by tolerant I mean that people have to stop judging one another."

"What's up with that?"

"With judging one another?"

"No. The rain. The rain that put out The Goddess Lounge fire. You don't think…you know…the anger of the gods…." The librarian gives a short chuckle.

And that's when things begin to disintegrate. No sooner does the librarian close her mouth than thirty conversations about The Goddess Lounge explode. And these are not friendly conversations either. For every friend or supporter of Grace Claire who thinks the Hollywood deluge was a work of supernatural powers, twice as many Moses' Disciples' supporters think it is the work of Satan. Every single kid on that bus is yelling at another one—except Pei. Pei is squinting her eyes at me and smiling.

I am lame enough to hope that arriving at the Antiquities Museum will distract everyone from this subject, but how can it? Stepping into this particular museum is like stepping into the age of the gods. The structure is designed to look like a first century Roman villa. It has colonnaded arches, a red tile roof, and an enormous reflecting pool surrounded by the statues of Roman gods. Statues. Mosaics. Coins. Pottery. Everything in this place glorifies the rulers of Mount Olympus.

And then there is Venus herself. The looted statue. The one everyone has come to say goodbye to, for the very last time. She has been placed in a large, otherwise empty room that is filled to capacity with gum-smacking thirteen year olds. The group of twelve girls I chaperone smell like grape lip balm and seem completely unconcerned that they are packed into this hall like sardines. They press tightly against one another, each neck warmed by the hot breath of the girl behind her. I have to hold my purse in front of me so that it won't knock into anyone, and now I'm regretting that I didn't clean it out before I left because it is so heavy that the strap is cutting into my shoulder and it really hurts. When we reach the exit the girls agree: "That statue isn't so great. It's only a hunk of rock."

And here, unbelievably, I must differ. This is no mere hunk of rock. The face that launched ten thousand school buses is exactly like the photo that's been tormenting me from billboards, bus boards, banners, and newspaper advertisements: "Venus: Say Goodbye for the Very Last Time." And, as in the photo, the face is lovely. Smooth, milk-white skin. Gentle eyes and a small, pert mouth. A flawless chin with nary a marble wobble and a long, gazelle-like neck. Any plastic surgeon would be happy to sculpt such a beauty. But the body! That tiny, little detail the advertisements neglect to display? That is something else. It's mammoth. It's seven feet tall at the very least. Big and thick. Strong. More like a stylized Soviet peasant than one of today's anorexic runway models. No. This goddess has girth. Linebacker shoulders. A trashcan size waist. Legs like telephone poles. And hips. Real hips. Hips that curve and roll. Hips that gave birth to heroes and gods. And if there is any doubt that this is a body to worship, rather than to hide, it is dispelled by the stone toga that clings to her body like a wet tee shirt, each marble fold, each marble wrinkle a siren song to lust.

"Just a statue." That's like saying oxygen is just an element, mother's milk just a beverage. It occurs to me that this statue is life itself. It's sex, hunger, strength, power, love, kindness—yes, kindness. Right there in the face. Right there in the smooth, welcoming, outstretched arm. Kindness. Generosity. Forgiveness.

This is not the Venus I thought I knew. This is not a goddess who fucked around, turned lovesick couples into lions, and jealously sent pretty girls to the underworld. She is not reckless sex and irresponsible choices. She is not narcissism and self-absorption. This is someone else entirely. Who? I don't know. All I know for sure is that she is huge and powerful.

I shuffle through the crowd in knocked down, bowled over wonder. But I'm not so far gone that I don't realize that things are getting grim. The more the field trip attendees stroll the museum and its garden, the more they take in the anatomically-bountiful works of art, the more people begin to murmur, whisper. The docent does not help. A tall, older gentleman who tends to spit while talking, he speaks so enthusiastically about the homoeroticism implicit in classical art, that the students decide he must be gay, and thus another political symbol around which to orient their response to the culture of ancient Rome.

By lunch, two self-identified camps have taken root. At the lunch tables on the left: Pei and the Moses' Disciples supporters huddle together and thank God for their food. At the lunch tables on the right: the religious-freedom supporters circle protectively around Grace Claire, who seems to blink absolution at whoever looks her way. I've got to admit, it's kind of working for her. Her group is bigger than the Moses' Disciples one, and I only have to linger nearby for a few minutes to hear two kids refer to Grace Claire as brave, one refer to her as heroic, and about five boys say she's even hotter now that she's a goddess girl. You know what? She really does have this under control.

Not wanting to mess with the hot-goddess-girl-thing Grace Claire has going for her, I decide to take another look at the art collections. I stroll the rooms of marble Zeuses, Poseidons and Apollos. I walk by athletes, heroes and deer. And goddesses. A sisterhood of goddesses. Roman. Greek. Even Egyptian. Dianas, Junos, Athenas and Isises. There are goddesses and muses I haven't even heard of, but all of them, each and every one, are so strong and so lovely and so different. I make my way to the second floor and wander deeper and deeper into a series of smaller, out of the way rooms, rooms quite deserted by the crowds flocking to see the looted goddess of love. It's so still here. There's floor-polished and climate-controlled order and peacefulness. It's such a relief, really, after the sweaty crowds of the Venus room.

Alone in an alcove is a small marble statue—headless, female, maybe three feet tall—that reminds me of the mammoth Venus. Its stone tunic clings suggestively to its body, but it has one bare breast and a clearly-defined pelvis. A sign at the base of the figure says, "Venus Genetrix. Literally meaning Venus the mother. Ancestress of the Roman people. A goddess of motherhood and domesticity. Marble. Roman. AD 100-200."

I blink. Motherhood and domesticity? A more detailed accounting of the work hangs on the wall. Sliding the straps of my purse into my fingertips, I begin to read:

"The Venus Genetrix (meaning Venus the Mother) celebrates the goddess's role as protectress of Rome, where she guided her mortal son Aeneus after vigilantly safeguarding him throughout the Trojan War. After propagating a family that would one day include Romulus and Remus and Julius Caesar, Aeneus was made a god when Venus convinced Jupiter to grant her son the greatest honor any human could receive. She is said to have personally washed Aeneus's body in the River Numicius (a necessary step in cleansing him of every human impurity) and warming his lips with nectar and ambrosia. She watched over Aeneus's descendents, and the vast empire they built, with loving attention and motherly care and protected Romans in times of need."

Enlightenment can be reached through years of study or it can hit you like a pie in the face. Some people get PhDs. Some people see light bulbs. For me, my aha moment is electric. It shocks every cell of my body with a jolt that makes even my hair feel feverish. And here's the truth that does it: I am Venus Genetrix. I am the overprotective mother who can't stop herself from loving her perfectly mortal—and thus imperfect—child. I would do anything for Grace Claire. Given the chance, I would guard Grace Claire in battle, guide her across great shores, and even wash away her pain and suffering and death. All I need is a Jupiter who would let me. And then, before that truth finishes rolling through me, another truth jolts down my spine: I am also the mammoth Venus. I am not a child-like wraith, not a pale, wilting lily. I have hips and breasts and a body that is strong and useful and that could destroy a man's Lexus in the blink of an eye. And then a third truth slams through me. I am every Venus. The Botticelli ones. The skinny ones. The fat ones. The sexy ones. The maternal ones. I am all of them, and they are all one and the same Venus. Because that's what women are. That's what women's bodies prepare them to be. Love. Death. Sex. Strength. Pleasure. Joy. Abundance. They are life. Women's bodies give life. And, in the process, women's bodies are *alive*. That's what Venus is. That's what she represents. That's why the Greeks and Romans worshipped her and built monuments to her. In a daily world of small and large, meaningful and pointless deaths and disappointments, Venus not only gave life, but she lived it. She loved. She ate. She ruled. She protected. And not once was Venus a hero. She was always a goddess.

The last truth—the biggest one of all—passes through me. Venus never wanted me to sleep around or hurt others. She never wanted me to stop being a good mother, or to be selfish, or to care only about sex or men or looks. She wanted me to live. So that's what I say. I say, "She wanted me to live."

I throw open my purse and finger inside it for the necklace. My hand crisscrosses the bottom of the bag like a spider—up, down, feeling this way and that. I brush past my phone (inconsequential), my wallet (useless). Finally, the smooth pearls knock against my fingertips. I grab my old goddess necklace and fasten it to my neck. "I've been dead," I say. "But I'm supposed to live."

From behind me, a voice purrs, "Well, it's too late for that."

It's Ashley. She looks uncharacteristically frumpy in flats, pleated khakis and an oversized blue blazer. "You missed your bus," says Ashley. "It pulled away ten minutes ago. Funny how they forgot about you."

I step backwards and scan the rooms behind her. "There's no one there," says Ashley. "The guard went to lunch." She holds out the lapels of the jacket. "I took this from the staff room. Pretty ugly, huh? And see this?" She holds up an Antiquities Museum badge with a woman's face on it. Like Ashley, the woman in the picture has long blond hair and fair skin, but she's at least fifty pounds heavier and twice as old. "You'd think people would notice the difference, but basically people are stupid. Don't you think, Penne? That people are stupid?"

I open and close my mouth and glance again toward the back of the gallery hall, but Ashley is right. The hall is empty.

"Do you think I'm stupid, Penne?"

"No," I say, sightlessly fastening my purse as I shuffle toward the back of the statue.

"Really? Hmmm. Because I figured you thought I was totally stupid. How else to explain William?"

"William?"

"You should have known I wouldn't let you be with him. You both should have known."

"I'm not with him."

"He was at your house."

"He brought me my dog."

"You were at Dashed Sails."

"I like the music."

"He likes you. He thinks he loves you."

"No."

"Yes. It's your fault. You did this to him. You made him want you when he's supposed to want me." Ashley flips back her hair and takes a step forward. Even now, in this delusionary state, she still holds onto the details. The hair. The nails. Perfection. She really does look like a goddess. "You tricked him—you and your Venus ways. Fine. You wanna play the Venus card? I'll play the Hera card. But remember: Hera is queen. She wins."

Ashley pulls a long knife from inside her jacket. It is a kitchen knife—a quality kitchen knife, the long, thin kind used to carve roast beef. A dull red sheen covers the blade. "We were supposed to get married. You ruined everything."

"I didn't." I twist the straps of my purse in my sweaty palms and take another step until I'm directly behind the statue.

Ashley holds the blade up to her chest and steps forward. "Hera turned Zeus's sluts into animals, but I guess I'll just have to carve you like one, you ugly, old whale."

It's the name that wakes me from my panic. Ugly old whale? I am not an ugly old whale—no more than that Venus who stands downstairs. I am strong. I am useful. I was dead once today and, damn it all to hell, once is enough. It is my turn to live, and no skinny, deluded cheerleader is going to stop me. I say to myself, "focus"—and I focus. I say to myself, "stop this crazy bitch"—and I do.

With a flick of my wrist, I wrap the leather straps of my purse once more around my hand. From the back of the gallery I pick up the sound of shouts, footsteps and a garbled voice from a Walkie-talkie. "Repeat: Suspect…female…security jacket."

Ashley hears the voices too. "Oh, no," she whispers. She flings back her thick curtain of blond hair, and, for a moment, it waves like a hundred hissing serpents. Her face hardens into a hideous mask, and, as a phalanx of burly male security guards run toward us, she lunges at me, the knife held high. She says, "This is for Hera, so don't try to be a hero."

Rolling my arm in a wide vertical arc, I swing my purse at Ashley. Its heavy contents clang violently as the bag soars through the air. The din of banging cell phone, journal, first aid kit, wallet, lipstick, hairbrush, and loose change hiss and wheeze like a thousand wasps. Splat. The purse crashes against Ashley's perfectly chiseled cheek, sending her reeling backward, straight into the rounded ass of the Venus Genetrix. The statue wobbles. It teeters sideways, delivering another blow to Ashley, who drops her knife and falls to the floor. Then, just when it seems that the protectress of Rome is about to crash to the floor, the statue teeters back in place and stops. Unharmed. Not a two thousand-year-old hair out of place.

"I am *not* a hero," I say glaring down at Ashley's crumpled form. "I am a fucking goddess."

For what seems like an eternity, but must only be seconds, a roaring silence descends on the hall. The security guards—mere mortals, after all—stand frozen like runners in a race, legs and arms extended, panting mouths open wide. Then Ashley utters a soft moan, and the room comes to life.

One of the guards turns to me and says, "What the hell have you got in that purse, lady?"

"Just the usual," I answer, hanging the bag back around my elbow.

A second guard, older and less easily impressed than the first, says, "Well, you're lucky. That's for sure. You should see what this gal did to a guard downstairs."

The police come and with them come throngs of LA news trucks and helicopters. I bypass them all. I make my statement to the police and have Georgie pick me up and take me home. The goddesses are with us, too, because we make excellent time. Even so, the media beats us. Women with dangerously tight shirts and men wearing volumizing-hair products stake out my doorstep while cameramen and producers have turned my driveway into an impenetrable maze of backlights and slithering cords. But I have fought a goddess already. I am not about to be put out by scavenging carrion. Plus, I have Georgie with me, and Georgie is only too delighted to take the limelight and promise "exclusive" interviews about her daughter's "traumatic run in with a knife-wielding art terrorist." And if that doesn't work I have my dogs, who are barking and jumping behind the fence, sending dog spit fifteen feet in front of them and looking happier than they have in weeks.

I swing open the door and walk straight into Owen. Grace Claire stands next to him, the phone cradled in her neck. "She doesn't really like Fox News," I hear her say. "I doubt she'd be interested, but maybe..."

"What the hell is going on?" Owen says. He motions to Grace Claire and then to the reporters outside. "We've been worried sick. You weren't on the bus. You didn't call. And then all this commotion. You wouldn't believe the things people are saying."

"Owen," I say. "We need to talk."

Chapter Twenty-Three

Owen is gone. He moved out yesterday, after the reporters ran off to cover a high-speed chase on the 105.

Grace Claire is cool with it. She might be a little disappointed, but she said she figured Owen wouldn't be with us long.

"It's obvious that you can barely look at Dad without barfing," she said. "Clearly, you have some forgiveness issues. But I get it. He was a jerk to you. You have to process that. Quan Yin doesn't think you're ready to move on to sending him feelings of loving kindness yet."

"No," I told her. "I'm not, but I am ready to move on. It's time."

Owen is less cool with it. When I told him that he had to leave he put on this wide, indulgent smile. He couldn't believe it. "But…I love you," he said.

Having crafted a lifetime of illusions in the name of family harmony, I know a thing or two about the art of pretending. So it was easy not to believe Owen. He didn't love me. It was a lie, a peacemaking lie, a practical lie, but a lie nonetheless. For a moment, my mind passed over the thousand lies that got me to this place. Owen's lies. Ashley's lies. And most especially my own lies, the ones I fed to myself. So well intentioned, so sympathetic, so nice.

I said, "Owen, if I believed you, I would feel sorry for you because Misery and Grief are the handmaidens of Love, and they would follow you forever. But luckily, you don't love me. Whatever pain you're experiencing won't last long."

"You didn't really say that." This from Nancy. We're making up a vat of homemade Play Doh before the kids arrive at school. I'm telling her everything because, frankly, I can still hardly believe it, and hearing the words makes it real.

"I did say that," I tell her. "I really said that."

"Wow." She leans back against the kitchen sink, a look of wonder framed by her beautiful mahalo hair. "Wow. What did he say?"

"He didn't say anything. He just stood there. And then I went in the kitchen to get the dogs dinner."

"And?"

"And then I made dog biscuits."

"What?"

"Lucy and Pablo really like those dog biscuits. They're into them. And, you know, they have had a hard time of things lately. They're very sensitive. They need comfort food.

"Plus, to be honest, I wanted to give Owen space. I heard him go into Grace Claire's room to talk to her. Then I heard him rummaging around upstairs. Then he went. I'm not sure where."

"Wow."

"I know. It's totally wow."

One of the assistant teachers enters, and Nancy and I move out into the classroom to get things ready for the morning. Later, after snack, right after I've helped a dark-eyed boy Velcro a loose shoe, Nancy comes up to me and says, "I still can't believe the day you had yesterday."

"I know."

"Listen, some of us are doing happy hour again tonight. Why don't you come? It'll be fun."

"I can't." I pause, and a familiar look of resignation begins to pass across Nancy's face. "I have something I need to do," I say. "But how about next week? Uzume, Bast and Freyja are taking Grace Claire to hear Sally Ride. She's giving a lecture at Cal Tech. They think she needs a goddess."

Nancy's eyes open wide. "It's a date."

By the time I pick up Grace Claire at the food bank, it's already getting dark. The dogs need affection, Grace Claire has homework, and I haven't even thought about dinner. I'm tired and still dazed from yesterday, but that thing I have to do: it has to be done.

Grace Claire is in her room unpacking her backpack. She has her hands around a history book as big as a medieval bible. When I say her name, she gives a surprised start and her hair rustles behind her. I say, "I have to go out for a while. How do you feel about staying home alone? Well, with Lucy and Pablo."

The book slides out of her fingers and she jumps back to avoid it landing on her foot, but she's already stopped thinking about her nearly-squashed toes. She is shining like I haven't seen her shine in years. For a minute, I see a younger Grace Claire, a girl who is only possibility. It's all I can do not to want to put her in a jar and stick her on a shelf: safe and unchanging. But, the thing is, people change. The person Grace Claire will one day settle into isn't written yet, but that's her journey, that's her tale. I can't write it for her.

Her voice joyous, she says, "Really? You mean it? I can do that. I'd love that."

I get in my car and head for the freeway. Although it's rush hour, I don't worry about traffic. I know Venus will clear my path. When I reach William's office, I don't worry about the security guards. They don't even see me. I don't think about the bitchy receptionist. She's long gone.

I make my way through a maze of cubicles and tired workers getting ready to head home. William is holding his phone to his ear when he sees me coming. He freezes for a minute, says something and then quickly hangs up. In just a few steps, he's outside his office and has me by the elbow.

"Come with me." He swings me around and takes me back to the elevators. I say, "I want—"

"Wait."

He leads me out the building. I try to speak, but he stops me again. "Not yet," he says.

He walks me about half a block until we reach a little garden plaza near the Downtown Library. It's dark, and all around us commuters rush for the Metro and cars snake end to end toward freeways. Besides a secluded fountain proclaiming, "Evil deeds do not prosper; the slow man catches up with the swift," he puts his hands in mine and says, "I'm sorry. It's my fault. I wanted to keep you safe, and I didn't." He shakes his head. "I tried to call. Yesterday."

"It's ok," I say.

"I think about you. All the time. I didn't want it to be this way, but I didn't think I had a choice."

My hands reach up to his face. I want to tell him to let it go. That it doesn't matter. That the only choice that matters is choosing to embrace existence or worry through it. We can be heroes or we can be gods. Either way, we're adventure stories waiting to unfold. I want to tell him all these things. But in the end, I don't need to. He tastes it in a kiss so deep, so true that Venus herself scatters its essence in the heavens where it floats like a string of pearls on a sapphire sky, immortalized forever, a new constellation: Penne Genetrix. Penne, the mother.

Acknowledgments

Not all books may need a village, but this one did. Cindie Geddes and Judith Harlan at Lucky Bat Books and Cathy Perlmutter and Alan Weinstein provided technical expertise and extensive advice. Laurie Allee, Teresa Atwater, Katherine Bleakley, Petrea Burchard, Susan Carrier, Kate Folkers, Paula Johnson, Kim Ohanneson, Victoria Patterson, Nancy Spiegel, Desiree Zamorano, and Steve Finnegan all read and commented on earlier drafts of this book. Steve Finnegan, who is possibly the best husband ever, deserves credit for his constant encouragement and support, as do Elizabeth and Mary Finnegan, excellent daughters who are in the process of becoming amazing goddesses. The faithful readers of my blog Finnegan-BeginAgain have kept me company in the virtual world, and I wish I could hug every one of them, except maybe the weird guy who kept posting comments about Icelandic travel. Finally, my Camp Scripps sisters were the ones who got me thinking about goddesses and the ways in which owning your own life is wrapped up in owning your own fun. I love them all. I dedicate this book to them and the rest of my village.